PRAISE FOR

T0244803

Where They Lie

"The tragic crash of a small plane sets an Oregon social worker on the trail of even greater tragedies behind it . . . A well-paced exposé of dark family secrets."

—*Kirkus Reviews*

"The plot takes many twists and turns and keeps readers guessing until the surprising end. For fans of Harlan Coben, Riley Sager, and Linwood Barclay."

—*Library Journal*

Or Else

2023 EDGAR AWARD WINNER FOR BEST PAPERBACK ORIGINAL

"Hart remains a suspense writer to watch."

—*Publishers Weekly*

"*Or Else* is a thriller/suspense tour de force. Joe Hart has knocked it out of the park with a start-to-finish roller coaster ride of perfectly executed twists and expertly timed chills. Deep character development and rich narrative seals *Or Else*'s place as the not-to-be-missed domestic thriller/suspense of the year."

—Steven Konkoly, author of the Ryan Decker series and *Deep Sleep*

"The perfect thriller for a rainy afternoon, *Or Else* draws you into a web of small-town secrets, lies, and intrigue and doesn't let you go. Hart's well-rendered setting and characters resonate like people and places you've known. Loved every minute of this absolute page-turner!"

—D. M. Pulley, bestselling author of *The Dead Key*

"Joe Hart has written compelling stories before, but it's in *Or Else* that he shows off just how good he is. This book checks all the boxes for me: a (seemingly) quiet, small-town drama—filled with those little quirks and secrets nobody wants to talk about—that quickly blossoms into something big, sinister, and menacing. Hart doesn't pull any punches on some serious issues, either: love, infidelity, family conflict . . . there's plenty to think about right up to the explosive ending. This is the thriller you'll be recommending for the foreseeable future."

—Matthew Iden, author of the Marty Singer series and *The Winter Over*

Obscura

"Joe Hart is a tremendous talent, and with *Obscura*, he has taken his storytelling to the next level. This is a genius work of science fiction, brimming with thrills, scares, and most importantly, heart. I devoured this book, and you will too."

—Blake Crouch, *New York Times* bestselling author of *Dark Matter* and the Wayward Pines series

"Outstanding . . . Fans of Blake Crouch's Wayward Pines series, with its combination of mystery, horror, and science fiction, will find this right up their alley."

—*Publishers Weekly* (starred review)

"This gripping book will be a must-read for fans of SF-based mysteries such as John Scalzi's *Lock In* and Kristine Kathryn Rusch's Retrieval Artist series, as well as aficionados of stories about science gone wrong, too far, or both."

—*Library Journal* (starred review)

"The pacing is excellent from beginning to end."

—*Los Angeles Times*

"Those seeking an off-planet sci-fi thriller with a haunting plotline will devour Joe Hart's *Obscura*, which reads quick and is jam-packed with terrifying surprises."

—The Real Book Spy

"For the reader who likes hard science fiction with some mystery and suspense thrown in, *Obscura* should hit the spot. It's not merely sci-fi, but a thriller wrapped in the deadly solitude of space with a determined heroine who refuses to give up."

—*New York Journal of Books*

NEVER COME BACK

ALSO BY JOE HART

The Dominion Trilogy

The Last Girl
The Final Trade
The First City

The Liam Dempsey Mysteries

The River Is Dark
The Night Is Deep

Nora McTavish

Where They Lie

Novels

Lineage
Singularity
EverFall
The Waiting
Widow Town
Cruel World
Obscura
I'll Bring You Back

We Sang in the Dark
Or Else

Novellas

Leave the Living

Short Story Collections

Midnight Paths: A Collection of Dark Horror
Something Came Through: And Other Stories

Short Stories

"The Line Unseen"
"Outpost"
"And the Sea Called Her Name"
"The Exorcism of Sara May"

Comics

The Last Sacrifice

NEVER COME BACK

A THRILLER

JOE HART

THOMAS & MERCER

Published by Thomas & Mercer, Seattle

www.apub.com

Amazon, the Amazon logo, and Thomas & Mercer are trademarks of Amazon.com, Inc., or its affiliates.

ISBN-13: 9781662515316 (paperback)
ISBN-13: 9781662515323 (digital)

Cover design by Shasti O'Leary Soudant
Cover image: © David Jensen / Alamy Stock Photo

Printed in the United States of America

There are some secrets which do not permit themselves to be told.

—*Edgar Allan Poe*

1

She wasn't listening.

Allie Prentiss stood in her dining room looking young and pretty in her skirt and cutoff sweatshirt, one hand on her hip. Confident. Sure this would turn out the way she wanted it to. She had no idea.

"Ten thousand," she said. "Or I tell them."

"We agreed on five."

Allie smiled a little and looked out the window onto the meager backyard behind the house. It was early spring, and the leaves from last fall were a brown carpet before the dormant forest. There were streams and rivers flowing out of sight, but they could be heard now that the snowfields above town were melting, the runoff roaring in hidden hollows. "I know what we agreed on, but things have changed. I need more."

"Because you flunked out of school."

That seemed to hurt her. Her face tightened into a mask. "One class."

"That class doesn't cost ten thousand to retake. It's not even one thousand."

"That's not the point. I have other things to pay for."

"And that's not my concern. It's five thousand or nothing."

She smiled again, wider this time. The prettiness was gone, leaving only cold calculation. "I don't think you want people knowing what you tried to do."

There was a heavy brass paperweight on the bookshelf nearby. It was in the shape of a large sphere with a square base. It shone dully in the room's cold light. "How about we call it all off? Forget we ever met one another. Just forget this happened. I can do that. Can you?"

Allie came closer. The cheap floor creaked beneath her, and the wind gusted outside, prying around the eaves as the day darkened. Her perfume was faint but there, sweet and infuriating. "No," she whispered. "No, I can't."

A blur and her head rocked to the side as the paperweight slammed into it.

Blood. A spatter fanning out in the air and falling to the floor. Allie fell with it.

She dropped to her side and rolled groggily, as if awakening. She croaked something that tried to be a scream and failed. The paperweight came down on the back of her head.

Something gave there.

Allie shuddered, legs stiffening, but one arm came up, trying to pull herself away, young strength unwilling to be quelled. She slid to the low coffee table and grasped its edge, trying to pull herself up with a shaking, blood-slicked hand.

The paperweight came down again.

And again.

And again.

A dog barked distantly, and someone shouted for it to be quiet. The dog obeyed, and there was only the wind.

2

It was raining again.

Long, slanting spates of it dashed against the front windows of my office. Spring rain, expected but not entirely welcome. At least not by me. Not after almost two steady weeks of it.

I stood looking out at the street. A few cars splashed by, along with one harried person beneath a red umbrella. There hadn't been much foot traffic today, the same since the weather turned from hopeful spring sunshine to steady dour downpours.

But I really couldn't complain.

Since hanging out my shingle as a family advocate the prior fall, work had been slow but steady. Mostly thanks to the referrals from a few dedicated friends at state child protective services from which I'd resigned after the Volk tragedy. Working for myself had its benefits. One of them being I no longer had to remove children from abusive households and was able to help those who had already started the process of rebuilding their lives, or at least wanted to. The stress of continually falling short, always feeling like the bad guy, had lifted, only to be replaced by the stress of running my own business.

The phone rang.

I turned away from the window and moved past the cramped waiting area to the partitioned office at the back of the shotgun space. I couldn't afford a secretary yet, so I was wearing that hat as well.

Someday soon I'd be able to hire someone. My thoughts strayed to Daniel Stellsgard, a tall, dark, and handsome assistant district attorney whom I'd been quietly flirting with for the last six months. He'd make a great secretary but probably wouldn't take the pay and position cut. But hey, a girl could dream. The number on the work cell wasn't a local area code, but I picked up anyway. No telling how far people had to travel to get the kind of help I dealt in.

"Sanctuary Family Advocacy, Nora speaking." Nothing. Dead air. No, wait. Faint breathing and maybe some background noise like distant traffic or wind. "Hello?" A slight intake of breath, but still no reply. "Listen, call somewhere else if you're trying to get off, like the state police. I'm sure they'd be interested in obscene phone calls."

I hung up and sank into my desk chair. It was almost closing time. I was glad. It had been dead all day, and there was nothing more tiring than boredom. From the lower drawer on the left I pulled out a slim bottle of bourbon and took a quick shot. Like I said, being my own boss had its benefits.

As I was contemplating dinner, probably the excellent Thai place around the corner for the third time this week, the front entrance whooshed open, and the sound of people stepping inside filtered through my half-open office door. I fumbled the booze bottle into the drawer and took a couple of hurried swallows from my coffee tumbler before going out to the reception area.

A young man and woman waited for me there, dripping rainwater from soaked clothes. They must've parked in the nearest free lot a block away and walked. Neither carried an umbrella. "Hello," I said, stepping forward and holding my hand out to the woman, who accepted it. "I'm Nora McTavish."

"My name is Gayle Pearson. And this is my husband, Joel Pearson." I shook hands with Joel, who met my gaze for a second before looking away.

4

"What can I do for you?"

"Our daughter was taken away. My grandmother took her, and we need to get her back," Gayle said, her voice trembling near the end.

"Okay." I reassessed them. "Well, let's have a seat in my office. Can I get you something to drink? Coffee? Tea?"

"No, thank you."

"Do you have a Pepsi?" Joel asked.

"Yes, I do, actually."

We went into my office, and while they situated themselves, I gathered a soda from the mini fridge as well as two towels I kept in the closet for when I got a wild hair to go surfing directly from work. I handed them the towels, and as they dried off, I found a general intake form and set it on my desk before facing them.

"Now, tell me about your daughter. What's her name?"

"Ivy Josephine Pearson," Gayle said. "Her middle name is for my mom. She died in a car crash when I was eighteen."

"I'm sorry to hear that. How old is Ivy?"

"She's three, and she loves butterflies and chocolate," Joel said, sipping his Pepsi. "And her favorite color is pink."

"She's with my grandma," Gayle continued. "My grandma's name is Arlene Jones. My name used to be Jones, but then we got married, and now it's Pearson."

Gayle and Joel each had some type of developmental or intellectual disability. Over the years at CPS, I'd had experience with multiple people with different disabilities. In almost every case they'd been reported for child neglect or abuse that in the end turned out to be false accusations. The public generally believed eugenics was a despicably antiquated notion, but in the legal realm it was still alive and well, with between 40 and 80 percent of intellectually disabled parents losing custody of their children at some point or another.

I scribbled some information onto the intake form and said, "Why does your grandma have custody of Ivy now?"

"She's always wanted Ivy. She told me we shouldn't be in charge of raising her, that we could barely take care of ourselves. We went to court, and the judge said Ivy had to stay with her until we could prove we were good parents. They don't think we're smart enough," Gayle said. Her eyes swam with tears. "But see, we are good parents. We love her very much and miss her."

Joel had begun digging in a worn canvas bag he'd brought in with him, and after a moment set a framed photo on my desk of him and Gayle standing on either side of a pony. A tiny girl wearing a pink sundress sat in the saddle. Ivy wore enormous sunglasses in the shape of two hearts. Mine melted at her smile. "She's beautiful," I said. But Joel was placing another photo beside the first, this one of a Christmas morning where a grinning Ivy was half-buried beneath colorful wrapping paper. Another picture of Ivy and Gayle in bathing suits wading in the ocean, both of them laughing. Another of Ivy on a swing set, legs kicked out, Joel behind her with his arm extended.

"These are all wonderful," I said as Joel reached into the bag again. "I believe you're good parents. You don't have to convince me." Both of them seemed to relax. "I just need to ask a few questions, and we'll go from there, okay?"

Gayle was twenty-four and Joel twenty-six. They'd been married for four years, and from what I could gather, they'd lost custody of their daughter six weeks ago after an incident in a grocery store. Apparently, Ivy had been sitting in the grocery basket of their cart instead of in the child seat, and an employee had approached them, asking them to secure her properly, which they did. Three days later CPS arrived at their house and removed Ivy from their care, citing endangerment. The necessary paperwork had already been filed by Gayle's grandmother Arlene, and Ivy had been remanded into her custody. A subsequent hearing ruled in favor of Arlene keeping Ivy until Gayle and Joel met a number of parental requirements.

"She's been gone one month and fifteen days, and she has to come home because the fairy parade at the flower gardens is soon, and we can't miss the parade," Joel said.

"We're going to try and get her home, okay? When you went to court, who represented you?"

"No one," Gayle said. "We went and talked to the judge ourselves."

"All right." I sat back from my desk. "Here's what we'll do. I'm going to get you a lawyer, and we'll—"

"We can't afford it," Joel said, sitting forward. "We both work, but I only make twelve dollars and seventy-five cents an hour, and Gayle only makes thirteen."

"Don't worry, the lawyer I work with helps on cases for free sometimes, and I think she'll help you."

"And what do you charge?" Gayle asked.

I paused. My business could definitely use a cash infusion, but there was no way I was taking money from these two people. "I help for free sometimes too. I won't charge you anything." Gayle looked at Joel, and he reached out to hold her hand. I cleared my throat. "Okay, so here's what we'll do."

Twenty minutes later I watched Gayle and Joel hurry away through the rain. They were still holding hands. I returned to my desk and skimmed the notes and intake form. I emailed Sharon Weisman, the attorney I'd mentioned to the couple, and attached the necessary information. The first step would be to petition for a new hearing since Gayle and Joel had already completed most of the court's parental requirements, all of which appeared redundant because none of them actually applied to the family's situation. Instead they were designed to disqualify parents because of IQs instead of their ability to care for their child. It boiled my blood.

Love doesn't abide by test scores and judicial rulings. It transcends them.

From what I knew so far, the very best place in the world for Ivy was at home with her parents. But there were a dozen things we needed to do prior to seeing a judge. When I had as many wheels in motion as I could, I shut the office down and was about to head out into the rainswept evening when the work cell rang. I half expected it to be Gayle or Joel calling with a question, but it was the heavy breather again. I almost didn't answer, but the couple's unwarranted plight had set me off, and I wanted a target to aim my anger at.

"Listen," I said, "there's this thing called caller ID, and it's made life a whole lot harder for perverts like you, so I'd suggest—"

"Nora?"

A woman's voice. That and my name together knocked me back a step. "Oh, yes. Sorry, I thought—never mind. Who is this?"

A long pause in which I thought she'd hung up, then she said, "I don't know if you'll remember me—it's been over twenty years. I . . . I tried to talk when I called earlier, and my voice just wouldn't work." She laughed shakily. "This is Theresa Grayson, but I was always Tess to you."

And just like that, I was eight years old again.

3

Sunshine and wind.

Those were the first two things that came back. The ocean. Running through sand with the waves crashing around our ankles.

Paul ahead, alive and strong and faster than the rest of us, then Tess and I with Stephen right behind.

Gulls wheeling in the salt air over our heads, feet freezing from the sea, the fading taste of lemonade, and a strip of endless beach. That moment forever in the memory of a child.

"Tess," I breathed. "Really?" It was all I could say.

"Yeah, it's me."

I sat in the nearest chair, the weight of the past coming down with me. "I can't believe it."

"I know, I'm so sorry for calling out of the blue like this."

"No, I mean, how else would you call? I didn't know if you were even still alive."

"I'm not sure what to say. It's been so long."

There was a break in the clouds, and the sun washed the street for a second, bleaching it a shimmering white, then it was gone, and the rain resumed. "I looked for you," I said. "After your mom died, I figured you went to stay with your father's relatives, but I didn't know his name since they were never married—"

"You don't have to explain. It's my fault." She paused. "I didn't know what happened to you and Stephen and . . . and Paul, for a long time. It was kept from me. And when I finally found out, I didn't know how to . . ."

"I understand. I do." And I did. The atrocity my father committed was national news, and I didn't blame anyone, friends or family, for not keeping or renewing bonds afterward. Tragedy has that effect on people, it leaves them without a compass. "So where are you?" I said. "What are you doing these days?"

There was another long pause, and for the second time I wondered if we'd been disconnected, wondered if it was fate separating me again from the closest thing to a sister I'd ever had. Then there was another sharp intake of breath, and when Tess spoke, she was crying. "I'm here, in Oregon. And I'm sorry, but for some reason I couldn't get you out of my head since this all started."

"All started . . . Tess, what's going on?"

A quiet sob. "I need help. I really need your help."

———

At home I parked in the carport and sat there for a time in a daze, looking at the rain dripping from the eaves. Then I rushed inside and listened to the comforting click of Merrill's nails hurrying toward me.

"Hey, hey, you, did you have a good day?" I said, kneeling to pet my rescue mutt, who was pretty much my whole world. He slathered my face with kisses, and I laughed. It felt good.

When Merrill was fed, I started to pour myself a glass of wine but hesitated and made tea instead. It would be too easy to blunt the edge of Tess's call with booze, too easy to keep the memories from coming back full force. But that was what I needed. I needed to remember it all.

Before our mother abandoned us to the monster who was our father, she had a friend named Diedre. She was more than a friend really, almost like an extension of the family. Like our parents, Diedre had always been there on the periphery of our lives, and so had her daughter, Theresa, who was exactly my age. Even though our father never allowed Diedre or Theresa in the house, our mother used every chance she got to visit them with us in tow. I recalled hundreds of beach days and just as many other outings to movies and parks, sleepovers in Diedre and Tess's small but neat home a half hour away from our own. While the four of us played, our mothers would sit shoulder to shoulder and watch, all the while in deep conversation punctuated by laughter. I remember that the most, the sound of their mingled laughter.

All of us kids got along well, but Tess and I were the closest. We shared secrets and slipped away from my brothers sometimes just to be alone together. Things were different with her. I loved Paul and Stephen, but another girl my age was like finding someone who spoke your language in a foreign country.

Then one day a trucker fell asleep at the wheel and crossed the centerline into Diedre's car as she was going to work, and everything changed.

The life went out of our mother. She grayed around the edges and quit talking. Amid our father's constant anger and violence, she retreated and retreated until one morning she was gone.

I hadn't thought about Diedre or Tess in years. It's funny how vastly important things can dim and fade with time until they're ghosts of themselves, and then not even that. As young as I was and under the pressure of our threatened existence, I'd forgotten the toll Diedre's death had taken on our mother.

Did I hate her any less for leaving us? Absolutely not.

But now things had changed. And I had a decision to make.

I paced to the tall windows in the living room and looked out at the trees and the ocean in the distance. The last of the storm was breaking up over the water, and the sun had notched into the horizon, spilling itself onto the sea.

I made a quick phone call, then turned out the lights and went to bed, only to lie there staring up at the ceiling where shadows grew and receded as night came on fully.

We like to think our choices are the result of the very best calculations, a reflection of who we are. But in truth some decisions are made before we even know of them. They're part of the landscape ahead, just waiting for us to arrive.

4

Stephen's house smelled of freshly brewed coffee when I stepped inside early the next morning, and it gave me life.

"In the kitchen," Stephen called as I came in with Merrill, who immediately padded away into the next room like he owned the place. When I entered the kitchen Stephen was on all fours wrestling with Merrill over a chew toy. "There's an excellent Guatemalan medium roast in the carafe," he said as Merrill growled playfully and yanked at the rubber ring Stephen held. "Just got a shipment yesterday."

"Smells amazing. Where do you want his food and whatnot?" I asked, balancing the box of Merrill's supplies on my hip.

"Over in the corner. Are you going to stay with Uncle Stephen? Are you? Are you?"

"He's not your uncle, Merrill, don't listen to him."

"So you were very abrupt and cagey on the phone last night," Stephen said, letting Merrill carry off the ring. "What's the deal? You on the run from another sordid past I'm not aware of?"

I poured a cup of coffee and added a dollop of cream. Drank. Ecstasy. "I got a call from Tess yesterday."

For a second there was only blankness on my brother's face, then a light came on. "You mean Tess, as in Tess from when we were little, Tess?"

"Yeah."

"Whoa. God, I haven't thought about her in forever."

"Right?"

"Craziness. I can barely remember her. Okay, the mystery deepens. What did she want?"

"Help. She needs help." We sat at the table as Merrill reexplored the house and settled onto the dog bed Stephen kept for when he came over. "So, the abbreviated version is this—Tess Hannover lived with her father's parents after her mom died and eventually made it back to Oregon. She married a guy named Neil right out of college and became Tess Grayson. They had a daughter, Kendra, and Neil secured a job teaching English and literature at Ridgewood University."

"I've heard of it, it's in midstate, right?"

"Yeah, up in the mountains at the end of a glacial lake, all very picturesque and hipster-chic."

"Go on."

"So a couple months ago a college student at Ridgewood named Allie Prentiss was murdered. She was bludgeoned to death in her rental. She'd recently flunked out of a lit class, and guess who the professor was."

"Tess's hubby."

"Correct. Prior to that Tess suspected Neil might've been stepping out on her so she filed for divorce. He'd been acting weird for a while, distant and moody. Some people said they spotted Neil and Allie talking a few times, and Allie's neighbor saw his car on their street the evening Allie was murdered."

"Not a great look."

"Terrible. So Neil is arrested on suspicion of murder, but it looks like he's going to get released after a seventy-two-hour hold, except some incriminating evidence is found at his family cabin and a trial date is set for this fall. But here's where it gets weird." I took a sip of coffee. "A couple weeks ago something comes to light about the evidence found at the cabin. Seems like it may have been tainted in some way, and one of the detectives on the case gets suspended. The DA drops the charges against Neil, and he's released. The first thing he does is petition for joint custody of Kendra."

"Oh, wow."

"Tess is obviously going to fight it, but she said she started thinking of us, of me, when this all went down and called asking if I could come help advise her in an unofficial capacity. I think she mainly wants some moral support."

Stephen blew out a long breath, and Merrill pricked his ears. "That's . . . a lot. So how long do you think you'll be gone?"

"No idea. It all depends on the court's timelines for custody. There's an initial hearing set for tomorrow morning, and she wanted me to be there."

"Such a blast from the past." Merrill stood and padded over to Stephen, resting his head on his leg. Stephen stroked his fur. "I remember us at the beach, and that's about all. Just a snapshot of running in the sand. But it's a good memory. We had fun with them, right?"

"We did. Diedre was Mom's closest friend. Maybe her only friend."

"She must've meant a lot to her since Mom hung us out to dry once Diedre was dead."

"Must've," I agreed. But my gaze had unfocused, and I barely heard him.

———

Stephen walked me out and gave me a long hug before I got in my car. "Don't worry about Merrill. We always watch Kurosawa flicks and eat too much popcorn."

Merrill had followed us out, and I knelt to scratch his ears and kiss him between the eyes. "You be good for Uncle Stephen."

"Oh, *now* I'm Uncle Stephen."

"I'll be back soon." One more kiss, then I stood and started to climb into the car.

"Hey, tell Tess hello from me. I can't really recall her, but it's nice to have at least one good memory from before."

Before and after, the continental divide in our lives. And I was about to cross back over.

I waved as I drove away, feeling my throat clinch a little when Stephen held up one of Merrill's paws to help him wave back.

Then I was on a street leading east, which brought me out of the city and onto a highway heading toward the mountains. As trees crowded in on either side of the road and civilization fell away, my mind turned to the one thing I'd omitted telling Stephen about Tess's call. For now I didn't want to say anything since I had no idea how he'd feel if he knew. I had no idea what *I* was feeling, for that matter. A barrage of emotions.

Disbelief. Anger. Disgust.

And longing.

I couldn't ignore that last one. Because if there was one thing I knew about myself, it was that I needed to know. It was what drove me, what had always driven me.

As the first mountain pass appeared ahead, I thought about what Tess had said and pressed the gas a little harder.

I think I might know where your mother is.

5

The town of Mutiny appeared in the flatlands ahead, the buildings dwarfed by the mountains beyond.

I'd been driving for the better part of three hours when the first signs of the town revealed themselves in a smattering of structures. In my rearview there were endless grasslands beginning to green. Ahead the mountains soared up in white-capped glory, overshadowing the buildings crawling ever closer.

Mutiny wasn't large, but like any college town, it boasted all its most attractive attractions on Main Street. I counted four breweries, three pizza joints, five tourist traps, and at least three chocolate shoppes—two *p*'s and everything.

People ambled between stores. A few cars crossed the wide intersections, and a couple of college-age kids blew by on mopeds, their laughter fleeting. Before I knew it the town proper had dwindled and nature took over again, and as I rounded a bend its unrestrained beauty caught me off guard.

A glacial lake sat at the southern end of town, its waters flat and eerily green in the sun. A vast moraine rose dramatically on the lake's left side, a crowning of the glacier that had birthed it. I was so struck by the view I almost missed my turn as my phone squawked directions.

A small development was nestled at the foot of the moraine, hemmed in by a forest of pines. Two parallel streets formed a U of homes, all the yards spacious and well kept. Tess's was a nice two-story set back from the street near the bottom of the U. A waist-high hedge lined the front walk, and a large SUV was parked beside a sleek Lexus in the drive. A kid's bike sat between the two vehicles.

I climbed out, stretching my legs and back, and breathed in the air. It had a different quality than the coast, lighter, maybe sweeter if I had to admit it. A second later the front door of the house opened, and a woman appeared there.

It was like I was looking back in time.

Tess was a copy of her mother, only taller. Same straight dark hair, same gorgeous heart-shaped face. And when she smiled, I blinked, a sense of the past overlaying the present.

She strode down the walk biting her lower lip and held out her arms as she neared. "I can't believe you're here," she said. "I really can't believe it." Then she was hugging me, and I was hugging her back, the rush of emotion much stronger than I'd anticipated. "Thank you. Thank you for coming."

"You're welcome," I said as we stepped back from one another.

She took me in. "You look exactly like I thought you would."

"I'll take that as a compliment."

"It is."

"And you look like your mom. I hope it's okay saying that."

"More than okay." Tess smiled. "God, it's so good to see you. Come inside."

The house was open concept, which I immediately appreciated, and nicely furnished. There seemed to be an emphasis on the kitchen, a comfortably sprawling space featuring a long counter with a half dozen chairs and a large reclaimed oak table beyond. A man sat drinking coffee at the counter. He was our age and dressed in a nice suit, his coat hanging from the back of a chair. His tie was loosened, and the top two buttons of his collar were undone. He was lanky and handsome in a rough-hewn way.

"Nora, this is Jacob Leighton—my attorney and very close friend," Tess said.

I shook hands with him. "Great to meet you."

"Likewise. Tess has told me a lot about you."

"Uh-oh."

"All good things, rest assured." He appraised me. "So you were in state child services?"

"Yes, for quite a few years, but I'm a family advocate now."

"Utmost respect for anyone who's worked in CPS. Tough job."

"It can be."

"Well we're very glad to have you on board. We were just finishing up the parenting plan for tomorrow's hearing. If you can think of anything else to add, be my guest." He grabbed his coat from the chair and started for the entry. "Gotta run, but I'll call you later," he said to Tess.

"I'll walk you out," Tess said.

"Great to meet you, Nora."

"You too."

I was left alone for a moment to take in the rest of the house, get a feel for the family who lived here. Or at least the remnants of it. A living room opened off the kitchen into a dining/sitting area giving unimpeded views of the backyard and surrounding woods through floor-to-ceiling windows.

"So . . ."

Tess had returned. We stood facing one another, an awkward silence almost thick enough to touch. We took each other in again, the moment so surreal neither of us knew what to say. Finally we both laughed.

"Weird, right?" I said.

"So weird. But good weird. I'm really glad you're here." We both smiled, and she finally looked away, gesturing at the view. "What do you think?"

"It's beautiful. Reminds me a lot of my place, actually."

"We were the first ones in the development when it was built, got our choice of lots, and picked this one. It's the quietest. I love the sound of the wind in the pines." Tess's expression darkened.

"Jacob seems nice," I said.

She brightened again. "He's the best. Great lawyer and better friend. We've known each other since college. Actually all of us have been friends since then. Until now." Her smile became brittle, and she blinked back sudden tears. I took one of her hands. "God, I'm sorry. I told myself I wasn't going to break down in front of you. At least not the moment you walked through the door."

"It's fine. That's why I'm here. Let's sit."

We sat in a pair of comfortable chairs upholstered in white linen. Tess perched on the edge of her seat and dabbed absently at her nose with a tissue. Her posture, the way her hair fell across her face, even the way she moved reminded me so much of Diedre I couldn't look away. To think the little girl I'd shared secrets with had become this woman was jarring. "I pictured us catching up and reconnecting when you got here, not spiraling into all this right away."

"We'll catch up later, don't worry. We have time."

"I don't really know where to start. It's all been a nightmare."

"You told me the basics about what happened with Neil and this student who was killed. What were things like leading up to it?"

Tess let out a long breath. "I don't know. Tense, I guess. For the last year or more it wasn't good between us. Little stuff at first. You know when you're in a relationship and something subtle changes and you can't quite put your finger on what's different? Like that. Then I started noticing how quiet he was. He wouldn't answer me sometimes when I'd ask him something. He was miles away. He quit touching me. I didn't know what was wrong. I thought it was me."

"Before that things were good?"

"They were great. We were . . . really happy." Her voice cracked. "Sorry, God, I'm sorry."

"Don't apologize, it's okay."

"I guess I still feel like I did something wrong. I don't know. I tried restarting the relationship. Nothing worked. Even Kendra sensed it." Kendra. I glanced over my shoulder, and Tess must've read my mind. "She's at school. She'll be home after her art class."

"Was he different with her too?"

"Yeah. More remote. They used to do a ton of things together. Always bike riding or hiking the moraine, kayaking, lots of outdoorsy stuff. We'd do weekends up at our cabin, just the three of us. But all that stopped, and he kind of slipped away." Something changed behind Tess's eyes, her gaze growing distant. "I saw him watching her one night."

"Watching her? Kendra?"

Tess nodded. "One night I woke up, and he wasn't in bed. It was like three in the morning. I went out in the hall, and he was standing at the door of her room, just staring at her in the dark."

A chill settled between my shoulder blades and traveled downward. I recalled footsteps in the dark when I was young, coming closer and stopping at the door to my room. Unmoving for what felt like hours. How terrified I'd been, waiting for something to happen. What, I didn't know, couldn't get myself to imagine.

"What is it?" Tess asked.

I sat up straighter. "Nothing. Just thinking."

She studied me for a second, then went on. "I said his name, and he startled, like I'd caught him doing something terrible. Looking back it really scares me. With what happened to that girl . . ."

"Was he ever violent in any way? Aggressive?"

"No. I mean, we fought, but it was just raised voices. Normal stuff."

"Did you ever suspect him of abusing Kendra? Sexually or otherwise?"

Tess recoiled slightly. "No, nothing like that."

"Sorry, I'm trying to cover all the bases here." I changed tack. "You said on the phone you thought he was having an affair."

She nodded, sniffling again. "He spent longer hours at the university. He'd shut his phone off and just be gone. When I asked him about it, he said he was just driving around, trying to clear his head. But this girl, she was only twenty-two, a few students had seen them talking in the halls, in the parking lot. One of the custodians said he saw Neil getting into her car one day."

"I'm sorry."

"It's the least of all this. I could handle my husband cheating on me, but him being a murderer is . . . I cannot let him have custody of Kendra." She swallowed and her gaze hardened. "I won't."

6

Transcript of *Poe, the Man and the Myths: A lecture series with Professor Neil Grayson*, Part 1—presented by Ridgewood University in coordination with College Partnership Programming.

Tragic. That single word can sum up much of Edgar Allan Poe's life. Tragedy seemed to follow him almost from birth. After his father abandoned him, and his mother died while he was only two, Poe was fostered by a wealthy merchant family in Richmond, Virginia. And so, one would think, he would've had as good a chance as any to find success and happiness. But it was not to be.

Much of his life has been written and rewritten, and I won't digress into a drawn-out biography. That's not what this series of lectures is about. Instead we'll study the artist through his art. We'll interpret both the famous and more obscure works to see if we can gain some kind of insight into the mind behind them.

It's said that writers especially imprint part of themselves on the page. And if that's true, Mr. Poe appeared to be a deeply unhappy person. Did that unhappiness drive the genius to creation? Must an artist suffer to make good art? Is there meaning in melancholy, or for so many people is suffering simply a default human condition?

Doubtless, his sadness and obsession can be felt throughout his work. It ripples outward and has found its way here to us, nearly one hundred seventy-five years later.

I would say that is the very definition of haunting, wouldn't you?

7

Reacquainting yourself with someone you used to know is like recalling a dance you haven't tried in a long time.

At first it's awkward and clumsy, you're stepping on each other's feet, you're out of time. But then slowly muscle memory takes over. You find a rhythm. The old moves return like the echoes they are, and pretty soon you're both moving together, and the music makes sense.

That's how it was with Tess and me. She made us lunch, and while she chopped lettuce and cold chicken for a salad, we chatted in starts and fits. By the time we sat at the table, I'd learned a little more about the intervening years of her life.

She'd moved to Boston after her mother was killed, living with her father's parents—a strict but kind older couple who raised her and didn't balk too much when she wanted to return to her birthplace after graduating high school. They even put her through college, where she got a business degree and met Neil her senior year. Before they had Kendra they'd gone on a tour of Europe, went skydiving, and even summitted Mount Hood.

"All on Neil's dime," she said as we ate. "His parents were fairly well off before they passed away. Our cabin was theirs too. They lived in Portland but came here a lot when Neil was young. Anyway, enough about me and my woes. You haven't said two words about yourself."

"I mean, you can read about our family on Wikipedia under *mass shooters*. Not much else to tell." Tess blanched. "Sorry. It's been a part of my life ever since it happened, so I'm a little calloused. I say shit like that without thinking." It was true. But there was also some self-defensiveness in being abrasive. A way of filing off the edges before they cut you. Because after a while explaining how your father locked you and your two brothers in a tiny closet for the better part of a month before taking a high-powered rifle to the roof of his office building to mow down coworker after coworker becomes imprisoning, not freeing. Especially when your older brother starved to death making sure you and your younger brother survived. Not really the kind of thing you want to relive any more than you had to.

"No, it's okay. Like I said before, I'm ashamed I didn't reach out sooner. You must think I'm a monster since I only got in touch when I needed help."

"Oh, definitely." I held on to a straight face as long as I could, then laughed. Tess's look of horror collapsed, and she joined me. "Listen, I know how hard it is to deal with other people's tragedy. Who knows what to say? Most times there isn't anything. I don't blame you at all."

She nodded and took a long sip of water. "That's what I try to tell myself now. Why my friends quit calling and I get looks in town." Her eyes took on a fresh sheen of tears. "I feel so alone now. I don't know what to do."

I took her hand, squeezed it. "We'll figure it out, okay? Don't worry about what other people think; they're going to think it, anyway. I learned that young."

Tess dried her eyes and stood, leaving the room. I wondered for a second if I'd said the wrong thing, but then she was back, holding a stack of folded pages and what looked like postcards or glossy photos. She set the pile down between us. "I didn't know how you'd react on the phone, so I kept it brief on purpose. But these"—she tapped the papers—"are letters from your mom to mine. There's a few postcards from the times she left your dad, and some photos. They're yours now."

I stared at the letters. Couldn't look anywhere else. There was a tightening in my center bordering on pain. All the years wondering . . . and now there might be answers sitting a few inches away. Did I really want to know them? Would it change anything?

I reached out, pissed at the tremble in my hand, and touched the pile. Then pushed it gently toward Tess. "I think I'm good. For now, at least."

Her faint smile faded. "You really don't want to know?"

"Oh no, I really do. But there are things better left alone. And I think this is one of them."

"But if you just read, you'll see there was more—" She'd started to unfold the top letter, and I covered her hand with my own.

"Tess? No."

She sat back, crestfallen. No words.

I glanced around. Maybe this had been a mistake. I wanted to help, but not at the cost of torpedoing my own life.

"I can't say I get it because knowing what I know now there's things you have to experience to really understand," Tess said. "But I'll tell you what—these will be here whenever you want them. In the meantime, is it too early for wine?"

"Never."

She grinned. "I'm glad because there's a red blend I've been leaning on pretty hard for the last few months. It's been my only true friend." She stood and disappeared into the walk-in pantry.

I found myself reaching to touch the letters again, then pulled my hand back to my lap and kept it there.

———

The sun moved into the backyard, and we followed. We sat and drank wine on Tess's patio, and as the alcohol did its work, the comfortable flow between us resumed.

I filled her in on my life, the *Reader's Digest* version, anyway, ending with my becoming a family advocate.

"I followed that Volk thing while it was going on," Tess said, pouring herself a second glass of wine.

"Everyone did."

"What happened with that girl and her family, it was so terrible."

"You don't know the half of it."

"Didn't I see something recently about the mother who survived—Kaylee? Wasn't there another scandal?"

"Apparently, she cheated on her new husband and made threats against him and his girls. He divorced her, and it was very messy. She lost a lot of sponsors and subscribers from her channel. Last I heard she shut her account down and left the state."

"I don't mean to be judgmental, but she seemed like the worst."

"The very worst." I drained my glass and Tess refilled it. "Enough of that, and not to bring everything up again, but are you ready for the hearing tomorrow?"

"We think so. The parenting plan we've got is really good. I mean, this is Kendra's home, she needs to stay here. And with all Neil's been accused of—"

"You know you can't rely on that. Since the DA dropped the case, anything to do with it will be inadmissible in the custody hearing."

Tess sighed. "Jacob said the same thing, but I mean, Neil's guilty. Everyone can see that."

"Doesn't matter."

"I think it does." Tess leaned forward. "This is a small town, and God knows people talk. The judge isn't insular. There's no way he'll give Neil partial custody. Maybe supervised visits, but we're going to fight that too."

"And Kendra? How has she been coping with all this?"

She looked down, turning her wineglass in circles. "That's something I was hoping you could help with. She won't talk to me about it.

Whenever I try, she pretends she didn't hear and changes the subject. I've brought her to therapy, but same thing. Like a vault." Tess's throat worked soundlessly. "I'm really worried about her. I don't know what to do. Maybe you can give me some ideas, or maybe talk to her?"

"I'm not sure I'll have any better luck, but I can try."

"Thank you. Really, I don't think you realize how much it means to have you here."

I was about to reply when the sliding door opened and a girl stepped outside. Her hair was dark like Tess's, but it curled about her head in a mass a few clips attempted to hold back. Her wide eyes were a stunning shade of green, drinking in everything she looked at. And now she was looking at me.

Kendra was home.

8

"Honey, this is Nora. She's who I told you might come to stay for a while."

Kendra glanced from me to her mother, then back again. "Hi," she said.

"Hi, Kendra. Nice to meet you."

"Why don't you get yourself something to drink and come sit with us?" Tess said.

"I'm not thirsty."

"Are you hungry? There's—"

"Can I have my tablet?"

"It's kind of rude to hide inside when we have a guest."

I shook my head. "It's okay. Really."

Tess sighed. "Go ahead. How was art—" Tess started to ask, but Kendra was already sliding the door shut behind her. "Yeah, like that."

"Don't worry about it. I think she's reacting like any nine-year-old would to all this."

"You think so?"

"I do. Kids have defense mechanisms like all of us. Probably better than adults. Maybe because their imaginations haven't been chipped away yet."

"I hope you're right. I just want her to be like she was before."

"She may not be." Tess's eyes snapped up to mine. "And you can't really expect her to."

She deflated. "I guess not."

"But that isn't to say things won't get better."

Tess reached for the last of the bottle, then stopped. "Probably shouldn't get sloshed the night before a custody hearing, right?"

"Wouldn't be a good look."

"Let's get you settled then."

I hesitated as she rose from her seat. "Oh, you were thinking I'd stay here?"

"Of course. Why, were you planning on getting a hotel room?"

"Yeah, actually."

"Oh no, you have to stay with us. I'm not going to have you come all the way here and then spend money on a hotel. Absolutely not. There's a guest bedroom just sitting there empty."

I started to say something else, to protest a little more, but Tess was already moving toward the house. I followed.

The guest bedroom was down the hall from the living area, nice and open, high ceilings with a view of the street. "This is really great. But I think I might be more comfortable in a hotel," I said.

Tess stood in the doorway, hands clasped together. She was smiling tightly, looking past me out the window. "Okay, if that's how you feel. I don't want to force you into anything. But . . ." She bit her lower lip. "I was really hoping you'd stay. It would make me feel so much better to have someone else here."

What at first I'd interpreted as disappointment was really something else. Nervousness. Fear. "Is something wrong?"

She brought her gaze back to me. "I've seen his car out there a few times at night," she said. "At the end of the street."

"Neil?"

She nodded. "He parks so he can watch the house. I've called the cops, but he's always gone by the time they get here." The same chill from earlier returned and crawled down the back of my neck. "I know there's nothing I can do, I've tried. Jacob told me there's no basis for a restraining order. But I keep thinking of him watching Kendra sleep." She breathed out a laugh. "The only solace is knowing his handgun is here in the house. Not that it makes me feel much safer. But you staying would."

I looked at her and saw the little girl I used to know. My friend, alone and afraid. Something inside me fought for a second and died. "I'll go get my bags."

———

The neighborhood came to life as the afternoon wore to evening. A few cars turned into drives, and children ran in yards, enjoying the warming spring air. Dogs barked and people sat on porches. The sun slid behind the highest peak, draping the valley in shadow.

I sat at the little desk in the guest room before my laptop. I'd heard back from Sharon Weisman, who was more than willing to take on Gayle and Joel's case and had even secured an open slot for a hearing next week. *Given the current info, I think we're in a good place to get their daughter back,* Sharon wrote. *Am meeting with them tomorrow and will fill you in. Are you getting the feeling the grandmother was following them and waiting for a mistake to pounce on?*

Yes, that was exactly what I thought. I was pretty sure someone had tipped off the grocery-store employee about Ivy being in the shopping-cart basket, and I was positive that same someone had alerted child services to the incident. A picture was slowly forming of Gayle's grandmother Arlene. Someone unable to keep from meddling in a situation where they weren't needed. I'd met a hundred Arlenes while at CPS. And the frightening thing was most times they won. Because the law was slanted away from the marginalized and toward the privileged.

Who do you think wrote the laws to begin with?

"Supper's ready!" Tess called. I shut my laptop and went to eat. As I made my way down the hall, something I hadn't noticed before caught my attention. There were very faint rectangular outlines on the wall here and there along with tiny holes near their tops.

Framed pictures had once hung there, and it took me all of a few seconds to guess what they'd been of. Family photos of Neil and Tess and Kendra together in better times. Now all taken down and stored away or maybe even tossed out with the trash.

"Hope you don't mind, I ordered in," Tess said, opening a few steaming cardboard containers on the table. "There's this great Chinese place in town we adore. Don't we, Kendra?"

Kendra sat at the end of the table, holding her tablet. "It's really good," she said without looking up.

"Sounds great," I said, taking a seat.

The food was fantastic—soup dumplings with a side of sour soup and stir-fry. The conversation—not so much.

Tess attempted to draw Kendra out of her shell while the girl remained polite but removed. She answered questions with one or two words and ate mechanically, all the while glancing my way as if to make sure I wasn't getting any closer. Tension was another guest at the table.

"Is tomorrow about whether or not I get to see Dad again?" Kendra asked, breaking a spate of silence.

Tess and I shared a look. "Well, it's like I said before, honey, we're going to talk to the judge and see what he has to say," she said.

"Do I get to tell him what I think?"

"Right now we're figuring out if—"

"Because I think I should get to decide."

"Well, there will probably be a day soon when we can talk about that, but at this point the adults have to figure out what's best."

Kendra surveyed her mother for a beat, then sank back into the e-book on her tablet. "Do you like to read, Kendra?" I asked, trying to shift the dynamic.

"I like to be called Kenny," she said. "And yes. I read."

I ignored the faint irritated sound from Tess's direction. "What are you reading now?"

"Edgar Allan Poe."

"'Once upon a midnight dreary, while I pondered weak and weary,'" I said in a creepy whisper.

Kenny's eyes brightened. "'Over many a quaint and curious volume of forgotten lore.'"

"'While I nodded, nearly napping, suddenly there came a tapping...'"

"'As of someone gently rapping—'"

"'—rapping at my chamber door,'" we said in unison, and broke out laughing. I glanced Tess's way. Her expression was strange, something between amusement and confusion.

"My dad taught classes on him," Kenny said.

"Oh, that's interesting."

"He's his favorite writer of all time. He did a lecture on him, and it's on YouTube with like fifty thousand views."

"Impressive."

Kenny paused, working up to something. "Do you have a favorite story by him?"

I pretended to think. "Probably 'The Tell-Tale Heart.' What's yours?"

"'The Cask of Amontillado,'" she said without hesitation, her voice rising in excitement. "When Montresor takes Fortunato down to the catacombs and chains him to the wall and starts sealing him in, brick by brick, and Fortunato yells, '*For the love of God, Montresor!*'"

"Okay, that's probably enough," Tess said and stood from the table, taking her half-full plate with her. "We don't yell at the table."

Kenny's eyes dimmed. She picked at her food for a second, then grabbed her tablet and left the table. A second later she was up the stairs, and the faint thump of a door closing echoed down.

Tess stood leaning over the sink, head tilted forward.

I brought my dishes over and set them on the counter. "When did she start wanting to go by a nickname?"

"I don't know. A few months before Neil was arrested. He thought it was fine, but I never cared for it."

"I thought it might've been in reaction to everything. A shift in identity to protect herself."

"No."

A silence grew. "She was just opening up."

"I know."

"Probably a way to feel like she's still connected with her dad."

"I know that, it's just—she doesn't know this, but Neil gave Allie Prentiss a book of Poe's works. He even inscribed it."

"Oh. I see."

"But that's not the worst of it. The book was the evidence they found at our cabin." Tess straightened and faced me. She was very pale. "It had her blood on it."

9

The courtroom was what you'd expect of any rural mountain town like Mutiny.

It was set up church-like, with pews backing two modest tables for the prosecution and defense. Low cheap ceilings and lots of wood paneling, especially behind the judge's bench. I took everything in along with the low babble of the dozen or so people in the room as Tess's hand found mine and squeezed. I squeezed back. She looked like she hadn't slept five minutes the night before.

We sat at the left-hand table with Jacob nearest the aisle. Across from us was Neil's lawyer, a woman named Yolanda Beech, and beside her, Neil himself.

I'd seen pictures of him on the web, but they were somewhat grainy, all except his staff photo for the university, and that was at least three years old. He was a compact man with sandy hair and wire-rimmed glasses. His features were angular, partially from weight loss, I guessed, and his eyes were the same electric green as Kenny's.

He glanced my way, and we shared a look before his counsel touched his shoulder, whispering something into his ear.

"All rise," the bailiff said. We did. "The Honorable Judge Rein presiding." The judge entered—a white-haired man of about seventy, stoop-shouldered in his robes. He settled onto the bench. "Be seated."

"Good morning," Rein said, shuffling through sheaves of paperwork. "Today we're reviewing case number 48324, complaint for custody of a minor between Theresa Jane Grayson and Neil Elliot Grayson. I believe I have all the necessary documents submitted by both counsels unless either of you has something to add?"

"No, Your Honor," Jacob said. Neil's lawyer echoed the same.

"I am to understand mediation was attempted to come to an agreement?"

"It was, Your Honor," Jacob said. "The parties couldn't find common ground."

Rein made a quiet sound in the back of his throat. "It appears Theresa Grayson is petitioning for full custody."

"Correct, Your Honor," Jacob said.

"And Neil Grayson is petitioning for shared custody?"

"Yes, Your Honor," Beech said.

Rein considered the paperwork before him for a time, then looked up. "Mr. Leighton, I'm not seeing anything disqualifying here for a ruling of partial custody. Would you care to enlighten me?"

Jacob stood. "Your Honor, if you'll note, Mr. Grayson has been unemployed since March twenty-fifth of this year. My client is concerned about financial support for their daughter as well as home stability."

"Mrs. Grayson, you're residing at 4500 South Lake Drive, correct?"

Tess shifted in her seat. "Yes, Your Honor."

"And Mr. Grayson, where are you living?"

Neil was slow to answer, and when he did his voice was a rasp. "My family's cabin. Your Honor," he added.

"And this cabin is the other residence listed on page two?"

"Yes, Your Honor," Jacob said.

The judge was silent for a bit, flipping papers back and forth as he read. Tess was no longer holding my hand, but I could feel the thrum of her body beside me.

"Mrs. Grayson," Rein said, "you and your daughter have stayed at the cabin in question before while you and Mr. Grayson were married, is that correct?"

"Yes, Your Honor. But—"

"And were the furnishings suitable at that time for your daughter?"

Tess hesitated. "Yes, Your Honor."

"And has anything changed in the interim you're aware of?"

"What's changed is he killed someone," Tess said.

There were a few quick intakes of breath in the room, and a murmur flowed through the people behind us. Jacob closed his eyes as the judge banged his gavel.

"Order!" Rein said. The room quieted. "Mrs. Grayson, I'm not sure if your counsel informed you that any prior criminal charges that have been dismissed are inadmissible in this hearing, but if not, he made a vast oversight."

"How can you just ignore the fact a woman's dead?" Tess said, starting to rise from her seat. I grasped her shoulder and pulled her back down.

"Mrs. Grayson, you'll keep your personal accusations to yourself while in this court, or I'll have you removed. Is that understood?"

Tess opened her mouth, glanced first at me, then at Jacob, who shook his head. Finally she nodded and shrank into her seat, staring down at the tabletop.

"I need an affirmation from you, Mrs. Grayson," Rein said.

"Yes, Your Honor," Jacob said. "She understands."

Rein gave our table a death stare, then went back to the paperwork. The seconds ticked by, the room filling with undeniable pressure as if we were descending through atmospheres. Finally Rein cleared his throat and looked up. "Mr. Grayson, it appears you are liable for child support and alimony per the conditions of your divorce. Given your lack of employment, do you foresee being unable to fulfill these obligations?"

"No, Your Honor," Neil said.

"Then without any other objections it is the court's ruling that Mr. Grayson will be permitted partial custody as per the parental plan submitted by his counsel beginning next week on the fifteenth following the filing and recording of this petition."

The gavel banged down again.

———

"I can't fucking believe it," Tess said.

We sat on the veranda of a small café a few blocks down from the courthouse. The air was crisp, and a breeze toyed with the umbrella over our table. In the distance Lake Carver glittered in a thousand points.

"We knew this was going to be a tough one to win," Jacob said.

Tess shook her head. She'd been doing it on and off since the ruling, denial pulling at her like puppet strings. "He's a murderer, and they're going to let him spend time with Kendra alone." Tears welled up in her eyes, and she finished off the tequila sunrise she'd ordered.

"He's still a person of interest," Jacob said. "You never know what might happen in the future."

"I was on the city crime-prevention committee; I know the DA. He's a coward." Tess signaled the waiter for another drink. "He won't do anything."

I played with the straw in my iced tea, beginning to wish I were anywhere else. Beginning to wish I hadn't come at all.

"Listen, we can appeal. Especially if we notice anything wrong after he gains custody," Jacob said.

"Oh yeah, we can try to fix things once he loses it again. Did you ever think it might be too late then?" Her drink had arrived, and she gulped half of it down.

"Hey," I said, "let's take a step back and reassess. There are still options, and Jacob's laying them out for you." Jacob shot me a thankful look.

"Take a step back? Are you serious? You can't be. I thought you of all people would be furious."

"It's upsetting, but getting drunk and making a scene in public won't solve anything."

Tess seemed to come back to herself and glanced around at the tables half-filled with people. Some were openly staring. The fight seemed to go out of her, and she slumped. "Take me home," she said quietly. "Please."

———

The house was empty and quiet when we got there, Kenny still mercifully at school. I was grateful she didn't have to see her mother wobble to the kitchen counter and pour herself a brimming glass of wine.

"You probably shouldn't do that," I said, picking up her suit jacket from where she'd let it fall on the way in.

"Yeah, probably not," she said, sitting on one of the stools and taking a long sip. Her hair had come undone from several pins, and mascara pooled beneath her eyes. She looked beaten.

I sighed and sat next to her. "I'm really sorry."

"Me too." She looked down. "It's so strange to realize your life is insubstantial. So thin it can come apart at any moment. I don't know what to do."

"You do what Jacob says. You can appeal, and there's a possibility things will go your way."

"And if they don't?"

I had nothing to say to that. Sometimes the wicked won. The end.

"This can't be real. It's not fair."

I thought of my mother leaving. My father killing and dying. Paul gone forever. "I'm not sure fairness and life coexist too often."

Tess drained her glass and stood. She swayed in place, and I put an arm out to steady her. "Here, let's lie on the couch. You can rest before Kenny gets home." I led her to the couch, and she sank into it, kicking off her heels.

"Thank you," she said, reaching out to touch my face. I kept from recoiling. Not because I didn't want her to touch me, but because I hadn't expected it. I still had trouble with physical contact at times but pushed it back now. "You've been so good, so strong."

"Just rest. We'll talk when you wake up."

"Wait." She grasped my arm as I started to move away. "Options. You said we have options. You know what to do, you get kids out of bad situations. Right?"

"Sure. But that's not—"

"You know how. You know what questions to ask, and you could—you could expose him. You could figure out a way to keep Kendra safe."

Internally I was already packing my bags to get back on the road. As much as I'd wanted to reconnect with Tess and possibly learn more about my mother, this wasn't what I'd had in mind. Moral support? Sure. Reminiscing? Fine. Weaponizing my experience against her ex-husband? Not so much.

"I really don't think that's a good idea."

"But you said you'd help me." Tess's words were merging, slurring into one long plea.

"I did, and I want to. But this—"

"I'm afraid. Afraid of what he'll do to her when they're alone. So afraid . . ." She was drifting, drifting, gone. Her hand loosened from my arm, and I laid it by her side. She snored softly.

I stood there, half of me down the hall and gathering my things. It would be easy to pack up and go while she was passed out. Instead I went to the counter, eyed the bottle of wine, and poured myself a glass as large as Tess's. Drank. I looked at my friend, then gazed out the front window to the street where Neil had parked and watched the house he used to live in, watched the family he used to have. I thought of him standing at Kenny's bedroom door while she slept, thought of a blood-flecked book cover.

"Damn it," I said, and drained my glass.

10

Transcript of *Poe, the Man and the Myths: A lecture series with Professor Neil Grayson,* Part 4—presented by Ridgewood University in coordination with College Partnership Programming.

In "The Tell-Tale Heart" we're told the narrator has committed a perfect crime. Their oversensitivity has driven them to murder the old man with the vulture eye, and now his body lies beneath the floorboards where no one will think to look. Not even when the police come calling and set their chairs above the very place the corpse rests.

But what really caused the narrator to commit murder? We're told there was no motive other than the vulture eye, which can be interpreted as God, the conscience, or the universe itself. To me the tell-tale heart in the story doesn't belong to the victim, but to the killer. The act of aggression and murder is the result of a secret, possibly a secret even unto themselves. Secrets drive all of us in both obvious and subtle ways, and here the secret drove them first to murder, then to madness and confession.

On the other end of the spectrum is "The Cask of Amontillado." Here the narrator's motive to kill Fortunato is also a secret—some unnamed offense to his family. And in this instance, he gets away with the crime. Montresor's satisfaction overshadows any guilt from beyond the grave, and a new secret arises in the form of a bricked-up alcove in a catacomb—a very symbolic image indeed.

Did Poe have secrets? Many, I'm sure. He was as mysterious and unknowable as any one of us here today.

11

I paused the video, and Neil Grayson froze on the screen, half leaning against a podium in the middle of a small stage.

I'd spent the last couple of hours sitting at the kitchen counter, watching the lectures Kenny had mentioned the night before. They were from the prior fall, and Neil looked like a different man. His clothes didn't hang from him, and his manner was easy and engaging, the type of professor who you'd remember years after graduating. He was handsome, too, with longer hair and an inviting smile. I could see why Allie Prentiss might've been drawn to him.

It was chilling watching these videos now knowing what had happened to her. What he'd been accused of doing. I pictured that same smile on his face as he battered the young woman to death, blood speckling the lenses of his glasses, the whiteness of his teeth.

A chime sounded beside me, and I flinched.

Tess's phone. She'd left it on the counter next to her empty wineglass. There was an incoming call from *Devon* on the screen. Tess shifted on the couch but kept sleeping. The phone went quiet. Ten seconds later a voice mail icon appeared. A minute after that a text message from the same person. Where are you? Call when you can. I felt a little dirty snooping on her phone. But only a little. It was lying right out in the open; anyone could see what was on the screen.

Turning back to the computer, I reflected on the lectures I'd seen so far. As someone who enjoyed Poe's work, I thought they were engaging and insightful if not on the indulgent side. Neil seemed to not only idolize Poe and his work but almost identify with him. There were small key moments and words he used that crossed the border of scholarly into brotherly territory. But I did find his interpretation of "The Tell-Tale Heart" interesting, and maybe significant.

Because I believed in a darker heart. One residing in all of us. It beats in time with our own but holds secrets instead of blood. Our desires, our deepest urges, our truths. It whispers to us, and sometimes we hear it clearly. Sometimes we listen.

What did Neil's darker heart tell him? And why?

A hand fell on my shoulder.

I spun, knocking it away, and Tess stumbled back, eyes wide. "Whoa, sorry—just me."

"Shit." I relaxed. "Thought you were still sleeping."

"Passed out, you mean. God, I'm thirsty." She went to the fridge and got herself a glass of water. Drank it down. "Sorry about losing it."

"Understandable."

"Is it?" She sighed. "You were right earlier. I need to step back and reassess. There has to be something we can do."

I toyed with my empty wineglass. "Before you fell asleep you asked if I could use my experience at CPS in any way."

"Oh God, did I? That's not fair to you. Forget it."

"No, I want to help. And I think I can."

"Really?"

"Maybe. There's a few things I can check into. No promises, though."

Tess swallowed thickly and came around the counter to hug me. I hesitated, then hugged her back, still not used to embracing or being embraced this much.

"Anything would be amazing."

"That's setting the bar pretty low."

She laughed. "What do we do first?"

I closed my laptop. "When does Kenny get home?"

———

Over the static hush of the shower running, Tess was talking to someone.

I paused at the juncture of the upstairs hallway near the main bedroom door. Behind it Tess murmured, but the words were lost in the hiss of water.

I moved on, feeling the earlier dirt of reading her text level up to grime. Whoever she was speaking with wasn't my concern. My concern was behind the bedroom door in front of me. I took a breath and knocked.

"Come in," Kenny said.

Her room was spacious with a single dormer looking out onto the street, a cushioned reading nook before it. Her bed sat against the opposite wall beside an ornate writing desk. A bookshelf above the desk almost overflowed. Some clothes dripped from a hamper and pooled on the floor. Kenny sat against the foot of her bed, tablet on her lap, a stylus in one hand.

"Hey, there."

"Hi."

"Mind if I sit down?" She gestured to a large beanbag, and I sat, sprawling slightly as the stuffing shifted beneath me. Kenny tried remaining stoic but giggled. "Way to make an old person feel old."

"You're not old. You're the same age as my mom, aren't you?"

"That's right."

"She said your birthdays were only four months apart."

"Yep. And when is your birthday?"

"Next month. I'll be ten."

"That's a great age," I said, unable to stop the rush of memories from my ninth year. Darkness. Hunger. The reek of filth. The fear. "Sorry, what?" Kenny had said something, and I'd been far away.

"I said do I get to see my dad now?"

Shit. "Well, that's really something you and your mom should talk about."

"I saw an empty wineglass in the dishwasher when I got home. Mom always has wine when she's nervous, so that must mean I get to see Dad again."

Double shit. "How would you feel about that?"

"Good. I mean, I miss him."

"I'm sure it's been really hard with all that's happened. How is school going?"

"School sucked before. The other kids don't like me. Now they just stare." She looked out the window. "Sometimes I think it's easier this way."

I regarded her and tried another tack. "What's your favorite thing to do with your dad?"

No hesitation. "Be up at our cabin."

"What do you do there?"

She brightened. "Lots of stuff. We hike and have bonfires. Ride bikes. There's this really awesome lookout nearby where you can see the whole valley. And if it's raining or whatever Dad makes a fire in the fireplace and cocoa, and we stay in and read."

"I was going to say I'm really impressed with you reading Poe. Not many kids your age would like his stuff."

"Sometimes I don't know the words, but I look them up." She paused. "Dad lets me read whatever I want. Mom doesn't like it, but he said that was one rule he grew up with he wanted to hand down to me. I can read any book in the house."

"That's pretty special."

Her expression dimmed, and I waited as she looked down at her lap, one hand spinning the stylus. "He didn't do it, you know. He didn't hurt that girl."

I kept my voice even, casual. "You don't think so?"

"He couldn't."

"Why?"

She stayed quiet so long I thought she wasn't going to answer. Then she said, "We were fishing one time, and I caught a lake trout. It was huge. Dad had to help reel it in. And when it got to the boat, it was all wore out and floating on its side. Dad took the hook out and started pushing it back and forth through the water, like this—" Kenny mimed holding a fish, pulling and pushing it through the air. "He said it would help wake it up. He kept moving it like that for a long time, even after I thought it was . . . but it finally started moving and swam away. He didn't give up."

Kenny opened her tablet to the drawing she'd been working on—a mountainscape with a castle nestled among the peaks—and resumed shading in some foothills. I was still forming my next question when she said, "I looked you up online."

"Oh."

"Do you think my dad did something bad because yours did?"

It was like a cerebral uppercut. I reeled internally. "No, I don't think that."

"So you think he's innocent?"

"I didn't say that, either."

She quit drawing and looked at me. "You're on my mom's side, though, right? That's why you came to stay."

"I'm on your side. That's actually what my job is."

She seemed to absorb this. The kid was whip-smart. As adults we tend to overlook children's insight, how truly keen they can be. I think that's because if we gave them as much credit as they deserve, we'd have to start thinking of them more as individuals and less as things to be molded into smaller versions of ourselves.

"If you're on my side, you'll believe me about my dad."

Movement out of the corner of my eye. Tess was there in the doorway. "Hey," she said. Her hair was wet and had darkened her T-shirt where it lay on her shoulders. "What's going on?"

"We're talking about Dad," Kenny said.

"Oh." Tess shot a look my way. "I thought we were going to wait until I was out of the shower for that."

"We were just getting to know each other a little better," I said, moving to the door. "I didn't say anything about court," I added, passing her. She seemed to relax. "I'll leave you alone."

I pulled the door shut behind me and went downstairs. Made myself a cup of tea. When it was ready, I took it to the front porch and sat on the steps.

The sky was overcast, clouds skimming the nearest peaks, the neighborhood falling into its evening routine. A few cars cruised past. Someone laughed loud and long. I turned over Kenny's words like rocks in a tumbler, looked for anything that stood out. There was nothing except for the kid being extremely perceptive.

Do you think my dad did something bad because yours did?

Christ. I hadn't felt that seen in a long time. I was setting my mug down when something caught my eye at the end of the street. Some flash of movement behind the windshield of a dark SUV parked near the development entrance. I stared at the car until the door behind me opened.

Tess came out and sat down. "How'd it go?" I asked.

"I told her, but she already knew."

"She's very smart."

"Too smart sometimes I think." Tess ran her fingertips over the step's edge. "She's happy she gets to see him."

"She doesn't think he did it."

"I don't know if she'd believe it even if she'd seen him do it. He walks on water as far as she's concerned."

"I don't know if that's fair."

She glanced away. "None of this is." After a drawn silence she said, "Did she tell you anything?"

"Nothing alarming. I didn't hear or see any signs of discomfort when talking about him."

"So what do we do next? We only have a little over a week until he gets custody."

"I have a couple ideas."

"You can tell me while I make dinner."

We stood and I touched her shoulder. "Hey, Tess?"

"Yeah?"

"Do you—" I shot a glance down the street. "Never mind." I followed her inside, giving the empty spot where the SUV had been a lingering look.

12

The patio outside the campus café was empty when I sat down with my coffee.

Ridgewood University sprawled around me in every direction. Most of the college's buildings were low stone constructions ceding to the grandeur of the surrounding mountains. On the west side the land sloped away dramatically to the lakeshore where a college park thrummed with some kind of activity that seemed to include most of the student body.

I sipped my drink and scanned the walkways and central court the café sat adjacent to. Only a few people moved through the early spring light, most heading in the direction of the park, where a collective cry rose and fell. I rubbed my eyes. Sleep had been sparse the night before. Looping dreams of searching for something in murky water. Over and over my hands went below the surface only to come up empty, black liquid running between my fingers even as I tried holding on to it.

Tess had been distant at dinner, answering in a few sentences and only becoming engaged once Kenny was in bed and I told her my idea for a path forward to keep Neil from gaining custody. Before we'd both turned in, I noticed how drawn she looked, how she'd seemed to age years since the morning's verdict.

A clack of approaching heels caught my attention.

A young woman with long dark hair made her way toward my table. She wore a sweater belted at the waist over leggings and knee-high boots. A leather bag was slung over one shoulder. I stood.

"Melody?"

"Mrs. McTavish?"

"God no. Not *Mrs*. Probably never that," I said, shaking hands with her. She indulged me with a polite smile. "Do you want anything?"

"I'll grab a coffee."

While Melody Townsend ordered at the nearby window, I organized my thoughts. She came back and swept her hair dramatically over one shoulder before taking a sip from her cup.

"Thanks so much for meeting me on short notice," I said.

"It's fine. There's really not much going on other than the spring jamboree down at the lake. Classes are all canceled for the day." She assessed me. "So you're a friend of Mrs. Grayson?"

"I am. I'm also a family advocate, like I mentioned on the phone."

"I'm not really sure what I can help with. I already told the police everything I know."

"I wanted to get your insight on some things concerning Mr. Grayson since you probably knew him better than anyone on campus."

She glanced away across the court, then half shrugged. "Okay."

"How long were you his assistant?"

"Two years. I applied right after I started working on my PhD."

"You must be close now."

"I get my doctorate in a few weeks."

"Exciting."

"I mean, yeah, but this whole thing has totally colored the experience. Being a murderer's protégé isn't quite the résumé boost you'd think it is."

"So you think he's guilty?"

She looked startled. "Of course. I mean they saw him in her neighborhood when she was killed. He had a book with her blood on it."

"Well, I wanted to ask you about before all that happened—was there anything in your time knowing him that stood out to you? Anything strange? Did he ever behave oddly or violently?"

"No. That's what makes it so much creepier, right? I mean he was totally normal up to that point."

"So he never did anything to make you feel uncomfortable?"

"No. And, I mean, I wouldn't have been surprised. Do you know how many faculty members hit on students? Like I could've put myself through college if I had a dollar for every time a professor said something suggestive to me." She rolled her eyes. "But Professor Grayson—he never made any moves, and he could've since we worked late lots of evenings. He walked me out to my car when it was dark. I always felt really comfortable around him."

I absorbed this. "Did you ever hear anyone else talk about him? Any rumors?"

"Nothing until this spring. A few kids mentioned seeing him and the Prentiss girl together a lot. But like I said, no one would've raised an eyebrow if a professor was hitting on a student. It's against university policy, but it happens quite a bit."

"And did you notice anything around that time? Did his behavior change in any way?"

Her expression darkened. "I mean, he was different the last year. Quieter. Still helpful and an absolute brain whenever it came to lit and whatnot, but different. He seemed—" Melody searched for a moment. "Just really sad. Like he was sinking inside himself. I don't know . . ."

Another tapestry of shouts rose in the distance. The sun slid behind a cloud. I tapped my fingers against the tabletop. This was everything I already knew. "And there's nothing else? Something you might've brushed off or overlooked?"

She started to shake her head, then paused. "Well, there was one thing."

I sat forward. "Okay."

"I mean it was probably nothing. I actually forgot about it until now. It was this winter. I figured out later what day it was, but at the time it didn't register. I was supposed to help grade some papers, and we were going to go over my thesis, but when I got to his office, he wasn't there. His coat was gone and so were his keys, so I knew he wasn't just somewhere else in the building. But—" She glanced around again.

"Go on. It's fine," I urged.

"There was a folded piece of paper along with his wallet and wedding ring on his desk, and it looked . . . weird."

"Weird how?"

"Everything was right in the middle of the desk so you couldn't miss it. The paper, the wallet, and his wedding ring were stacked perfectly on top of each other. It looked really strange, like he'd spent time arranging it." She cleared her throat. "Then he was there all of sudden, coming through the door and scooping it all up. He said he'd run uptown and forgotten his stuff."

I processed this. "You said you figured out what day it was. What did you mean by that?"

Melody straightened and toyed with her coffee cup. "I heard later a sheriff's deputy came by his office before I was there. That was the day he got served his divorce papers."

———

"Suicidal?"

Tess paused in putting the groceries away. She hadn't been home when I returned from the university, and I'd waited outside for the better part of an hour before she arrived looking harried but more herself than the night before.

"Very likely," I said, sitting down at the kitchen counter. "His behavior, along with the way he arranged his personal effects, paired with the timing of your divorce points to suicidal ideation." Tess looked away. "Listen, I'm not saying you drove him to it, just that all the factors indicate he was, or more importantly, *is* suicidal."

"So you're saying—"

"If we can prove he's suicidal, then we can get a stay of custody."

"For how long?"

"Maybe weeks, maybe months, years, who knows? The point is if we can prove he's a danger to himself, then he's a danger to Kenny by proxy."

Tess moved to one of the stools and sat. "I guess it fits. I just never thought he was hurting like that." She looked up. "But then again I never thought he'd kill someone either."

"People are unknowable, even the ones we love."

Her gaze grew distant. "So what do we do?"

"We build a case. We find out if he was seeking treatment and subpoena his therapist. We talk to his friends. When we think we have enough evidence we file an ex parte, which is basically an emergency application for sole custody. If we do this before he gets custody, we can put a hold on it."

"Isn't Melody's testimony enough?"

"No. It's circumstantial at best. If we had the piece of paper his wallet and ring were on top of, then maybe."

"You mean a suicide note."

"Right. But without professional testimony or hard evidence, it won't work."

Tess sat still for a moment, then started nodding. "I'll call Jacob, he can come for dinner tonight. We'll go from there." She reached out and laid a hand on my arm. "Thank you. This is the most hopeful I've felt in a long time."

I told her she was welcome. Helped put the rest of the groceries away and retired to my room. When the door was shut, I told myself it was a breakthrough, exactly what we needed to keep Kenny out of Neil's custody and in Tess's. The right thing.

So why did I feel so wrong?

13

Night is a stealthy assassin in the mountains.

At first it clings to the ridges and foothills, then eases down and settles into the valleys before deepening its hold to squeeze the last light out of evening.

We'd dined in the backyard beneath a string of softly glowing lights. Jacob had arrived shortly before six, kissing Tess lightly on the cheek before commenting on Kenny's newest drawing on her tablet, which she promptly tucked away. The food was good—short ribs braised in a sweet, tangy sauce, and fresh green beans. Tess poured generous glasses of white wine, and soft music came from the outdoor speakers. Even Kenny's mood seemed to improve, and she told us how her art teacher had complimented her on the latest technique they'd learned.

At Kenny's bedtime Tess disappeared inside, leaving Jacob and me alone. "Gorgeous night," I said when the silence bordered on awkward.

"It really is. Hard to believe we live here sometimes. Think we take it for granted." He sipped his wine. "So Tess mentioned over the phone what your idea was. It's good, it might work."

"I know it's not common, but there's precedent."

"Definitely. I'll get the paperwork going and reach out to the local psychiatrists."

Another pause. "Tess said Neil didn't have too many friends, that you were probably one of his closest."

Jacob sat forward, brow furrowing. "I guess I am. Was. We've known each other since college. I couldn't believe he had something like this in him."

"You never noticed anything before?"

"Nothing to make me think he could kill someone, no. I mean, Neil always had a flourish to him. A little showy, liked attention. But that was part of his charm. He was a presence in the room. He could talk intelligently about almost any subject, but get him on books?" Jacob made a sound like a jet taking off. "Gone."

So was my wine. I set the empty glass down. "I keep coming back to motive. If they were seeing each other, what would make him kill her?"

"Maybe she was threatening to tell Tess? Say something to the university? Could've been blackmailing him for money, who knows?"

"But wouldn't a smart guy like him know he'd immediately be a suspect?"

"He had everything to lose if she came clean. His relationship, his job, his reputation. His whole world would've crumbled. In the moment when faced with all that, he snapped."

I could see it. A man of status in the community. Perfect family, perfect life, suddenly upended by depression and a scandalous affair. He gets pushed to the edge, and instead of holding on, he goes over it.

Except . . .

"Nora?" Tess stood half in, half out of the house. "Kendra asked if you could say good night." She looked bemused and a little annoyed. "I told her she'd already said good night before coming in, but—"

"It's fine." I was already up and moving past her.

"I think she might want to talk more," Tess said. "About, you know . . ."

"The more she opens up, the better."

Tess nodded, but the irritation was still there. I got it. What mother wouldn't want to be their daughter's confidant? The one they always ran to when they were afraid? The one to protect them?

My eyes snagged on the stack of letters and pictures still sitting on the kitchen counter.

Well, there were always exceptions.

Upstairs, Kenny was tucked in, holding a hardcover loosely, a finger curled in, keeping her place. I sat on her bed. "I received a good night request from this room. Was it you who ordered, madam?"

She smiled but it faded. "I wanted to ask you something."

"Okay."

"After what your dad . . . what he did . . . how did you—"

"How did I move on?" She nodded. I took a beat, measuring the best answer. Weighing the truth. "Well, I had my brother, Stephen, and I really focused on taking care of him." I studied her young face in the low light. "But I'll be honest, I hid from it for a long time. I pretended like our lives started the moment we were put into foster care. Like it hadn't happened at all. Except my older brother, Paul, wasn't with us. I think I could've hidden from it forever if he'd still been alive. So after a while I did the opposite. I learned as much as I could about what happened. Why it did. How."

"Did it help?"

"It did. Some."

"What else helped to make you how you are now?"

I looked into her wide beseeching eyes. How do you tell someone who's broken they'll never be fully mended again? How do you say the strength on the outside camouflages the pain within? "There's some things that come along in life that change us forever. Good and bad. And there's no stopping them. It's *how* we change that's important. What we become afterward."

She absorbed this. I could almost hear the gears turning. Such a smart kid. "So I could be like you someday?"

"Better." Another smile. A yawn. I rose. "You should get to sleep. Your mom will be mad if I keep you up all night."

"Is Jacob still here?"

58

I paused at the doorway and looked back. "Yeah. Why?" A half shrug. "Do you not like him?"

"He's okay." She shifted. "I just don't want Mom to marry him."

I came back to the bed. "Honey, I think he's just a good friend. I wouldn't worry about that."

"They were kissing."

I took a step closer. "Kissing? When was this?"

"Last week. They thought I was asleep, but I came downstairs to get a drink. They were in the entry, and they were kissing."

Hot lead settled in the bottom of my belly. "Well, sometimes adults kiss. Sometimes it's a friend kiss." She seemed to believe it about as much as I did.

"He's not going to be my dad."

I reached out and smoothed her hair back. A gesture that seemed to surprise us both. Kenny looked up at me. "Your dad will always be your dad, okay?"

A faint nod. Another yawn.

I said good night and made my way out of the room in time to see a shadow retreating down the stairs. The back door opened and shut. Silence.

14

The Milky Way streamed in a billion points overhead.

The elevation combined with the lack of smog and light pollution heightened the stars to surreal levels of brilliance. Jacob was right, it was hard to believe people could live in places like this and not be in awe.

Jacob.

He'd taken his leave a few minutes after I'd come down from Kenny's room. I'd looked for signs of which one of them had been inside eavesdropping, but there was no way to tell. They both looked comfortable and in midconversation, so I'd said nothing.

The flames from the outdoor fireplace danced off my wineglass. It was half-full again, Tess refilling us both before she'd walked Jacob out. When she came back, I stiffened, seeing what was in her hand.

She set my mother's letters and photos down on the table between us. "I thought maybe you'd want to look through these now that you've settled in."

"Like I said, I'm really not ready for that."

"I know, but if you'd just let me explain—"

"Tess, please."

"I wouldn't push if I didn't think it was—"

"Kenny said she saw you and Jacob kissing."

Tess looked like she'd walked into a wall. Her mouth opened, then closed, and for the first time that night I realized she was more than a little tipsy. She was drunk. Maybe she'd been sneaking drinks while inside. "What?" She blinked and shook her head.

"She said she came downstairs last week and saw the two of you in the entryway." My heart was trying to breach my chest in hard, heavy beats.

Tess started to shake her head again, then sat back in her chair and sighed. "Damn it." I waited, and after a moment she went on. "It was nothing. Jacob was over discussing the hearing, we had a couple drinks, and when I was letting him out—he kissed me." I waited. "Maybe I kissed him back a little, I don't know. It was nostalgia or something."

"Nostalgia?"

She sighed again. "We were a thing for a while before I met Neil. That's how we all knew each other in college. Jacob and I broke up, Neil and I got together. We stayed friends. That's it."

"Until now."

"Nora, it was nothing. Really."

"Kenny was worried you're going to get married."

Tess huffed a laugh. "She doesn't need to worry about that."

"I said the same thing."

She stared into the fire. "I know it looks bad, but you have to believe me."

"It does. And I do."

Quiet settled in. Somewhere distant water was rushing in the dark. A gust of wind guttered the fire.

"I guess I can't blame her, though. She's a snoop, just like me." A smile surfaced. "Remember when I found my mom's hiding spot for all our Christmas presents?"

I laughed. "We took the dolls out and played with them at least ten times before she wrapped them up."

"And we knew every single present just by the shape on Christmas morning."

"Mom was so exasperated," I said. And she was there suddenly in my mind, clear as if I'd seen her yesterday. All smiles and eyes lit up. Happy.

My attention was pulled to the stack of letters and photos like gravity. I couldn't look away. Couldn't think. Tess's voice brought me back.

"I never grew out of it. Neil even had to hide my engagement ring in a secret spot at the cabin so I wouldn't find it." She touched her naked ring finger absently. Her laughter faded. Smile died. "You never know what's coming, do you?"

"No. It's probably a blessing."

"I wonder sometimes. If we knew, then we could change it." Tess stared into the fire, and after a few moments her eyes closed, head nodding forward. I rose and helped her up.

"Let's get you to bed."

We made our way through the house and upstairs to her room. "Sorry," she mumbled as she sat on the bed and I helped her get undressed.

I pulled a blanket up over her. "It's okay."

She was half-asleep already. Mumbling. "Your mom loved you. And my mom too."

I stood listening to her deep, even breathing for a beat, then left the room and went to my own. I lay on top of the blankets for what felt like hours, looking at the ceiling, following the gentle travel of light and shadow as a car passed.

Hatred is comfortable. It's a suit of armor we wear to protect us from the real threat.

Fear.

People hate to be afraid. And they hate others to quell that fear.

I was no different. I was afraid of what was in those letters. What the pictures portrayed. They might show me some of the woman I remembered when my guard was down. The woman I caught a glimpse of in the mirror from time to time.

I climbed from bed and padded through the empty blue-black of the house. Outside the fireplace was still burning bright.

I picked up the stack of paper and photos, gave it a look, then tossed it into the flames.

15

Two, maybe three hours of sleep, and I was up again.

I shut the front door behind me and jogged away from the house in the predawn gray. Up the street and out of the neighborhood. The moraine swelled on my left, but I headed straight, crossing the mostly barren highway toward the lake.

In the early light the water was flat steel. A walking trail hugged its eastern border, and I ran its inner edge, leaving tracks in the light frost. My lungs smoldered. Thoughts churned.

I'd almost gathered my things and left instead of going for a run. It was beyond tempting, and as a bonus, the excuses were there. I'd come and helped Tess as much as I could. If the current plan didn't work, she'd have to adapt to the fact Neil would gain custody. My mother's letters were gone. There was nothing else here for me.

Then why hadn't I left?

The answer was probably still asleep in her bed, those striking green eyes closed. The kid was growing on me, tugging at my heartstrings whether she knew it or not. And why? Did I see something of myself in her? Sure. But that was nothing new. There'd been dozens of kids like her over the years; afraid, embittered, used, beaten, cynical, vulnerable. I helped them all as much as I could.

But I didn't get attached.

I crested a rise and slowed, breath pluming in the air. The lake extended in both directions, crisp silence. No one in sight. I leaned against a guardrail and let my pulse slow.

Family was the reason.

I'd spent most of my life longing for Paul's presence and living with his ghost. And just when I'd begun to believe it would only be Stephen and me for the rest of our lives, Tess walked back in, bringing my mother's memory along with her.

Family—the one thing you can't seem to escape whether you want to or not.

When I got back to the house, I was still ambivalent about leaving. But walking in the door brought the smell of frying bacon and eggs. Tess was at the stove, and Kenny sat at the counter.

"We wondered where you got off to so early," Tess said. Something in her eyes told me she was almost as surprised to see me as I was to still be here.

"Couldn't sleep, so I decided to go for a run."

"Breakfast is almost up. Hope you're hungry."

"Nora, we're going to show you one of my favorite spots today," Kenny said as I sat down beside her.

"Oh yeah?"

"Yeah. It's the best. You won't even believe it."

Tess gave me a long look. An unsaid question there. I wavered.

"Can't wait," I said.

———

Kenny's favorite place was four thousand feet above us.

The mountain towered over the parking lot when we stepped from Tess's car, but I only had a second to take it in before Kenny grasped my hand and towed me toward an open-walled building where a sky tram waited.

We climbed into the gondola, and a minute later we were ascending the mountainside, the tops of forty-foot pines scrolling past on either side. The lake and foothills sprawled below in all their splendor. But Kenny's smile was what I kept coming back to. She'd talked almost nonstop on the ride over, and now, dangling in the swaying car over the side of the mountain, she thrummed with life. All eyes and smile. Her mood was infectious, and Tess joked along with her, being much sillier than I'd seen her so far—the mother beneath her current worry shining through.

At the top we exited, walked a trail to the mountain's summit, took in the panoramas.

"Over there's our cabin," Kenny said at one point, extending a finger to a swath of trees on an opposite mountainside. "Dad's there now." I glanced at Tess, but she was looking away.

We lunched at the restaurant attached to the tram station overlooking the valley. The view was stunning, the food less so. But Kenny made up for it. She was vibrant, and in turn Tess beamed.

Here was a snapshot of the family before.

The shard of a shattered life.

Because I noticed the looks the other patrons gave us as we entered the restaurant and sat down, saw their heads lower, heard their murmurs of conversation.

Guilt by association is still guilt. And murder is something people never forget.

When we finished eating, we took the tram back down, and like the loss of altitude, the mood followed. Kenny quieted. Tess only half smiled. By the time we were back in the car and heading toward town, the familiar pall had descended. The brief reprieve exchanged for reality.

"I was thinking I'd make those melts you like tonight for dinner," Tess said, summoning a brightness in her voice as she glanced into the rearview mirror. Kenny stared out the window in the back seat. "Does that sound good?"

"Sure."

"Just sure?"

"Yeah."

Tess frowned and said something to me, but I didn't hear. I was looking in the side mirror, which I'd adjusted. Under my breath I said, "What does Neil drive?"

"What? A blue crossover. Why?"

"Because we're being followed."

The dark SUV hung three cars back in our lane.

I'd noticed it a mile or two ago, then registered it as the same vehicle that had been at the end of Tess's street a couple of days before.

"What? Where?" Tess looked over her shoulder, and the car swerved a little.

"Keep it steady and straight. Let's make sure I'm not imagining things."

"Our turn's coming up."

"That's okay. Keep going into town."

The turnoff for the development approached, passed. The SUV stayed on track behind us.

"Mom? Where are we going?" Kenny asked.

"Just a little side trip, kiddo." Tess glanced at me.

"Turn right at the next street," I said, watching the mirror. Tess turned the blinker on. A second later the SUV did the same.

"They're following," Tess said. She was pushing the car over the speed limit, buildings rushing by on either side.

"Slow down."

"What are we going to do?"

"Make sure it's not a coincidence. Turn left up here, then hang a quick right."

Tess did as I asked. Still a good distance behind us, the SUV followed suit. There was no license plate on the front, and it was too far back to get a good look at the driver. Kenny craned around in her seat, trying to see what the fuss was about.

"Nora?" Tess said.

"Is the police station attached to the courthouse?" I asked.

"Yes."

"Go there and pull into the parking lot."

Tess navigated through town. The dark vehicle hung behind like a shark. Never too close or far. The courthouse appeared ahead.

"What do we do if they follow us in?" Tess asked, turning on her blinker.

"We circle the lot and call the cops. Don't park."

Tess swung into the lot. At the same time the SUV turned on an opposite street and accelerated. A moment later it was out of sight.

16

"But who would it be?"

Tess sat opposite me at the dining table, arms crossed, cupping her elbows as if she were cold. Maybe she was. I felt a slight chill thinking about how whoever was driving the SUV knew exactly when to break off the chase. And clean too. I'd only gotten the first two numbers of the back license plate—six and four.

"I don't know. But I doubt it's the first time."

"What do you mean?"

I told her about spotting the SUV in the neighborhood earlier in the week, and the last of Tess's color drained away.

"I'm assuming the newspapers and TV stations have bothered you already," I asked.

"Oh yeah. They hovered for a couple days after Neil was arrested. But they lost interest pretty quickly, and only a few came back when he was released."

"Kenny said the kids at school mostly just stare, but have you gotten any threats?"

Tess sat back, glancing toward the stairs at the mention of her daughter. We'd given her a nonanswer on the ride home as to the detour. She'd responded in kind, beelining to her room the moment we stepped through the door. "No, no threats." But there was something in Tess's voice I didn't like. I waited, and after a second she shook her head. "It's probably nothing, but there were a few calls over the last couple weeks. A random number, and when I answered they hung up. It did scare me, though, because Kenny will answer my phone sometimes when I'm not in the room. I've told her not to, but . . . well, you know her. So I ended up blocking the number."

I thought about sending the number over to my friend Abe Foster at the state police. He could trace whether it was a registered account or a burner phone and go from there if I convinced him it was a threat. But was it?

"Anything else?"

"Other than Neil parked out in the street every so often? No."

"He doesn't really have a reason to follow you."

"He doesn't?" Tess barked a laugh. "Okay."

"The court ruled in his favor. As far as he knows he's getting custody next week. Why would he follow you and jeopardize that?"

"Because he's a psychopath?" I fanned the air with my hands, motioning toward Kenny's room. Tess took the hint and lowered her voice. "You think he's suicidal—aren't there a lot of cases where the husband kills his family, then himself? I mean given what happened to you, I'm surprised that wasn't your first thought."

I sat back from the table and looked out the window. Let a response die inside me.

Tess sighed. "God, I'm sorry. I'm just so fucking worried. And scared. I haven't been sleeping. I've been drinking too much. This is tearing me apart. *Us* apart." She glanced at the stairs again and swiped away tears.

"It's okay. I get it."

She grimaced and reached out for my hand. I gave it to her. "I know you do. That's why I'm so thankful you stayed. After last night I thought you'd be gone this morning."

"Me too."

"And I'm glad you took your mom's letters. Whenever you want to talk about them, I'm here." She squeezed my hand once and stood. "I'm going to check on Kendra."

When she was gone, I glanced out the back windows to the blackened firepit and the ashes dancing within it.

———

The afternoon dissolved in a few answered emails and a phone call to Sharon Weisman confirming our prehearing meeting with Gayle and Joel. Everything was set.

I texted Stephen. Asked how Merrill was. He replied with a selfie of them at a dog park near his place. Both their tongues lolled out the sides of their mouths, and I laughed. I needed it.

My head was a storm cloud of thoughts.

Foremost being who could've been tailing us. Who might be watching Tess and Kenny. And if the phone calls were nothing or something.

"Nora?"

I jerked. Tess stood in the doorway, one hand on the knob. "Sorry, I was totally gone."

"Dinner's almost ready."

"Be right there." I closed my laptop and followed her, even though eating was the last thing I felt like doing.

Dinner was ham-and-cheese melts on slider buns with a side of fries. Kenny picked at her food, and Tess watched her. The atmosphere was that of a funeral. Near the end Tess's phone pinged a couple of texts in a row, and she sighed, rising to check it. I studied her as she read them and turned slightly away, typing a response.

Kenny dipped a fry in ketchup, leaving it standing upright with four others. I got her attention and crossed my eyes while sticking my tongue out. She sighed but smiled a little.

"Do you think I could totally impose on you?" Tess said, coming back to the table.

"Sure."

"I spaced about the crime prevention committee meeting tonight. It shouldn't be more than a few hours."

I clocked what she was saying and glanced at Kenny. "Uh, sure. That's fine."

"Great. Sorry. I'd skip, but they're sticklers about attendance."

Kenny and I cleaned up while Tess went to get ready, reappearing ten minutes later with a hint of makeup and trailing faint perfume. She kissed Kenny on the forehead. "Be good and do everything Nora says."

"I will."

"Be back soon." Then she was hurrying out the door and gone.

We were alone.

I was half-amused at feeling flustered. How many tense and heart-breaking situations had I gotten through, and now spending an evening entertaining a kid had me nervous. "So—" I said.

"So—" Kenny echoed.

"What do you want to do?" A shrug. "Play a game?"

"Like what? Monopoly?"

"Do you like Monopoly?"

"No."

"Oh. Okay."

A sheepish smile. "But I like cribbage. Do you know how to play?"

I cracked my knuckles. "Kid, I'm the cribbage queen."

———

I'd never lost at anything so badly in my life.

She skunked me the first game and double skunked me the second.

"Where did you learn to play like this?" I asked, tossing down the third useless crib in a row.

Kenny giggled. "Mom and Dad and I always play at the cabin. They taught me when I was seven."

"Ages ago," I said, starting to deal.

"Where did you learn?"

"A boyfriend taught me in college. He was a card shark. Played everything from Texas Hold'em to Go Fish. He won a pretty big tournament in Las Vegas a few years ago."

"Too bad you didn't stick with him," Kenny said without looking up.

I barked a laugh. "Yeah, I guess so."

We played a couple more hands before Kenny declared she was starving and raced into the kitchen to make popcorn. I stood and stretched, gazing out the windows at the backyard. It was getting dark.

I drifted.

For a second I thought the sound pulling me back was the kernels popping in the microwave, but when I looked at Kenny, she was facing the entry.

Someone was knocking at the front door.

"I'll get it," I said. She started to follow, but I held out a hand. "Stay here, okay?"

I had a number of ideas who it could be as I peered through the window beside the door—a delivery person, a neighbor, Jacob. But I was wrong.

It was Kenny's father.

17

Those moments of pure indecision.

Pulling us in different directions. Pulling us apart.

Half of me was reaching out to make sure the door was locked, the other half intending to open it.

What were my options?

Call the cops? On what grounds? Neil wasn't restricted from being here. There was no restraining order. Nothing in the divorce decree or legal proceedings I knew of.

He knocked again.

"Nora?" Kenny called from the kitchen.

"Hold on," I said, and stepped outside.

Neil was even shorter than I'd estimated in the courtroom. Up close I stood at least an inch taller. And the gauntness of his features was more prominent, skin stretched over bone. He wore a T-shirt and faded chinos. Hands empty, no weapons I could see.

"What are you doing here?" I asked as he took a step back.

Neil surveyed me. "I—I just want to see my daughter. That's all." I opened my mouth to reply but he said, "I know Tess isn't here."

"Stalking's against the law, you know."

"I'm not—" He sighed and closed his eyes. When he reopened them, they were awash with pleading. "I've been staying away out of courtesy, I didn't want to make waves, but I haven't seen her in person in months. Please. Just five minutes. Tess doesn't have to know."

Beyond torn.

I weighed what to do, what to say.

But then it was decided for me as the front door opened and Kenny burst past me into her father's arms.

"Dad!"

I could lie and say my throat didn't tighten watching him drop to one knee and sweep her into a tight hug. I could say there was only suspicion as a tear slipped from one of Kenny's eyes. I could say I was alarmed by it all.

But I wasn't.

I was moved.

Neil let out a half laugh/half sob and stood, spinning Kenny around in a circle. He set her down and held her at arm's length. "You're taller!"

"No I'm not," Kenny said. Then burst into tears for real, leaning into him again.

I glanced around, seeing who else was witnessing the spectacle. The street was blessedly empty. Not even a car rolling by. But it wouldn't last for long.

Neil was looking at me over Kenny's shoulder. Asking a question.

"Go in the backyard," I said, after a beat. "Get out of view."

They did.

I went inside.

———

Father and daughter sat in patio chairs pulled up facing one another. Kenny was speaking animatedly, waving her arms over her head while Neil grinned. I stood watching through the tall back windows, one hand holding my phone, the other the mace I'd retrieved from my room.

Neil laughed at something Kenny said, and I wondered what the hell I was doing.

Betraying my friend.

Possibly endangering us all.

Following my instincts.

The last held sway. At least for now.

I checked the time. They'd been in the backyard for ten minutes. And Tess could be home any moment. I opened the sliding door and stepped outside. Both of them glanced my way, and Neil must've read something in my body language.

"Okay, mouse," he said, standing. "I gotta get going."

"Already? You just got here."

"I know, but—" He threw another look my way. "I'll see you next week."

"Are we staying at the cabin?"

"You know it."

Kenny beamed and hugged him. I felt like a prison guard overseeing visitation period. They parted, and Kenny headed my way. Neil went around the side of the house toward the street, pausing before he was out of sight. "Thank you," he said, and was gone.

We went in.

Kenny retrieved her popcorn, and we sat at the table, our latest hands splayed out near the cribbage board. We stayed that way for a drawn moment before I said, "Mouse?"

Kenny smiled down into her bowl. "My two front teeth came in before all my other ones. Mom and Dad said I looked like a little mouse."

I picked up my cards. She did the same. We started playing.

"Are you going to tell my mom?" she asked after we counted our hands.

"I don't know." But I did.

"Please don't. She'll be really mad."

"This isn't about her being mad." *It's about what's right*, I was going to say, and stopped myself. How did I know what was right? I knew how Tess felt, what she believed along with the rest of the town. Knew the suspicion surrounding Neil. But there was also the light in Kenny's eyes when she spoke of her father. There was the way Neil had come alive the moment she'd run into his arms. There was real love there.

But even killers had people they loved. And who loved them.

"Let's just finish the game," I said.

We did. I lost.

Afterward we started a movie, some Disney number I tuned out as soon as the opening credits rolled. I didn't come back to any semblance of presence until the door opened a half hour later and Tess called out from the entry.

"Hey, how'd it go?" she asked, coming into the living room.

I could feel Kenny looking at me. Waiting. Pleading.

"Fine," I said, summoning as much of a smile as I could. "Everything's just fine."

18

Home.

Coils of tension I hadn't realized were there released the second I walked through the door. My house was cool and open, welcoming the way only home can be. The only thing missing was the click of Merrill's nails coming to greet me.

I'd left early in the morning prior to Tess or Kenny rising, leaving a very brief note for them on the kitchen counter. I was needed at home. I'd be back soon.

It wasn't a lie. But I had other reasons for leaving.

The first was simple and selfish. I'd had a hard time looking Tess in the eye after lying to her. Something as straightforward as being there for a long-lost friend had become a web of complexity. And secondly the pressure of the past was too much too soon. Even with the letters gone, there were still Tess's intentions of clearing the air, of discussing our history, and right now I didn't have it in me.

Might not ever have it in me.

So I ran.

Ran home to my sanctuary. Alone again. Sartre was right about hell and other people. I'd even go so far as to say the only safe place was alone. And sometimes not even then.

Our problems can always be traced back to ourselves. Nothing in the natural world even comes close.

Because we aren't natural.

I sighed, pressing my hands to my face. "Too existential for this early in the morning," I said to the empty house. Whatever my feelings about people, nature was the opposite. Something I needed. Craved.

I changed into my wet suit and went down to the beach. The waves came in like always. Like old friends. I got on my board and paddled out into them. The water was still very cold. I floated for a while, savoring the numbing chill, then rode a few waves in before going back to the house to shower.

Comfy clothes and a cup of tea. Sitting in front of the windows, I longed to go pick Merrill up and bring him home. But if my suspicions were correct, I'd just be dropping him back off at Stephen's in a couple days, and that would only confuse and depress him. So I settled for a text to Stephen asking how they were. They were fine. Had just come back from a walk. They were good for as long as I needed.

I hoped it wouldn't be much longer.

———

The following afternoon Gayle and Joel Pearson listened wide-eyed as Sharon Weisman went over the outline a second time.

"And if the judge asks you a question, what do you say?" Sharon said.

Gayle glanced at me, and I nodded my encouragement. "We say 'yes, Your Honor,' or 'no, Your Honor,' like that."

"And how do we keep our answers?"

"Short," Gayle and Joel said in unison.

I smiled at Sharon. "They're good."

"I think they are," Sharon said. "Okay, so the last thing the judge might say is you have to have a person come to your home and check on you and Ivy a few times after you get her back. They'll probably have some training for you too."

"Training?" Joel asked.

"For parenting. They'll give you some ideas and tips on how to parent Ivy."

"We know how to be her parents," Gayle said. "We've always been her parents since she was born."

"It's a formality," I said. "They have to do it because the judge says so. It doesn't mean you're bad parents. You aren't."

Gayle and Joel shared a look. "If we have to," she finally said.

We finished up and gave them the final documents regarding the hearing process, then sent them on their way. "They're wonderful," Sharon said, watching them join hands and walk down the street outside my office. "Thank you for bringing me in on this one. Makes all the other shit worthwhile."

"Thanks for helping. It shouldn't have happened in the first place."

A smile crept onto Sharon's face that could've cracked ice. "Oh, I'll make the other counsel wish they never would have answered the phone."

"I don't see any hiccups, do you?" I asked as she gathered her things from my office.

"None. They've completed everything that was mandated, which was all bullshit in the first place, and there's nothing I've found the grandmother can use. All the social activities they've done with Ivy are excellent, the kid's on track as far as education, her health is great, and the home is stable. They're better parents than most people. You hop on the stand, and we should be golden."

I took comfort from Sharon's confidence. Everything appeared to be in Gayle and Joel's favor, but I wanted it airtight. I wanted the hollow longing in their eyes to go away and never return. Their family hadn't deserved this. The world was hard enough without other people making it more so.

When Sharon was on her way, I set about catching up from my absence. There were a half dozen files to scan and email, a few voice mails to answer, and papers to organize. Around the time my desk was starting to reappear, and my thoughts were turning toward home, the door to the street opened, and someone stepped inside.

"Be right with you," I called and set the last of the paperwork aside. An older woman waited in the reception area. Feathery hair an unnatural shade of violet encircled her head. She had rounded features and a set of scowl lines so deep on either side of her mouth they didn't budge when she attempted a smile.

"I was just admiring your photo here," she said, motioning at a black-and-white seascape on the wall. A solid shaft of light cut through thick clouds and flooded a section of beach in the picture. "A break in the storm," she read from the title plaque at the bottom, eyes twinkling. "Goes well with the name of your company I'd say. Sanctuary. Very fitting."

I tilted my head and held out my hand. "Thanks. I'm Nora McTavish, how can I help you?"

The woman reached out to shake with me, at least six gaudy rings adorning her fingers. "I hope you can help me a lot—my name is Arlene Jones. I think my granddaughter's just been in to see you."

My hand retracted on its own accord. An unconscious recoil.

The forced smile tilted, almost fell from her face. "Well, I see you know who I am," she said.

"What are you doing here?"

"Like I said, looking for help."

"I'm representing Gayle, Joel, and Ivy. You have no business here. Please leave."

"Well I thought I could shed some light"—she motioned to the photo, still trying to smile—"on this whole mess and maybe we could clear it up without having to go to court. Wouldn't that be easier for everyone?"

"I'm sorry, but that won't—"

"You see I'm not sure you really understand the whole picture. I love my granddaughter, I do, and she means well, but she's not mother material."

"Well it's a good thing a judge is making that decision and you aren't. Now if you'll excuse me—"

"No, see I've been picking up after her her whole life whether she wants to admit it or not. I've always been there to help, and believe me, she's needed a lot of it over the years. I always told her mother that Gayle needed a firm hand given her condition. But she wouldn't listen. She gave her too much freedom, and wouldn't you know it, she went and got herself pregnant." Arlene huffed. "Since her mother passed Gayle's become my burden, and I've tried to keep her in check, but now . . . Well to get to the heart of the matter, there's things you should know about those kids."

"I know they love their daughter very much and she was taken from them without cause."

The first hint of indignation appeared as spots of color on her face. "Without cause? They left that little girl unattended in a shopping cart. She could've fallen and hurt herself and—"

"They didn't leave her unattended. I've seen the video the grocery store provided. I also spotted someone who looks very much like you stalking them from aisle to aisle right before siccing an employee on them."

Arlene blinked, a hand going up to her throat where a well-worn gold cross hung. She rubbed it like someone trying to summon a genie from a lamp. "I was nowhere near the grocery store that day. I'll have you know my neighbor Willa Gustafson will vouch for my whereabouts."

"I don't care what Willa says because it doesn't matter. When we go to court you're going to lose because Gayle and Joel haven't done anything wrong."

"Can't you see they're unfit!" Arlene's voice had risen an octave. "They can't even take care—"

"Of themselves? Yet they both hold full-time jobs where their managers have offered to testify on their behalf. Their daycare provider says Ivy is happy, healthy, and well adjusted. They've passed every single mandated requirement set forth for them and jumped through hoops typical parents wouldn't have had to." I'd taken a step toward Arlene without thinking, and she retreated to match it. "Their only real problem I can see is standing in front of me right now."

Arlene shook her head slowly, still rubbing the cross. "You don't get to tell me about my life, you have no idea."

"Oh I'm thinking I've got a pretty good handle on it. Now get the fuck out of my office."

Hey eyes widened at my cursing, which only made me feel like doing it again. She turned slightly and primped her hair. "I see this was a waste of time. They seem to have found the perfect bleeding heart and bamboozled her." I stared holes through her until she smiled thinly and started for the door.

"You know, before you use *bleeding heart* again as an insult, maybe you should look up where the term came from," I said. "That is if you can stop rubbing the cross around your neck long enough."

Her hand strayed toward her throat, but she stopped. "Mocking the faithful is nothing new. We're used to it." She began pushing out through the door.

"Oh, Arlene?" She paused. "I may have missed it, but I didn't see anyone else listed as a caregiver besides you on the removal petition for Ivy." She stared at me, uncomprehending. "Where is Ivy right now if you're here talking to me?"

The indignation was back. "She's safe with Willa."

"Which violates the parameters of your custody. Temporary custody," I added. "I'll be making the court aware of that too."

Arlene struggled for a moment, then raised her chin. "Who said I was ever here?"

I pointed at the camera mounted high in the corner of the room. "Cameras really aren't your friend, are they?"

Her mouth opened and closed, a fish drowning in air, then she was gone.

I locked the door behind her.

The bottle of booze in my desk cried out, but I ignored it, still coming down from the adrenaline of telling Arlene off. I thought of Gayle and her mother growing up in the shadow of that woman and wanted to spit. "What a monster," I murmured, and gathered my things.

A light rain fell on the way home. The wipers were metronomic, hypnotizing. Slowly my anger burned off and was mostly gone by the time I hurried inside. I called out for Merrill not thinking and almost teared up. I poured a glass of wine and drank it, leaning against the kitchen counter, in three long swallows. Better.

A shower was calling my name. I needed to wash the day off more than anything. Another little splash of wine, and then I was moving toward my room when the phone pinged a text. The temptation to ignore it just until I'd showered was there, but I caved and checked it. My heart sank a little. It was Tess.

Jacob just called. He heard from Neil's lawyer.

Neil has never been to a therapist. What do we do?

19

Transcript of *Poe, the Man and the Myths: A lecture series with Professor Neil Grayson,* Part 5—presented by Ridgewood University in coordination with College Partnership Programming.

In "The Man of the Crowd" we encounter the theme of duality. Many critics argue the narrator is pursuing himself through London when he spots the old man who seems apart from all the rest of the crowds. He catches sight of someone out of place, something other, and is compelled to follow, to understand.

It is the same for our own motives. Sometimes they're clear, and the duality of ourselves inhabit the same space. We feel as one, though it's an illusion. At other times we're not sure of the why, and it frightens us. Mostly because we don't truly know who we are, or more importantly, what we're capable of.

20

It was long past dark when I rolled through Mutiny.

A series of texts with Tess all amounted to the same thing: Could I come back?

Yes. Sure. Of course.

What I'd really wanted was a quiet evening at home listening to some music and reading as the wind blew rain against the windows. What I got was a white-knuckled return drive through the mountains until finally the storm fell away in the rearview mirror.

The neighborhood was quiet and still when I pulled into Tess's driveway and parked beside Jacob's car. A few porch lights were on, but it was a weeknight, and people were battened down for the evening. Around the side of the house, firelight danced, and I went that way instead of knocking on the front door.

Tess and Jacob were seated around the fireplace. Kenny sat on Tess's lap, her tablet on a nearby table. She spotted me first, hopping free of her mother to greet me with an unexpected hug.

"Hey," I said. "You're up late."

"I was waiting for you," she said.

"I told her she could say hi, then it's off to bed," Tess said, starting to rise from her seat.

"Well if that was the deal you better get going," I said.

"I have something to show you," Kenny whispered into my ear. Then she released me and yelled a good night over one shoulder before disappearing into the house.

Jacob asked something from where he reclined in one of the chairs, and I brought my gaze back from the direction Kenny had gone when I realized he'd spoken to me. "Sorry, what did you say?"

"I asked how the drive was."

"Oh, fine once I got free of the storm."

"Thanks for coming," Tess said, embracing me even tighter than her daughter had.

"Of course." I was pleasantly surprised she smelled only of perfume instead of booze. We sat.

"So," Jacob said. "We're back to square one. None of the therapists in town ever had Neil as a patient, and I double-checked by querying his attorney, which was an unpleasant experience. But the paperwork was in order, and she had no choice but to confirm Neil hasn't ever gone to counseling, locally or otherwise."

I chose my words carefully, given Tess's beseeching expression. "It was a long shot, and we knew that. I'm sorry it didn't pan out."

"But isn't there still a way to argue it?" Tess asked. "Couldn't we bring Melody's testimony to the judge, and I could back it up with how odd he'd been acting?"

"It's conjecture," Jacob said. "Nothing more. Nora was right, we need evidence."

"The suicide note." Tess sat on the edge of her seat. "Something like that."

"Right, but even if he still has it, there's no way of getting it," I said.

"Not legally," Tess said.

"I hope you're not hinting at breaking the law in front of your attorney." Jacob said, shifting in his chair.

"We don't know what was on the paper," I said. "And I'm sure he didn't keep it. If you chose not to kill yourself, you wouldn't want a reminder lying around." Tess didn't respond. She only stared into the fire, flames reflecting dully in her eyes.

"You ever wish you could start over?" she said after a moment. Jacob and I shared a look. Tess finally seemed to come back to herself. "Have a clean slate and try again?"

"Everyone wishes that sometimes, I think," Jacob said softly.

"It's too bad you can't," she said looking off into the dark. "It's really too bad."

———

A half hour later Jacob left, and we went inside. Tess paused in the kitchen for a drink of water while I hauled my bag to the guest room. On the way back I found her glassy eyed and staring again.

"You okay?"

"Yeah, I think so." She put her glass in the dishwasher and stood very still, brow furrowed, before looking at me. "Do you ever think it's okay to do a bad thing to right a wrong?"

"Well, if we're talking about breaking into Neil's place to look for a suicide note, then I'd say no."

"I wasn't thinking that. I was just—" She chewed her lower lip. "I have some of his handwriting—letters, notes, that sort of thing. Maybe I could . . ."

I let the idea hang in the air between us for a long second before knocking it down. "Absolutely not." I lowered my voice, glancing toward the stairs. "*Forge* a suicide note and present it to the court? Number one he'd deny it and demand it be examined by an expert who would be able to tell when it was written—"

"But if we—"

"—and two, you'd be charged with forgery, leaving him with full custody. Is that what you want?"

Tess shrank, looking like a scolded child. "No, God no. I'm grasping at straws."

"Well grasp at different ones. None of this will help Kenny."

"If we had more time, a continuation or a stay, maybe then—"

"There's no reasonable cause."

Tears gleamed in her eyes, and she swiped them away. Part of me withered, seeing her hurting, breaking. But there was a point when acceptance was the only option. Even if it felt like a betrayal.

"Look, we'll figure something out. Or there'll be a development in the case, and things will change. I know it's really hard right now, but you have to be strong. For Kenny." She nodded.

"Thank you. For coming back. For everything."

"It's okay."

I was touched when she leaned close, her lips brushing my cheek. "Good night."

She went upstairs and I was alone. Emotionally wrung out. Road weary. And wired.

I readied for bed and lay there, listening to the house settle, to the blood beating in my ears. Then to something else. Soft footfalls coming down the stairs and toward my room. A knock. I opened the door to Kenny standing in her pajamas, clutching her tablet.

"What are you doing awake?" I asked, glancing at the time.

"I had to show you," she said, skirting into the room. She plopped onto the bed and opened her tablet, flicking between pages before glancing at me. "While you were gone, I did what you said. I went back and researched everything about my dad's case."

Oh no. What I'd said to her came creeping back. "Kenny, listen. I told you what helped me. But everyone's different. This might not be the best—"

"No, no, it's good, because I found something. Come look." Against my better judgment I sat beside her. "So I read through everything in the newspapers and online. Even the comments, which are always terrible." She handed me the tablet. On the screen was a news article titled Evidence recovered at accused professor's property. A picture took up most of the page, featuring a quaint cabin in a clearing beside a rocky outcropping leading up into thick pines. Four police cruisers were parked in front of the building, and crime-scene tape stretched tight, marking a perimeter. Two men stood on the cabin's deck in conversation. One was older, graying and heavyset, while the other was younger, tall with dark hair and a long black peacoat. Kenny tapped the younger of the two men. "He was at our house in the middle of the night."

"What? When?"

"The weekend my dad was arrested." Kenny looked down into her lap. "I couldn't sleep. I kept thinking about Dad sitting in some cell. Alone. I knew he wouldn't be able to sleep, either. I asked to call him, but no one would let me. Mom was crying all the time and . . ." She twisted her hands. "I was lying in bed, wondering what was going to happen, and I heard Mom talking to someone. I went downstairs, and he was in the kitchen." She nodded toward the tablet. "I don't know what they were talking about, but Mom seemed really worried. Then he left."

I adjusted the screen and stared, my heart first pausing, then skipping quickly like a flat stone across water.

"He's the detective who's been suspended too. Does it mean anything?" Kenny asked.

I heard her, but it was hard to register since I kept rereading the caption below the picture.

The cabin owned by Grayson where new evidence was found by authorities. Pictured are lead detective Lt. Carl Lowe (left), and Detective Devon Wilson (right).

21

Kenny touched my arm, and I took in her hopeful expectation. "What do you think?"

"I think . . . ," I said, rising from the bed, "that it's really late, and we both should get some sleep." I went to the door and opened it. The look on her face flickered and died. She picked up her tablet and moved into the hall, head down, feet shuffling. I stopped her.

"Hey. Did reading all this help you feel better?" She thought, then nodded. "Okay then. If nothing else, that means something. Hold on to it."

Some of her smile returned. Then she was gone in the dark of the house, her small footsteps retreating to silence. I shut the door.

Devon Wilson.

Of course I'd seen his name before, and it only took a space between heartbeats to recall where.

Tess's phone.

He'd called and texted her the day of the hearing. Unless she knew someone else by the same name. Someone other than the detective who had overseen her husband's arrest and had been at her house in the middle of the night in what appeared to be some kind of clandestine meeting.

Yes. Right.

The air suddenly contained ropes, all of them tightening around me. I sat on the bed and took a deep breath. All of this could be coincidence. There was any number of reasons for a detective to visit a suspect's spouse. I couldn't jump to conclusions. But I could start the wheels rolling on finding out the truth. I opened my laptop and typed a quick email, hesitated, then sent it.

Back in bed, sleep seemed even less likely. My mind did more than wander. It struck off on expeditions into the wild. Cut new paths. Strained to see what was over the hill, what shape lay just beyond the trees.

The subconscious is the great net. The collector. It knows the truth, but we don't know how to listen. Or we choose not to, which amounts to the same.

We miss things. The answers are there, but they slip by, and we go on, oblivious.

I quieted myself. Tried listening. Let assumptions slide away.

And dreamed.

Fire blackening paper, written words disappearing forever.

A bloody hand reaching, then falling still.

The shining lenses of my father's glasses obscuring his eyes.

A gunshot.

I bolted up in bed. The noise hadn't been in my dream. It had been real. I went to the door and cracked it open, listening. A quiet clatter of dishes in the kitchen. Coffee pot percolating. Normal morning sounds. I relaxed and made my way toward them.

Tess was bent over the stove, flipping eggs. She winced when she saw me. "Sorry, I dropped a pan. Did I wake you?"

"No," I lied. "Was just getting up."

"Good. Breakfast will be ready in a minute."

When she only set two plates on the counter, I said, "Isn't Kenny eating?"

"She's already gone. The bus comes pretty early."

"When's school out?"

"Two weeks." Tess uttered a quiet laugh. "Normally we'd be making plans for the summer. Trips, projects around the house, camp. Now . . ." She sipped her coffee. "I just don't see how we're going to be able to stay here. Everything's tainted. If I could I'd put the house up for sale and move as far away as possible. Start new somewhere else."

"It's natural. I thought about the same thing in college. Moving out of state where no one knew me. But it doesn't matter where you go if you're the same. Everything changes. So do we."

"I don't even know how to begin. The way everyone looks at us." She gestured at the street. "There's a neighborhood barbecue tonight. Everyone gets together each month, and there's kind of a block party. It used to be something we really looked forward to, but we haven't gone since . . . since everything."

"I think you should go. Both of you."

She blinked. "What? We can't."

"Sure you can. You and Kenny didn't do anything wrong. You're still part of the community, and if you're going to stay here, the community needs to remember that."

"Easier said than done."

"You mentioned a blank slate last night. This is as close to it as you're going to get. Start over like this is ground zero. Day one. Go out and show people you're not afraid. That you and your daughter are still part of this place and everyone better get used to it."

Tess sighed, smiling a little. "You haven't changed at all. You were always brave."

"No. Paul was. I'm just what's left."

She looked down, brow creasing, then smiled. "I had such a crush on him."

"Paul?"

"Oh yeah. I don't know if you ever noticed but I always sat next to him on the couch when we'd watch movies. If there was a scary part, I'd grab his hand, and he'd let me hold it for a little while."

We sat in the bittersweetness of the moment, then finished eating and cleaned up. While I was wiping the counter down, Tess said, "Can you stay? Until Friday when I have to let him . . . let him have her?"

"I've got a hearing I can't miss at home, but I'll come back afterward."

"I don't think I could be alone at first. It would be too—" Her voice broke as she looked around the house that used to be a home.

"I'll be here. Don't worry."

And I would. Because there was something hidden in all the turmoil and drama, something wrong. And I needed to know what it was.

I always needed to know.

22

Friendship is a tenuous bridge between two people.

We try to maintain it with trust, honesty, love. But sometimes we ask it to carry a heavy burden. Much more than it's ever supposed to. I felt invisible supports straining later that morning when my phone rang and I saw who was calling.

"Abe," I said, stepping into the backyard. Tess had gone into town to gather the necessities to participate in that evening's neighborhood get-together. She'd slowly warmed to the idea from when I'd mentioned it, and upon leaving the house she'd actually seemed excited. The sight gladdened me.

Now, listening to the hesitant silence on the other end of the line, I felt the opposite.

"What are you into now?" Abraham Foster finally said.

I had to laugh. "That's what I'm trying to figure out."

Abe was a state police detective. A veteran. One of the unwavering I counted as a true friend. And now I was asking something of him I shouldn't. I gave him the rundown, the general details of how I was connected to Tess, and by proxy, the murder of Allie Prentiss. He listened in silence, only making a soft grunt of affirmation when I asked if he was familiar with the case. "So I was wondering if you had any info you could share," I said near the end. "Nothing that would get you in trouble, I know it's an ongoing investigation."

There was a long pause. Anyone else might've hung up. Instead Abe said, "What do you want to know?"

"Devon Wilson looked to be the assist on the case under the lead detective. He was suspended right after Grayson was released. I can't find anything else about it, only that it was an interdepartmental matter."

"I'll touch base with a friend of mine. He retired last month, but he was the liaison on the case for the state. He won't bat an eye filling me in, so it shouldn't be a problem."

"Thank you, I really appreciate it."

"I know you do. That's why I'm doing it. And, Nora?"

"Yeah?"

"Be careful."

———

Abe's words boomeranged in my head.

Careful. That line we walk, telling ourselves if we stay on one side of it, we'll be okay. But when the truth is across it, there's really no choice. At least not for me.

I locked up the house and drove out of the development, the moraine sweeping up and away as I turned toward town. My eyes kept flicking to the rearview mirror, half expecting to see the dark SUV a few cars back, but there was nothing. Normal traffic. People going their own ways.

Pulling into the university parking lot, I scanned the buildings, picking out the English department where Neil had spent most of his days lecturing. Students flowed in and out of the doors, talking, laughing, hurrying. I imagined Allie Prentiss with them, a young, pretty blonde woman at the beginning of her life, the notion she'd only be a memory soon unfathomable to her. An impossibility.

I reset the dashboard tripmeter and pulled out of the lot, glancing at my phone as it directed me down the main thoroughfare, then left onto a narrow side road, which dead-ended in a small huddle of old houses. The buildings were set against a border of thick forest, their fronts sad and sagging. Peeling paint, broken steps. Ahead a cottage came into view set slightly apart from the other homes. Its windows were dark and unfettered by shades or curtains.

I stopped in front of Allie Prentiss's house.

The place where she was murdered.

The tripmeter read 1.3 miles. It had taken me four minutes to get there from the English department building.

Outside the wind had come up and bent the trees back and forth as if in greeting. Beckoning. I stood on the deserted street, then made my way up the short walk to the cottage's front door. A small window at head height revealed a cramped kitchen leading into a sitting room. The interior was bare. No carpet. Stripped of any personality, any remaining evidence. It was forlorn and lonely and settled a stone of heartache inside me to know a young life had been snuffed out savagely in this dismal place.

"It's for rent if you're looking."

I startled and turned, taking in the voice's owner.

A woman past middle age stood halfway down the walk. Her hair was tied up in a messy bun, and she wore a threadbare knee-length parka. One hand was cocked to the side holding a lit cigarette.

"I might be," I said, coming down off the front stoop. "Are you the landlord?"

A nod. A quick drag on the cigarette. "From out of town?"

"Yes."

"Look like it. Rent's seven hundred plus utilities. First and last months. Two hundred damage deposit, no pets. No smoking." The cigarette flared.

"Seems steep."

A shrug. "Average this close to campus. Probably won't find any cheaper."

"Is that mainly who you rent to? Students?"

"Mostly." She eyed me. "Guess I should be up front if you're serious. Kid got killed in this one a while back."

I feigned shock. "Killed?"

"Yup. Professor from the uni did it. Guess they were having an affair, and she wanted to end it from what I gather. Saw him parked right where your car is myself on the day of. He was sittin' behind the wheel there just staring at the place when I went by. Didn't think anything of it at the time. Gives me the willies now." She shivered, either from the wind or the willies. "Not surprising, though, I guess. Knowing the girl."

"Why's that?" I asked, trying to maintain an average level of interest.

"She had strict parents from the coast. Didn't want them privy to what she was up to. Older men, drugs, whatnot. We chatted some. She was friendly, nice enough, thoughtful. Brought me coffee a couple times when she got some for herself. But she was stupid, too, like all kids that age. A few guys came and went, then the professor started showing up. Never stayed long, though. Guess they got business over quick." She sniffed and spat onto the patchy lawn. "Men that age tryin' to hold on to something that's gone. Always leads to ruin."

"He was the only one who stopped by to see her?" If the question seemed out of place, she didn't show it.

"Like I said, other guys her age. Probably drug dealers. Who knows. This side of town's been going to hell for a while. I had a prowler back of my place down the street more than once this spring, and do you think the cops did anything about it?" She blew out a breath of disdain and pitched her cigarette butt. "Couldn't care less. Useless to the last of them."

"So you told them all this? About what you saw and what the girl said?"

"Absolutely. Told them everything. Even how happy she seemed right before the end."

"Happy?"

"Oh yeah. She was practically floating the last week or so before that teacher bashed her head in. When I mentioned she sure looked upbeat, she told me sometimes things just work out for the best."

"They work out for the best?"

"Yup. Eerie, ain't it, knowing she was dead a few days later? And to think they let the bastard back out of jail after arresting him." I was getting good at feigning shock. "Oh yeah, that's the kicker. District attorney dropped the case for some reason or another. Maybe they're friends, who knows. So the murderer's out walking free." She seemed to realize what she said. "Don't suppose you want the place now."

"It's definitely off-putting."

She drew a battered pack of smokes from her parka's pocket and lit up again. "Well, consider it this way—what's the odds of being murdered in a place that's just had a murder? Like being struck by lightning twice, right? So what do you say? I'll even knock off the damage deposit."

"I'll think about it."

23

Back in Tess's driveway.

Car off. Staring at nothing. Thoughts roiling.

I registered Tess had returned, her car parked inside the open garage. From time to time she was visible inside the house, an outline blocking the light as she passed by windows.

I'd idled through Mutiny for a time after leaving Allie's house, letting the landscape slide by without really seeing it. Driving always calmed me, beveled the edges off my mood. But today it didn't work. My mind was in upheaval, rushing from one point to the next and back again.

Allie had been using drugs according to the nosy landlord—not out of the realm of possibility given her age and the accessibility to substances these days. But her attitude before she died was what gave me pause. If the landlord was to be believed, Allie had been down, then upbeat shortly before she was killed. As if she'd seen light at the end of the tunnel before the final dark closed in. And what could it have been? Money, like Jacob had suggested? If Neil had promised to pay her off for keeping their affair secret, that tracked.

But—

I caught myself reentering the process I used when still working at CPS. Filtering the words of others to glean the truth. People were deceptive, purposefully and by accident. The key was discerning what was important, what insight lay within statements or details.

There were neighbors of abuse victims who thought kids were just clumsy and the bruises they noticed were from bike riding or skateboarding. Some people mistook a parent's affection for something more sinister.

Which only proved people didn't always know what they were seeing when they were seeing it.

What had the landlord seen without knowing it? And why was all of this suddenly eating at me? Gnawing maddeningly at the fringes of my mind.

My phone rang, pulling me back. It was Sharon Weisman. As soon as I answered she was already talking.

"That fucking grandmother."

"What happened?" I said, stomach sinking.

"She filed a continuance."

"Don't tell me—"

"And the judge granted it. The stupid ass."

"What was the continuance for?"

"She claims she's twisted an ankle and can't make it to court. She also filed an amendment to her custody, adding a . . . Willamina Gustafson to Ivy's care plan."

I seethed. "She's stalling."

"Well, no shit."

"She stopped by my office last night. Tried coercing me into dropping Gayle and Joel as clients. She left Ivy with this Willamina, and I called her on it. I've got her on camera."

"Well, isn't that interesting." Sharon's tone made me think of the cold flash of a shark's teeth as it surfaced for prey. "Can you send me the video?"

"I'll download it and get it to you this afternoon."

"That's the last nail in the coffin. She did the work for us." Sharon laughed. "Sometimes I wonder about people, and sometimes I just don't know."

———

Inside, music blared from the kitchen. Tess stood at the counter, swaying in time to the beat, a potato salad on the counter. The oven was aglow, a pie of some kind baking away.

"Hey!" Tess said as I entered. "Where'd you get off to?"

"Went for a drive. Took in a little more of the town." I clocked an open wine bottle near the sink already half-empty.

"Well I'm glad you're back." She poured me a glass, spilling a little as she handed it over "Oops!"

"Tess?"

"I'm so glad you talked me into doing this. Hold on." She tried opening her phone, but flour obscured her thumbprint. She punched in her code and cut the music off. "You're totally right, we have nothing to be ashamed of. Why should he dictate whether we have a life or not? We live here too. This has been our home just as long as his. He's the one who's supposed to be locked up, not us."

The front door opened and closed. I put a finger to my lips. Tess blinked, then nodded. Kenny appeared a moment later, eyeing the scene with apparent distrust. "What's going on?" she asked, setting her backpack down.

"The neighborhood get-together's tonight," Tess said. "We're going."

Kenny's brow crinkled. "I thought you said—"

"I know, but I think it'll be good for us. Don't you?"

Kenny glanced at me. "I guess?"

"Go get ready. Everyone will be out there soon."

Kenny threw me another look, then disappeared upstairs. When I was sure she was out of earshot, I said, "Do you think maybe she needs more time? I could stay in with her while you go out."

"No, she should come too. I want people to see we're not afraid."

But she was afraid. I could see it in the way she held herself, how she smiled and drank deeper from her glass of wine, how her eyes flicked away. And I wondered, not for the first time, how much she wasn't telling me.

A loud crack came from the street, and I jerked. Tess squeezed my arm. "Just fireworks. The kids always set them off."

Outside people milled in front yards. Kids scampered. A sparkler fizzled white hot, leaving an afterglow in the gathering dusk.

"Come on," Tess said. "Let's go out."

24

By the time we made our way down Tess's drive, the neighborhood was alive.

People moved in throngs across yards, and most of the families had gathered in the center of an empty lot between two houses halfway up the street. A ring of torches burned in a circle surrounding a row of tables laden with potluck. Couples lounged in foldout chairs, drinks dangling from hands. A game of horseshoes was in full swing while another group huddled around a set of cornhole boards, a collective shout erupting whenever a sandbag slid home.

I carried the potato salad while Tess held the still-steaming cherry pie. Kenny lagged behind, lugging a two-liter soda and dragging the toes of her shoes. As we approached the main throng of people, I studied faces as they turned toward us. The expected reactions were there.

Surprise. Disdain. Curiosity.

Tess, on the other hand, beamed. Her smile glowed as bright as any of the torches and didn't flicker. A force field conjured to protect her. It was the same when we were kids. Anytime something uncomfortable arose, a berating by one of our mothers, a disagreement during a game—Tess smiled until it was over.

Kenny hadn't inherited her mother's Kevlar grin.

She kept her eyes down, deeply interested in her feet and the ground beneath them. I nudged her with an elbow, giving her a wink when she looked up.

"Carol!" Tess called, setting the pie down on the nearest table. A blonde woman around our age wearing yoga pants and a long-sleeved T-shirt was moving toward us, trying out a tentative smile. Tess embraced her, and Carol hugged her back, saying something low into her ear that made Tess laugh. Kenny and I kept moving, depositing our burdens and hovering near the end of the table as a few more people gathered around Tess. Mostly they exuded warmth. Exclamations of how glad they were to see her. But there were a few holdouts lingering a good distance back, eyeing her as you would roadkill to distinguish what kind of animal it had once been.

Humans were an odd species.

Kenny seemed to be sharing the same sentiment. She searched the crowd, her too-intelligent gaze landing on one person then skipping to another, looking for something. I guessed what it was.

"Any of your friends here?" I asked.

She turned her attention to the forest surrounding the development. In the distance where more vacant lots were still for sale, a group of kids frolicked. Some unnamed game with mercurial rules. They dashed one way, then the other, then somersaulted. Then gathered to discuss something, and were off again, one leading the rest, who trailed like the sparks from the fireworks they held.

"I don't think so," she said.

There was a big pack of sparklers open on the table, a long-necked lighter beside it. I plucked one of the fireworks up along with the lighter. "Tell you what," I said. "I can either light this, and you can go run around with those maniacs, or you can have a sudden-onset stomachache, and I'll take you back to the house and we'll watch a movie. Your choice."

Kenny's indecision was palpable, and I hated myself for it since joining in the festivities had been my idea. Besides, this quest to reenter society wasn't hers. It was her mother's. But how many times does the parent superimpose on the child until they become carbon copies? Hadn't I seen it all my life? What else was abuse but a reservoir of trauma trickling down to the next generation?

She surprised me by taking the sparkler from my hand and holding it out. "I'll run, but not away."

I lit it and hoped the moisture in my eyes didn't shine too bright.

She flew away, a shadow showered in a magnesium glow. Beautiful abandon in the half dark.

The streetlights were coming on. Music followed. A few firepits belched flame. People mingled, a few danced. In the distance a storm slid over the mountains and descended, lightning flickering halfheartedly. I sipped a pilfered beer and tried to stay away from everyone. Across the lot Tess laughed loudly, reaching out to steady herself against the joke teller.

"So you're the long-lost sister?"

Carol, the first greeter of the night, stood a few feet to my right. I hadn't noticed her approach. She must've angled in while I was distracted. "Uh, we're not actually sisters. Really good friends."

"Well, she must think the world of you because that's what Tess told me, that you're sisters."

I must've been getting soft. Second time in an evening I almost started to cry. I covered it up with a long sip of beer, then stuck out my hand. "Nora."

"Carol. Nice to meet you." Her skin was velvet but the grip strong. We settled into the no-man's-land of newly met silence. "How long are you staying?" she finally asked.

"I'm not sure. Probably until next week."

"And you live on the coast?"

"Yes."

"Tess said you were a family advocate."

"That's right."

"Well, if this isn't the job for you, what is?" Carol's tinkling laughter was there and gone. "I'm sorry. What was I thinking?"

"Don't worry about it."

"It's just . . ." She waved a hand at the street-long gathering. "The truth is it shook all of us to our cores. Something like that, you don't think it'll ever happen in your town, your neighborhood. And then nobody knew what to do or say. So we stayed away, which was wrong. I knew it, I think we all did."

I hadn't expected anything else from someone like Carol. She seemed the perfect fair-weather friend and neighbor. But at least she was self-aware enough to quasi-apologize, even if it wasn't to the right person. "Well it looks like she's being welcomed back." As if on cue, Tess laughed again. It was good to hear. Better yet to see a few kids leaning toward Kenny, sharing what looked like an open bag of candy. "I hope they both find some peace now."

"Me too, me too. Before everything she was always so outgoing and cheerful. Always smiling. She's got this magnetism, you know? People just get pulled in." She paused, and her voice took on a different tone. "Say, you would actually know better than anyone. I was thinking of inviting Tess back to the crime committee. Do you think she'd be ready for something like that?"

Blood thudded in my temples, pounded in my ears. I was sure I'd misheard. "Sorry?"

Carol shot me a look. "Oh, she must not have mentioned it. It's the committee we formed a few years back. We liaise with the police and neighborhood watch. Tess was one of the founding members. Understandably, she stepped down from the board, and I took her place."

I was suddenly treading water, trying to keep my head above it in the here and now.

"—or do you think it's too soon?" Carol was asking.

"I—I think it's a great idea, but she might need more time," I managed.

"Yeah, yeah, that's what I was thinking too. I mean, I know it would take a little convincing for the rest of the board, but really there's no reason—"

Carol's voice became background static. Something to tune out. To lose myself in. Across the lot someone had poured Tess a shot, and she tossed it back without hesitation. The crowd around her now was larger, and they had a quality to them I couldn't put my finger on at first. Then the way they spanned out before her clicked. The way they all listened raptly, how intent their eyes were in the yellow glow of streetlight.

They were an audience.

Suddenly I could hear Tess over Carol's droning. Her voice raised two clicks with the alcohol.

"That's a really good question, Ben. No, I had no idea. No idea what he was. But I mean, is it always the wife's responsibility? Everyone has their troubles, but ours seemed normal. How was I supposed to know he was capable of something like that?"

I was moving, handing my beer off to Carol, who took it without pausing in her one-sided conversation. I beelined toward Tess, looking for Kenny and not seeing her.

"So he was a liar and a cheater? So what? Lots of people cheat. But not everyone kills their lover."

"Tess," I said as loudly as I could. She didn't notice. A few people looked uncomfortable, but most were fixated on her—their attention moths, her words flame.

"And to think a judge gave him partial custody of our daughter. *My* daughter." She paused to take a long sip of wine. I was ten steps away. Five. "You'll see, it's a huge mistake. He's a fucking monster."

As I reached Tess, I noticed a small form standing off to the left. Curly hair, wide green eyes watching. Taking in every word her mother was saying.

"Tess," I said, grasping her arm. The scent of booze rolled off her in waves. "I think it's time to go in."

"What do you mean? We just got here. Hey everyone, this is Nora. I'm so rude I didn't introduce you."

The abject horror on Kenny's face was too much. Like trying to look into a dying star. I glanced away and saw a man holding his cell phone out, staring at the screen, recording. He panned the phone away from Tess toward Kenny. Held on her.

I let go of Tess and started toward him. His eyes came up. Met mine.

Locked.

Then he was tucking his phone away and threading through a throng of people.

"Hey," I said, but he kept going. I picked up my pace, maneuvering around a folding chair. "Hey!"

He threw a half glance over one shoulder.

Broke into a run.

My body reacted without thought.

I chased.

Across the uneven architecture of the lot. Past a mound of gravel from some unfinished outdoor project. He sprinted ahead, a leaning figure crossing the threshold of where the neighborhood ended and true night began.

Behind us there were a few shouts, but they were distant. There were no more sparklers. No bangs of fireworks. Only the soft thud of our footsteps. Our breathing as we ran full out.

There was an urge to call to him again, to command that he stop. It was laughable. He wouldn't stop unless I made him. If I could catch him.

Ahead he angled between a home and the encroaching trees, disappearing behind the attached garage. I skidded to a halt at the border, searching the space where he'd vanished.

Pure darkness. But sounds within it. The snapping of twigs. Branches skittering across clothes.

I plunged forward, the image of him filming Kenny—recording her heartache—driving me on like a shovel of coal in a blast furnace.

A trail appeared behind the garage in a faint lick of lightning, narrow and overgrown, but there. I didn't hesitate, didn't look back. Knew if I did, I'd probably stop.

Down a decline into thicker brush. Distantly, water gushed and gurgled. The path jagged hard to the right, and somewhere below there was the unmistakable sound of rocks and gravel giving way, followed by a hissed curse.

I slowed, more to keep myself from suffering the same fate than considering the fact I was alone in the woods with an unknown man. He was fleeing me, but that could change in a second.

The path degraded into a steep goat trail—rocks protruding from the crumbling dirt like nubs of giant teeth. I clambered down sideways, listening intently after each step. Waiting for movement to come crashing out of the underbrush. For the impact of his body against mine. For the inevitable pain.

But there was nothing. Until there was.

Below a dirt road appeared in the headlights of a car flashing on, followed by the guttural thrum of the engine. Through the trees the vehicle's back end sank as its wheels spun. Another flash of vague purple lightning, and it materialized just enough for me to see the vehicle's general size and shape before careening out of sight down the access road.

A black SUV.

25

Adrenaline and shock have their benefits.

I didn't recall climbing back up along the path through the trees or making my way across the darkened edge of the development. There was the moment where I recognized the SUV speeding away in a bleeding glow of taillights, then I was holding Tess's upper arm and guiding her toward her house with Kenny in tow.

Tess babbled drunkenly the entire way back. *What happened? Who was that? Why did you run?* I didn't reply. Could barely hear her over Kenny's deafening silence. There was a track of tears down each side of her small face, which caught the light like safety reflective strips.

Carol angled toward us, still holding her drink and my beer. She started to say something but must've caught the look on my face and kept turning until she was headed back toward the largest firepit.

Then we were inside, the quiet of the house both soothing and thunderous. "Nora, what the hell's going on? What's the matter with you?" Tess asked.

I ignored her and steered Kenny away deeper into the house. "Why don't you go get ready for bed?" I said. She sniffled but didn't object. When she was safely upstairs, I went back to the kitchen where Tess sat on one of the stools. I leaned on the counter, granite cooling my palms and splayed fingers. Then I ran a large glass of water and handed it to her. She set it aside and stared. Waiting.

"It was the guy who was following us the other day," I led with, not really wanting to start there, but knowing anger wasn't going to grease any gears. "He was videoing you and Kenny. He ran when I saw him. There's a path behind one of the houses across the way that leads down to some kind of access road. His SUV was parked down there. He got away."

A little unease entered Tess's gaze, sweeping back some of the drunken cobwebs. "What the hell? Why would he be recording us?"

"I don't know." *But I have a feeling he got what he wanted* was something I didn't add.

"I think we should call the cops, don't you?"

"We could. But I didn't get his license plate again."

"You saw him, though, saw his face, right?"

I flashed back on the moment when he'd been there only a few paces away. Even then the light hadn't been great, his features tiger striped in a wash of yellow sodium arc and shadow. From what I could recall he'd been plain looking, average in a forgettable way. All except a dark mole near his temple just below the hairline, which may have been a fleck of ash or dirt.

"I don't know if I could identify him," I finally said.

"Well maybe someone else could. There had to be a dozen people there; someone must've seen him."

"Even if they did, there's no law against recording in public as far as I know. And I think everyone was a little preoccupied with you at the moment."

She blinked. "What do you mean?"

"You know what I mean. Unless you're too drunk to remember."

"I'm not . . . drunk," she said, attempting an indignant pause between words.

From one heartbeat to the next my anger boiled over. "Jesus, Tess, you were holding fucking court."

"You said we should get back out there."

"I didn't mean air everything to the neighbors. And I definitely didn't mean say things like that in front of Kenny."

"Like what?"

"Things about Neil."

"Why? They're true."

"Even if they are, it's deeply damaging to hear them from one parent about the other."

"Damaging. Wow, yes." Tess stood, swaying a little. "Look, I know you worked with kids a lot and saw terrible things, but you're not . . ." She bit her words off and frowned. "Never mind."

"No, what were you going to say?"

She gathered herself. "You're not a mother."

My jaw clenched, biting back a response I'd regret. "You're right, I'm not," I said.

I went to my room and shut the door, chiding myself for thinking Tess and I could reconnect so easily after all the years between. Time was a crucible, it molded people. And usually they were no longer recognizable on the other side.

The neighborhood get-together was winding down. Fires were extinguishing, and kids were being herded inside. Possibly because it was getting late, more likely because of the spectacle I'd caused. But I'd only reacted. It had felt as natural as breathing to chase the man who'd turned his attention as well as his phone on Kenny in a moment of utter vulnerability. I worried what I would have done if I'd had a weapon at hand.

Gradually my thoughts lost their adrenaline sheen and the entire evening came into sharper focus. The deeper significance of the man who'd been staking out the neighborhood and following us showing up at a block party to record a very personal moment between mother and daughter.

It reeked of predation.

I'd heard from more than one cop it was common practice to surveil an abductee or murder victim's candlelight vigil for someone who looked out of place. Someone there to watch others suffer. To lap at their grief.

In other words, the person responsible for the vigil in the first place.

Abe said he'd personally run down the killer of a young boy at the boy's funeral when he showed up to attend the service and fled after being approached by undercover state police.

Until that moment the idea of Neil's innocence had been like a city you'd heard of but never been to—there, but unfamiliar and not really real in the sense you could visit it. Tess was utterly sure of his guilt, and the whole scenario did look very bad for him. But wasn't there a possibility it hadn't been Neil? Hadn't the nosy landlord said other people had been in and out of Allie's home? There'd even been prowlers about. I wondered if a certain SUV had been in or around the vicinity leading up to Allie's death. I wondered if the landlord had seen it herself. And if this man had done the deed and Neil had taken the fall, was it unreasonable to think he might want to take a tour through the suffering he'd created? Be in the front row as a family was torn apart spectacularly?

I'd seen what human beings could do to each other—the only limits of violence and cruelty were their own imaginations.

A soft knock at the door drew me from my inward state. When I opened it, Tess stood there looking down. "I'm sorry. I really didn't mean that."

"Yes, you did." Her eyes flashed up to mine. "And you're right, I'm not a mother. In fact, the idea of being one terrifies me." I took one of her hands, squeezed it. "You asked me for my help. This is me giving it in the only way I know how. I've seen the fallout from families imploding. It's ugly. And the kids are always collateral damage. Always."

"I don't want that for her. I don't want any of this," she said, her voice low and breathless. "I don't know what I'm doing sometimes. Everything is wrong. It's like another life started the second I found out, and I've been trying to get back to the other one ever since. But it's not there anymore, is it? That life is gone forever."

She reached for me, and I held her. And then we were back to the single time I'd seen her after her mother died. It was at the funeral, and she'd worn a black velvet dress with a matching bow on one shoulder that had crinkled between us when I'd hugged her. Her tears the same wetness on my neck now as they were then.

Some things didn't change.

26

The faint hope Kenny would be sleeping when I checked on her evaporated.

She was awake and staring at cool-blue shadows pocking the ceiling. I sat on the end of her bed, choosing to take in the view outside instead of her expression, which was void of emotion. It was almost worse seeing her this way than crying. It spoke of a hardening that happens to all of us at some point when the secret that the world isn't ordered or kind finally begins to reveal itself. That some of the malice you thought was temporary appears to be permanent. Some people get to live in oblivion longer than others. It wasn't fair to have the veil lifted so young.

"I know you're going to say something encouraging," she said as I started to open my mouth to do just that. "Please don't."

"All I was going to say was, I'm sorry."

"For what?"

"For what happened tonight."

"It wasn't your fault."

"It was in a way. I told your mom you and her should get out and see people. Try to do normal stuff." She was quiet at this. "Your mom loves you very much. She's trying to do what she thinks is right. But sometimes people can be hurtful while they're trying to help. Sometimes that's when it's the worst."

Kenny finally looked at me, those too-bright eyes searching, combing for the truth, since that's what everyone is searching for at that age whether we know it or not. "I thought maybe you really were on my side, like you said. You let me see my dad. I hoped you'd believe me about him. But you're my mom's friend."

I started to protest, to try prying some reassurance from the tightness of my chest, but Kenny rolled over to face the wall and closed her eyes. I stayed immobile for a second, then rose and left her room, closing the door behind me.

Soft snores came from Tess's bedroom. She was lying face down, crossways on the mattress, still dressed, her shoes fallen to the floor beneath her outstretched legs. I watched her for a time, feeling a mingling of pity and rage. It was a bitter cocktail.

Downstairs the house was quiet, the neighborhood empty and serene. The first drops of rain were gentle, almost considerate, taps on the windows. The light over the stove was on, and when I went to turn it off, I noticed the black rectangle of Tess's phone on the counter.

Most of us think we can control what drives us. We like to believe the true engine running inside, turning the gears, making things go can be turned off when we feel like it. When the line approaches we've agreed to not cross. But that's not the way it is. That's not the way people are.

The code Tess punched in earlier floated behind my eyes, and a moment later my finger was hitting the same digits on her phone screen. It opened.

A creak came from near the patio, and I froze, every nerve singing. Just the house settling. More rain, coming down steadier now. I waited for another minute of unbroken silence before proceeding. My finger hovered first over the email icon, then slid to messages. There were none unread flagging attention, but the name I was looking for was only two down below my own and Jacob's.

Devon.

My pulse juddered in my eyes, in my temples. I still had time to change course. Instead I touched the message.

In for a penny and all that, I scrolled to the very beginning of Tess and Devon Wilson's exchange. My expectations were they'd start sometime around Neil's arrest. Instead they went back over six months, well before Allie Prentiss had met her end. To begin with, the conversation looked professional—dates exchanged, which I slowly understood to be for the crime-prevention meetings. A couple of jokes back and forth. Very genial, but nothing eyebrow-raising.

Then the messages changed.

They became farther apart in time. More cryptic.

I put the new feeder out today, Devon texted in late January.

See anything? Tess said.

Just chickadees so far.

The goldfinches are back, Devon wrote in February.

Lovely, Tess responded.

It was like that for a while. Truncated conversations of birds or birdwatching punctuated by sometimes weeks of silence. All the way down to when Neil was arrested. The messages stopped there until just last week—the very message I'd caught the day of the custody hearing.

Where are you? Call when you can.

And then just as I'd suspected, the final text in the string coming the prior Saturday evening around the time we'd been eating dinner.

You should see the hummingbirds, he wrote.

Bet they're beautiful, Tess replied.

I shut the phone off and placed it back where it had been. Retreated to my room. Inside I lay on the bed, listening to the rain chuckling hollowly in the downspout. And I thought about loyalty and how it was the closest thing to love without being one and the same.

Sleep crept in gradually. I pulled away from it in starts and fits before it finally grasped me fully. Dragged me under.

It was still full dark when I jerked awake to shattering glass and a rising scream.

27

For a second there was a complete dislocation.

I had no idea where or when I was. The shattering glass was a plate my father had thrown across the room when Paul had served him eggs that were overdone. The scream was my own as he wrenched my arm behind my back for muddying a new pair of shoes.

Slowly my sense of time and place returned, and I realized the scream wasn't a scream at all but the security system winding up. Then I was on my feet, half-conscious of reaching out to grab the doorknob to my room, still convincing myself this wasn't a dream.

The hallway was dark except for the weak flicker of lightning painting the carpet and walls deep blue, then gone. I took a breath, trying to come back to myself, trying to think. For half a second I tried blaming it all on a dropped glass or plate, but that wouldn't set off the security system. So therefore, a window had been broken.

Even as my sluggish thoughts began to catch up, a gentle breeze smelling of fresh rain and earth coursed past me. My phone. Where was it? I backed into my room and spent year-long moments searching before finding it in my crumpled jeans' pocket.

Somewhere in the kitchen a bright jangle of tones sounded. Tess's phone was ringing.

I punched in 911 and listened as the call connected and a woman's calm voice came on asking what my emergency was.

"I think someone's broken into my friend's home." I gave her the address as she asked if anyone was inside. I didn't know. Was anyone hurt? I didn't know. Police were on the way. She wanted me to stay on the line with her, but I disconnected, unable to hear anything over the wail of the alarm and her voice.

Out in the hall again, and now with the adrenaline fully flowing, my eyes felt like vacuums, sucking in everything, identifying all. The shapes of the banister going upstairs, the kitchen counter, the light spraying the undercabinet from Tess's cell.

And the sliding door, a fractured rim of glass inside the frame, a carpet of shards glittering on the floor with a misshapen island in their center. It took a moment to recognize the lump as a softball-size rock.

I panned the open space, searching for movement, for a shadow to rise from behind the long table or leap from beside the counter. Nothing. Just more breeze drifting in, smelling of the storm.

Then someone was coming down the stairs so fast and suddenly I flinched and cocked an arm back, ready to strike.

It was Tess, eyes shining to the whites, arms extended, a revolver shaking in her hands.

"What is it?" she half yelled over the alarm. "What's going on?" At some point she'd woken and changed into a loose T-shirt and shorts.

I pointed at the back entry, and her mouth opened a little, taking in the glass, the rock on the floor. Kenny appeared at the top of the stairs, and we moved in sync, both shouting at her to go back to her room. She did at top speed.

My hand found a nearby switch, and a lamp nudged back the dark enough for us to move through the room, both of us hesitant and careful. Tess made it to the alarm's control panel and silenced it. It was like my ears had been stuffed with mud. The quiet like an atmosphere. Tess grabbed her phone and answered, still pointing the gun around—its bulk so large in her small hand it looked cartoonish.

"Diedre. One, two, four, one, two," Tess said into the phone—her code to prove her identity to the security agency.

"The police are on their way," I said.

She nodded and spoke for another few seconds before hanging up. We assessed one another for a beat before wordlessly beginning to search the room. It didn't take long to realize we were alone, the closets and pantry revealing no one hiding inside. By the time we were done, fresh sirens were rising to the north, and a minute later the first cop car came gliding to a stop in the drive. I took the gun from Tess's trembling hand and put it in the bedside table drawer in my room. Outside, flashlights cut long white blades back and forth across the yard as officers made their way to the front door while a couple circled around the side.

Tess started to go let them in but paused. "It was him. I know it was," she said, the words like steel in her throat. When she'd gone to the entry, I turned in time to see a small shadow retreating for a second time from the top of the stairs to blend with the rest of the darkness.

28

There's an impotency in the aftermath of injury or violence.

You're at the whim of officials, whether it be the fire department putting out the blaze and cordoning you off from the smoking ruin that was your life, or medical staff separating you from an ailing loved one, leaving you in a limbo that's worse than any torture dreamed by man.

The police brought us all outside, where the rain had tapered to nothing, and we sat on a couple lawn chairs in the front drive between two of the cruisers while they swept the house. The neighbors who had just gone to sleep woke with a curious thirst slaked only by loitering in their driveways and discussing what might be happening at the local pariah's house. Tess tried cuddling Kenny in her lap, but Kenny sat in a separate chair wrapped in her own blanket, staring away into the retreating storm on the horizon.

I watched the two of them. Mother and daughter like opposite ends of magnets. Part of them wanting to come together but holding themselves back at the same time. I was lost in thought when I noticed something on the shoulder of Tess's T-shirt. But then a cop was giving us the all-clear, and we headed back inside.

A uniformed officer sat down at the counter to take Tess's statement while I swept up glass. "So, Mrs. Grayson—" he began, but Tess cut him off.

"I'm not married anymore. Just Tess is fine. Would you like some coffee?"

"Sure, that'd be great." The cop's gaze slid appreciatively to Tess's bare legs when she turned away. He saw me see him looking and cleared his throat, opening a voice memo app on his phone. "So, Tess. You mentioned you have reason to believe it was your ex-husband who vandalized your door?"

"I can't think of anyone else."

"Uh-huh. And why is this?"

"Don't tell me you're not aware of the situation, Officer. Your department is well versed on my husband and what he's done."

"Well, ma'am, it's not that I'm unaware of the uh . . . accusations, it's I need to understand the current crime. Has your husband been threatening you or your daughter?"

"No. But I've seen him watching the house from his car sometimes. And I'd bet my life he was here last night."

The cop frowned and stared at his phone. "I spoke to some of your neighbors, and they said there was a disturbance last night at a block party? Something about a guy being chased?"

"That was me," I said, setting the broom aside and emptying the dustpan. "There was someone videoing Tess's daughter last night. I spoke to him, and he ran. I chased him."

"You chased him."

"Yeah."

We traded stares for a long moment before he let out an extended breath. "Okay. And have you seen this man before?"

"We think he may have been following us at one point," Tess said. "He was driving a black SUV. Maybe a Tahoe or Blazer, I'm not sure."

"And could you describe him?"

Tess looked to me. "About six feet, hundred and fifty pounds. Maybe a mole on his left temple."

"Okey dokey, I think that's all I need."

"Well what's the plan?" Tess asked. "Are you going to pick him up?"

"Your husband or the guy from last night?"

"Jesus," Tess huffed. "My *ex*-husband."

"We will definitely follow up all leads and keep you posted."

Tess death-stared him out of the kitchen until we heard the front door open and close. "Can you believe that?" she asked as I set about finding something to pin across the glassless door. "I mean, really."

"They're crossing t's and dotting i's," I said, finding a large enough blanket at the end of the couch. "They dusted for prints and took the rock. If it was Neil, they'll figure it out."

"If," Tess muttered as she helped me tack the blanket across the door.

Kenny appeared a few minutes later looking none the worse for wear.

"I'm not sure if you should go to school today, honey," Tess said.

"We've got a test in science. I don't want to miss it."

"But if you're tired you won't be able to concentrate."

"I'll be fine." She ignored an offer from her mother for breakfast and retrieved a granola bar and a juice from the fridge instead before heading toward the entry. "Have a good day!" Tess called, but only received the quiet click of the door closing in reply. "She hates me."

"She doesn't hate you. She's torn."

"Amounts to the same. Coffee?"

"Of course."

We sat with our cups at the table, observing the way the blanket undulated with the wind, like the house was breathing. The storm had washed the sky a clean pale blue without a cloud left behind. Birdsong filtering in through the shattered door made me think of Tess and Devon's texts.

"You thinking of something spicy?" Tess asked.

"Why?"

"You're blushing."

"Probably still coming down from earlier." Which wasn't truly a lie. The crash from adrenaline can be a gradual descent. And when you hit bottom, you know it. I felt the beginnings of exhaustion tugging at me even through the caffeine. "What do you have going on today?"

"Well, I'll have to go see a glass company, I guess. Other than that, a couple errands around town. How about you?"

"My hearing got postponed, so I can stay a little longer."

She brightened. "That's great. And what you said last night really resonated with me. Kendra is my central concern. She's my world. So I have to be careful. Especially now."

After she'd gone, I lingered on those words and wondered exactly what she'd meant.

29

Sleep.

Deep, dreamless, senseless sleep. When I woke it was to a bell in my stomach pealing hunger and blinding sunlight only high elevations seem to be capable of providing. I meandered to the kitchen feeling like I'd been up all night and missing home. Missing my dog.

A chicken-salad wrap and side of fresh veggies helped fill the void in my center but did nothing for the homesickness. While I ate and watched the door's makeshift barricade ripple, I thought of what Kenny had said last night. How I was her mom's friend, and therefore not on her side. Not really. I thought about Tess speaking drunkenly to the neighbors and the sound the glass had made when the rock came through it in the middle of the night.

There was a shard I'd missed earlier underneath the couch, and I retrieved it, rolling the fractured pebble in my hand before depositing it in the garbage.

Upstairs I paused in Tess's bedroom doorway, but only for a second. Then I was inside and opening every drawer I could find. Rummaging and putting things back the way they were. All the while the heat of shame rose steadily from my center, burning outward like a fever. I beat it back by thinking of the messages on Tess's phone and what I'd seen on the shoulders of her T-shirt last night.

After searching everywhere I could think of in the main part of the room, I set upon the walk-in closet stuffed to the ceiling with clothes and shoes. What I was looking for I couldn't say. An addendum to the suspicions slowly forming in my lizard brain. I would know it when I saw it.

A cardboard box was stuffed near the back of the closet beneath some dresses. I pulled it out and sat back, drawing out the contents one by one.

It was the missing photos from the hallway downstairs. At least a dozen of them. Here was Neil and Tess and a much younger Kenny on their front lawn, Kenny toddling toward the camera with bright eyes while her parents leaned against one another, watching her with pure adoration. Next was a shot of the family on a hiking trip—Kenny maybe five years old, proudly sporting a miniature backpack. Neil and Tess knelt on either side of her, beaming. Here was a selfie Neil had taken while holding Tess close, their hair windswept with a panoramic mountain view behind them. I looked at this picture the longest, took in Tess's closed eyes, how she leaned her head against Neil's shoulder, her faint contented smile.

It hurt to look at them. How happy they'd been. Hurt to see these remnants of their life piled into a box and shoved out of sight. I pictured Tess sitting where I was now, reliving better times, unwilling to keep these reminders in plain view but unable to throw them away.

I replaced the box filled with the memories of a broken family and turned to leave, but something on a topmost shelf stopped me. I reached up, grasped the spine of a small photo album from between two shoeboxes, and drew it down. When I opened it, I was met with my eight-year-old self.

There I was, seated beside an equally young Tess at her childhood kitchen table. We both wore bilious yellow party hats, chin strings and all. Our attention was rapt by a pink cake with eight candles burning like a pyre. Tess's birthday. I remembered this. The next photo was us at the beach, and my heart clutched painfully at the sight of Paul knee-deep in the waves, so young and alive. I quickly paged past it to more and more snapshots of our overlapping youth.

Christmas.

Outings to the zoo.

The beach again.

A hike.

In one our mothers stood on a rock shelf overlooking a vertigo-inducing drop. Somewhere in the northern part of the state, if I recalled correctly. They were oblivious to whoever snapped the picture, standing there gazing out over a panorama of pine-studded mountains and river-lined valleys. Standing like they were the last two people on earth, surveying what was now their world.

I felt my brow dip at the last shot. It was Diedre and my mom again, standing somewhere on a sun-drenched beach, the sand so white it was like they floated on clouds. They were in bathing suits, both holding drinks aloft, wearing sunglasses much too big for their faces, my mother smiling hard enough to expose molars.

I had no idea where this was, but it wasn't a Pacific Northwest beach. Not with the tiki-hut bars behind them and the palms waving in a tropical breeze. But there was something more to the picture that gave me pause, something about the way they were standing that didn't compute.

Downstairs my phone rang, and I fumbled the album, picked it up from the floor, and placed it back where it had been before hurrying out of the room.

I missed the last ring by two seconds and saw Abe's number floating on the screen. When I called him back, he answered with, "You know not picking up, then calling back doesn't actually make people think you're busy. It just pisses them off."

"Hello to you too. And I am busy."

"That's what concerns me."

I waited the correct amount of time, then said, "So—yay or nay on the retired buddy filling you in?"

"Yay." The fear Abe would shut me down fell away. I had no other real resources to call on at this point. "But the usual disclaimer, you don't know this, we never spoke, and I'd advise you to find a different avenue to channel your attention."

"This avenue is kind of a one-way street if we're going to keep up the allegory."

"We're not. Okay—" Abe's breath rushed out in a long blast. "So your boy Devon Wilson really fucked himself good." I eased to the bed, glancing out the window once to make sure Tess hadn't returned yet. "You know the basics of the case, so here's the rundown. The lead detective, Carl Lowe, he arrests your friend's husband a bit prematurely from what I gather. He has him near the crime scene around the time of the murder, he's got DNA in the girl's apartment and in her vehicle, he has eyewitnesses seeing them chumming around campus. And the last text Allie sent was to Grayson. Something like, 'you need to come see me, now.' On top of that Lowe is nearing retirement, from another age, so to speak, so he sees all this as more than enough for charges and pulls the trigger. But the DA gets gun shy."

"It's all circumstantial."

"Right-O. So Neil Grayson is sitting behind bars with no charges actually backing it up. He's on a seventy-two-hour hold, then he's a free bird. You know what happens next."

"His cabin is searched."

"A second time, I might add, and the book with Allie Prentiss's blood is found in a little hidden nook beside the fireplace. Bingo-bango, we have damning evidence, and the DA changes his tune."

Tess's car appeared at the end of the neighborhood and drew closer. I stood and made my way toward the back entry.

"All goes as you'd expect for the next couple months," Abe continued. "Grayson sits in jail while his attorney keeps chewing away like a rat, and then there's a break." I peeled back the blanket hanging over the open frame and slipped through the gap, hearing Tess's vehicle pull into the garage. "I lose you?"

"No, keep going," I said, sidling around the patio furniture toward the wall of trees.

"Grayson's attorney digs up the crime-scene photos from the Prentiss place, and, lo and behold, there seems to be one missing. It's a particular shot of the girl's bookcase."

I came to a stop beneath a pine, well shaded from the sun, and let what he was saying sink in. "Let me guess, it was the one pic that showed the book they found at the cabin."

"Give her a prize. So here we have ourselves a problem, because there's an evidence photo of the book there after her murder, then suddenly it's found at the suspect's residence. The DA takes one look and drops the charges, and Grayson walks. Around that time internal affairs takes over, Devon Wilson goes on leave, and the waters get muddied."

"Nora?" Tess's voice floated through the blanket from inside. I stepped around the back of the tree and leaned against it.

"So what's your gut tell you?" I asked, lowering my voice.

"For two and two to make four, I'd say sometime during the seventy-two-hour hold, Devon Wilson gets antsy. He knows Grayson's going to walk unless there's a break. He goes back to the crime scene and searches for something useful, finds the book that was a gift from Grayson, which either has a small amount of blood spatter on it or he adds it himself, then hides it at the cabin and 'finds' it, cinching the charges."

"Then the lawyer digs in and sees a photo's missing."

"And Wilson gets popped. Now he could argue that Grayson went back to the crime scene to collect a trophy, but that's weak tea. So what we're looking at here is planting evidence, and that is what we call a 'no-no' in the business. If the good ol' boys club doesn't sweep it under the rug, he'll be fired and probably do three to five, maybe more. Won't ever be a cop again, that's for sure."

"Nora? You out here?" Tess called from the back door. I held my breath, waiting for her to spot me behind the tree, but there was nothing more.

"You okay?" Abe asked.

"Yeah," I said. "Hey, thank you for all this. I know you didn't want to do it."

"It was just bullshitting with an old friend, no skin off my nose. What worries me is you asking in the first place." There was a long pause. "I don't know if you're privy to the specifics of Prentiss's murder or not, but it was brutal. My friend said they collected skull and brain matter off the ceiling."

I winced, the entire contents of my stomach doing a barrel roll. "I'll be careful."

"I hope so. Because even if I don't know all the details, I know this—whoever killed that poor girl is walking free."

I hung up with him, feeling every inch of skin tingling like I'd just stepped out of a cold shower. Images of Allie Prentiss's living room before it had been cleaned and stripped crowded into my head. I shook them away before imagining what her body might have looked like and stepped around the tree, nearly running into Tess.

"There you are," she said, clocking the surprise I wasn't able to conceal. "Everything okay?"

"Yeah, fine."

She glanced around with a half smile. "What are you doing out here?"

"Getting some air. Trying to wake up. I had a nap and felt logy."

She nodded. "Well, the glass guy will be here soon. Did you eat yet? I'm going to make something."

"I'm good."

She stared for a second or two beyond comfort, and I wondered how long she'd been standing there, listening. "I'll make a little extra in case you change your mind."

I watched her move back to the house, relentless sun dappling the yard, the breeze lifting her hair. When she was inside, I let some of the tension ease from my muscles. Weakness replaced it.

What the hell was going on?

Some of the picture was revealing itself, and I didn't care for what it showed. For a time I stood still near the pine, not hearing or seeing anything around me. Then I headed inside, Abe's last words following me while sounding more and more like the warning they were.

30

The glass "guy" was a sturdy woman who arrived twenty minutes later in a large panel truck.

She worked quietly and methodically, taking the old door out of its frame before transferring it to her truck, where she began installing new glass. A short time later an apprentice arrived to help her set the fully renewed door into its track. By the time Kenny returned home from school, it was like the damage had never happened.

Tess mirrored the illusion.

Far from sulky and hungover, she operated on the opposite end of the spectrum. Any further indication of her earlier suspicion was burned away by easy laughter and her smile, which I tried gauging as genuine, or the armor she donned whenever things got rough. For once I struggled to determine which it was.

Kenny seemed to sense the change in her mother as well, and after a short meeting between the two upstairs, some of Kenny's cheer returned. She asked if we could play a game of cribbage before dinner, which I lost spectacularly.

Afterward I answered emails—one from Gayle and Joel being of particular concern since it sounded so panicked. I reassured them everything would work out, that the continuance was only a minor bump in the road. My words looked hollow and small on the screen, nowhere near comforting enough for two parents aching with their child's absence. I hit send.

Tess's extended apology for the prior night came in the form of dinner. She called it a *Signs* meal, cooking us each a different dish. For me it was pad thai, Kenny had chocolate chip pancakes with bananas and whipped cream, and glazed salmon with a single glass of white wine for Tess.

We ate at the kitchen table, and my eyes kept straying to the repaired door, the glass gradually filling with our reflections as the day gave way to evening.

"How was art class?" Tess asked Kenny.

She'd eaten two pancakes that made my stomach ache just looking at them and was hard at work on a third. "Okay. Mrs. Palmer said my hand sketches were some of the best she's seen in our grade."

"That's great!"

"Yeah," Kenny said, looking solemnly at the remains of her meal. "Hands are the worst."

"Well, you're extremely talented. And if you want to accomplish something, you can't give up. Isn't that right, Nora?"

I'd been consciously dipping in and out of the back and forth, catching every other word. "Sure is," I supplied with as much enthusiasm as I could muster.

"See, Nora used to work for the state and had to answer to lots and lots of people, and now she works for herself. She was brave enough to do what she thought was right." Tess's smile was still there, locked in, unwavering. Her eyes searched me. "And she's much happier now."

Kenny turned her attention to me. "So you're your own boss."

"Yes, but in a lot of ways that's harder than taking orders." I looked at Tess. "You have to know your own limitations."

Silence fell. Kenny looked between us, then resumed eating. We all did.

For a time there was only the clink of utensils on plates, muted chewing, then Kenny said, "Um, so I was wondering how Friday is going to work."

"Work how?" Tess asked without looking up.

"You know . . . like how am I going to get to the cabin to stay with Dad?"

Tess paused, her fork hovering between plate and mouth. "Well, I suppose we'll meet somewhere."

"Where?"

"Like a halfway point or something."

"But where?"

"I'm not sure, honey, but we'll figure it out."

"So have you talked to him?"

"No."

"Have your lawyers talked to each other?"

"I don't know."

"Well then, how will we figure it out?"

"Honey, please leave it to the grown-ups, okay? Don't worry." The edge in Tess's tone was final, and Kenny shot me a look before finishing her food. I could almost hear her unsaid reply. *Leave it to the grown-ups? When they're the ones who've made such a mess of my life? Okay. Sure.*

"Maybe after we're done, we can look at more of your art projects," I offered. Kenny shrugged halfheartedly, but I could tell she wanted to show off her work to someone. "I can even give you some tips about hands."

"Tips? What do you mean?"

"Well, I'm kind of an expert. Not to brag, but I've had two of them my whole life." I got a laugh from my stupid joke. Even Tess smiled, and this time it seemed fully her own.

While we were clearing dishes there was a knock at the door. Kenny ran to answer it before Tess or I could stop her, and a moment later Jacob's voice drifted from the entry. Kenny filed back through, barely pausing. "I'll be in my room," she said, already mounting the stairs as Jacob stepped into the kitchen.

"I missed dinner again," he joked, kissing Tess lightly on the cheek.

"I can reheat something," Tess offered.

"No, that's okay. Maybe just a beer."

While she retrieved a bottle and glass, Jacob eyed the repaired door, then looked at me. "Can't even tell, can you?" he said.

"No, the company did a great job." Tess had mentioned she'd looped Jacob in on the prior night's festivities.

Jacob poured his beer and sipped. "So, there's been a development," he said. Tess nodded toward the patio, and we went outside. When we were seated, Jacob continued. "The chief of police got ahold of me about half an hour ago."

"And?" Tess asked. She'd scooted forward to the front of her chair.

"They arrested Neil late this afternoon."

Tess lowered her face to her clasped hands as if a prayer had been answered. It probably had.

Jacob gave her a moment, then went on. "They pulled footage from a traffic camera on the highway, and he was identified leaving the neighborhood around the time of the break-in. And one of the neighbors said they spotted his vehicle prior to the alarm going off. When Neil was initially questioned, he said he was home at the time. Then he changed his story and said he was just driving through the neighborhood."

Tess looked to me with an air of vindication before turning to Jacob. "So what happens now?"

Jacob blew out a breath. "Well the custody arrangement will definitely be put on hold for the time being. He's supposed to see a judge sometime tomorrow or the next day about bail, which he'll definitely make. But this is our chance to file a restraining order."

"Do it," Tess said. "I don't want him anywhere near us again."

"Already in the works. And I asked a friend on the force to swing past on the regular, just in case."

While Tess absorbed this, I said, "So what are we looking at for charges?"

"Breaking and entering won't be an option since there's no evidence he actually entered. We can press vandalism, destruction of property, maybe violent intimidation. Any of those could keep him from gaining custody at the very least. But my guess is there won't be any jail time. Most likely a fine and some community service—that's, of course, if he's convicted."

"So the question," I said after a moment, "is how do we explain all this to Kenny?"

Tess and Jacob fell silent. The evening deepened, the sky bruising from dark blue to purple as the first stars emerged.

"It doesn't matter what we tell her, she won't accept it," Tess said after a time. "She'll retreat into her shell again."

"That's if we're the ones telling her," I said.

"What do you mean?"

"I think you should let her talk to Neil." She bristled at this, but I held up a hand. "Hear me out. You said yourself she won't believe he did this. Let him explain why he won't be able to take her this weekend. Whatever he wants to say, at least she's hearing the bad news from him. It takes a little pressure off of you."

Tess seemed to go to war internally. She frowned, picking at the arm of her chair. "It would be nice not being the bad guy for once."

"Exactly. And it might put some things in perspective for her."

We adjourned shortly after, and when Jacob said his good nights and headed for his car, I followed him outside.

"Hey," I said, throwing a look back at the house. Tess had mentioned a shower, but I wasn't sure she'd actually gone upstairs. Jacob paused, the door to his car open, one leg inside. "What do you think the odds are any of this holds up? Really."

He looked down the street and shook his head. "Not good. Especially not the way she thinks it will. If nothing sticks, he'll still get partial custody. This is only a temporary hold. And there was something else." He glanced at the house as if he had the same concerns as I did of being overheard. "I didn't say anything because I don't know for sure, but there was a rumor floating around the courthouse that Neil's lawyer filed something this morning before he was arrested. I have no idea what it was, but there was no reason his counsel should've been doing anything further on his behalf. He already got awarded partial custody, which is what he wanted. It makes me a little nervous."

I watched Jacob drive into the night, his taillights winking once, then gone. The neighborhood was battened down, quiet and serene. Innocuous. But there was always something hidden beneath a facade. Always something more to be seen.

You just had to know how to look for it.

31

Transcript of *Poe, the Man and the Myths: A lecture series with Professor Neil Grayson*, Part 7—presented by Ridgewood University in coordination with College Partnership Programming.

Ah! And now we come to Poe's most famous poem, and arguably his most famous work, "The Raven." I'm guessing most of you in the room and watching from home could recite the first few lines off the top of your head, it's that ingrained in American culture. On the surface it's about a person mourning the loss of someone they love— Lenore. It's a poem of grief written in a style that nearly sings off the page. But let's dive a little deeper.

When the narrator begins asking questions of the raven, what are they actually doing? They're questioning their own beliefs. Their emotions. Their motivations. They're wondering aloud about the future, but they're also wondering about what's going on inside them.

Haven't we all felt this way at one point or another? We're torn by our internal struggles and feelings when encountering great triumph or loss. We wonder if what we're feeling is normal or natural. If it's in line with society's expectations. We look outward for validation.

But what comes of great passion that's unmoored? What comes of untethered grief or anger? The future is shaped by our actions, and actions in turn are shaped by what we feel.

In the end there is no raven. There is only the chaos inside us.

32

There's never really a calm before a storm.

All that's skewed perspective created by going through something difficult. People are revisionists at heart; we like to rewrite both the good and the bad so they become the most joyous and the very worst experiences. All I know is when things get rough, everything before that point looks calm. But in the days following the break-in, we had as much peace as anyone could ask for.

Two days after Neil was arrested, Kenny and I went out on the lake in a pair of kayaks. At that point she was still blissfully unaware her father had been accused of the break-in and had spent a night in jail. Unaware their planned reunion was no longer.

The lake was calm and clear, the water visibility at least twenty feet down. On the far side opposite the highway, the mountains rose up from rock- and pine-infested banks to towering jagged peaks sawing at the sky. One lower stony shelf jutted so far out, it was being used as a runway and diving board for dozens of teenagers. Their cries of delight as they plummeted into the ice-cold water rang across the flat expanse.

We paddled toward the moraine, and I got my first up close view of it. The uniform curve of the land looked incongruent amid the rest of the surrounding nature. It was bare of trees for the bulk of its length, then gradually rose into a stand of pines, which became a full-fledged forest. Kenny pointed at its far end.

"There's a ton of awesome hiking trails up there. Dad and I've gone on most of them."

"Is it busy this time of year?"

"Not really. There's a lot of people in the summer. But the higher trails are always empty. It's really nice."

At the far end of the lake, the mountainside became wall-like, running sheer-faced upward for at least five hundred feet where it angled in slightly. Kenny gestured to a bare spot near the top. "That's the lookout by our cabin. You can see forever from there." There was a buoyancy to her, a vibrant light in her eyes that had been absent since the sky tram. I was glad to see it, and gladder still she'd wanted me to go with her on the lake. A truce had formed between us, forged by games of cribbage and strengthened by ignoring our conversation after the neighborhood block party.

Yet I felt a stab of guilt watching her gaze up at the lookout. Tess had helped orchestrate the outing so she and Jacob could fully weigh out the pluses and minuses of a call from Kenny to her dad. They'd verified he'd made bail the previous day, but Tess had still dug her heels in over Kenny speaking to him, even though it would mean a few turns off the vise for her in explaining the situation.

"I'm just worried what he'll tell her," she'd said the night before over cups of tea. "He could say whatever he wants, and she'll believe it."

I hadn't pushed the idea too hard, letting the notion of not having to break the news to Kenny build a weight of its own. It wasn't long until she caved.

As we started back to the boat launch, I receded, letting my thoughts move in time with the paddle strokes. I'd been torn from the first moment of arriving, pulled like gravity to reconnect with one of the few bright spots of my childhood only to realize it was so much more complicated than I'd expected. Trying to go back always is. And now there was Kenny.

I glanced at her—a few yards ahead and to my left, she was the epitome of wonder, of young intelligence, of promise. Everything I'd missed at her age. Everything I wanted to preserve in her.

And beyond all this I sensed something coming.

A dark and dangerous blot on the horizon. A boulder teetering, readying to roll downhill and crush everything in its path. And the worst was not knowing who had pushed it.

When we got back to the house and Tess mentioned the phone call to Neil, Kenny was predictably suspicious. She glanced from her mother to me, and back again.

"You want me to call Dad?"

"Yes. Don't you want to?" Tess said.

"Yes. But why are you letting me? Why now?" The kid didn't miss anything.

Tess sighed. "Well, there's been a slight change of plans, and I thought you'd want to talk to him about it."

"What change?"

"Just call him, honey." Tess held out her phone. Kenny eyed it with a slight distrust, as if it were some elaborate joke, then snatched it from her hand and scurried upstairs, her bedroom door thunking shut a second later.

"I really hope this is the right move," Tess said, sipping at a cup of coffee.

"It's probably the best peace offering you can give with the current situation."

Tess released another long breath. "I'm just relieved. We've got some breathing room with the custody on hold." I made no reply but thought of what Jacob had said regarding the chances any charges against Neil would stick. I knew Tess was operating in a fantasy state brought on by the upheaval of her life, but at some point reality would crash down.

We were quiet for a time, neither of us wanting to admit we were waiting for what was to come.

A door finally opened upstairs, and a moment later Kenny reappeared with Tess's phone. She handed it off without a word and headed for the back door, features betraying nothing.

"Honey?" Tess asked. "Are you okay?"

"I'm fine."

"Did you talk to him?"

"Yep."

"And?"

"And I guess I'm staying here this weekend. But you knew that already."

"Oh, honey . . ."

"It's okay, Mom. I'm fine."

Kenny gave a faux smile and went outside to sit in one of the chairs. "Damn it," Tess said. "That's almost worse than her being angry. No, it is worse." Tess started for the back door, then stopped. "I'm going to take a shower and then talk to her once she's had a little time." I nodded and waited until she was gone to join Kenny outside.

The day had become even more beautiful since leaving the lake, if that were possible. Everything seemed to be green and growing, and the sun was like a torch on my exposed skin, tightening it in that painful/pleasant way. Kenny sat watching a beetle crawling across the rim of the fireplace, its carapace an iridescent green.

"You were right," Kenny finally said. "Things are never going to be the same." I said nothing, the answer in my silence. "I knew everything was going to change when Mom and Dad were getting a divorce and Dad went to jail, but when he got released I thought maybe we'd figure it out. I'd be here sometimes and with him sometimes, and that was okay. Lots of kids have divorced parents. But it's not going to be like that, is it? They think he did that to the door, and now they won't let me see him."

I stiffened. "Is that what he told you?"

"He didn't have to. I knew Mom was going to blame him for it. She blames him for everything." Kenny started to weep, and something wavered, then collapsed inside of me. She was every kid hurting because of the adults in their lives, caught in the cross fire of egos and emotions of the very people who were charged with their safety and comfort. It wounded and pissed me off in equal parts. I left my seat and knelt, taking one of her hands. Held it. I let her cry. Sometimes that's exactly what everyone needs.

"I'm not going to be able to see him again, am I?" she finally said through tears. "It'll be like this forever."

"No, no, it won't. That's one thing you can count on. Nothing stays the same. Everything changes."

She sniffled, her eyes shining emeralds behind a layer of sorrow. "I guess that's what happens sometimes, isn't it? Things can keep changing for the worse."

I searched for something to say, but then she was standing and walking toward the house, head down. When she was gone, I settled halfheartedly into her chair. The green bug had trundled its way to the other side of the fireplace. It paused, then dark wings unfurled from its body, and it took flight, zooming away into the spring woods.

I envied it. Sometimes running away is a privilege.

———

The afternoon dissolved into evening, and long shadows crawled across the valley in dark tides. Tess fretted after attempting to engage Kenny through her bedroom door but was met by a feeble "Go away, please" when she tried the knob and found it locked.

Needing something to keep busy, I started dinner, whipping up a quick chicken in cream over penne pasta. Tess sat at the counter, watching blankly. When the food was ready, she asked Kenny to come down, but she said she wasn't hungry.

"Leave her be," I said as we sat at the table. "She'll be down sooner or later, and she'll talk when she wants to."

"I feel so goddamn helpless," Tess said, nudging a piece of chicken with her fork. "I wish I could explain it so she'd understand."

"Kids soak up more than we give them credit for," I said, diving into the meal. I was famished. "Give her time."

We were quiet for a while, only the clinking of our silverware filling the gap. At one point Tess rose and opened a bottle of malbec, pouring us each a glass. "I find myself wondering what my mother would do," she said, staring out the windows to the backyard. "She was always so sure of the future." She sipped from her glass, then laughed a little. "Ironic, isn't it? She was so hopeful and then something as stupid as a truck driver falling asleep changed everything. I think about that sometimes. What would have been if she hadn't died. I would've never moved away, Neil and I probably would've never met, Kendra wouldn't exist. None of this ever would've happened." She swirled her wine. "I can see why you hate your mom. It probably feels like she set everything in motion by leaving."

The last bite of pasta no longer looked appetizing. I sat back from the table. "I don't blame her for what my father did. I blame her for leaving us. For never coming back and for being a selfish bitch who only ever thought of her own happiness."

Tess didn't look at me. "That's exactly what I'm afraid of, that Kendra will grow up feeling the same way about me. But I keep telling myself all I've done, every decision I've made, has been for her. To keep her safe. Even if she hates me for it."

I always hid behind glib responses when presented with the idea of becoming a parent. I'd say something like, *It terrifies me*, or *I'm not* responsible *enough to be responsible for another human being*. But in reality, Tess and I shared the same fear. I felt almost as much loathing for my mother as I did for my father, and the only notion eclipsing it was becoming just like her. That the same cowardice flowed in my veins. Was somehow part of my DNA no matter how much hate I tried burning it away with.

After that we U-turned the conversation as much as possible, talking about Kenny's summer art program and a trip to visit the East Coast Tess had promised her. We reminisced, dredging up dozens of memories from the backwaters of our childhoods, leapfrogging recollections with one another's details. We laughed at the time Stephen had gotten into a sack of flour when he was four and spread it all over Diedre and Tess's kitchen, covering himself in the process. We got misty when I told her about Paul's St. Anthony medal and where it still hung on my success board at home, presiding over all the photos of families I'd had a hand in helping. We gelled in a way we hadn't since I'd arrived, and it felt damn good. Here was the woman my best friend from childhood had become, here she was—a resurrection of her mother in body and spirit. I kept my suspicions at arm's length.

We want to think the best of those we love. Because what does it say about us if they're not worthy of affection?

I can't say that I knew what was coming when I turned in later that night, squiffy on wine and feeling better than I had for some time. But in the early hours of morning when Tess's panicked voice started shouting Kenny's name and I surfaced from lead-lined sleep, I wasn't surprised. I just didn't know what shape tragedy had taken.

My door was barely open before Tess came hurtling down the stairs, shoving past me to glance into my room, eyes resembling some small animal running for its life from a predator. "What is it?" I asked.

"Is she in here?" was all Tess said, then she was hurrying on, opening the closets, running out onto the back patio, all the while yelling Kenny's name. By the time I caught back up with her and got her to stop, she was shaking, gaze still wild. "Gone," she finally managed, trying to pry away from me to look somewhere else. "She's not in her room. She's gone."

33

The window in Kenny's bedroom was still open like Tess had found it early that morning when she went to check on her.

I watched as a forensic tech knelt before it and dusted the sill for fingerprints in careful, even strokes. The rest of the room was unremarkably the same. Clothes still lay in small heaps. Her backpack hung from the back of a chair. Her bed was unmade and ruffled as if she'd only gotten up to go to the bathroom and would return any moment. The only glaring wrongness of it all was her tablet and stylus lying on her desk. I'd rarely seen it out of her reach since arriving.

Voices floated up from the kitchen, and I went down to find Tess hovering near the counter while Detective Carl Lowe sat at the dining-room table, his cell phone open to a voice memo app before him.

"And you're sure you didn't notice anything before?" Lowe was saying. "No warning she was going to do something like this?" He had a jowly basset-hound face with deep bags beneath his eyes. His scant gray hair was combed over a scalp dotted with liver spots.

"How are you so sure she ran away?" Tess said, cupping her elbows and rocking from foot to foot.

Lowe glanced at me, then resumed his almost disinterested focus on Tess. "Well, the window was opened from the inside. And we've got a partial shoe print in some mud from where she hopped down off the porch roof. There's nothing to suggest someone came into the house and took her."

"No one had to come in. Haven't you been listening to me?" Tess's voice rose an octave, and I stood beside her, putting a hand on her shoulder. "Her father could've been outside waiting. I told you she spoke to him earlier yesterday."

"And we've searched his residence," Lowe said. "There was no sign your daughter had been there. Mr. Grayson said he was home all last night, and his vehicle isn't on the traffic camera footage near the highway, which is the only way in and out of the area. Mr. Grayson was cooperative and seemed as upset as you are right now. He was leaving to go search for Kendra as soon as we'd finished questioning him."

Tess scoffed and turned away, busying herself with her third or fourth cup of coffee that morning. Lowe shifted in his seat. "Miss, ah—"

"McTavish," I said. "Nora is fine."

"Nora, you said Kendra was distraught after the phone call with her father?"

"Yes. She was disappointed she couldn't see him this weekend."

"But she didn't give any hint to this? Maybe threaten to run away?"

"Kenny's not really the type to threaten something. She just does it."

Lowe drew a long breath in and let it fizzle out of him like he was some great tired balloon. "Well, the good news is kids who run away are normally found within twenty-four hours in my experience. They get hungry or cold or afraid and come home. My guess is that's what'll happen here. In the meantime we've got patrols out with her picture and description all over the city and county. We put out a public announcement, and there's already two volunteer groups being organized for a search later today." He stood, scooping his phone up and shutting off the recording. "The weather's clear, and the temp's going to be in the sixties today. You said her jacket and hat are missing, so that's a good sign. She's prepared for the outdoors. We've checked the places you mentioned, the sky-tram facility, et cetera, and we'll keep checking them in case she shows up." He regarded Tess until she finally returned his gaze. "Panic only makes things worse in situations like this. Take comfort in the fact hundreds of people are on the lookout for your daughter. I'll be in touch later today."

Lowe gave me a half nod, then showed himself out. Tess shook her head, fear and anger tug-of-warring her features. "I can't believe this is happening." She tried bringing the coffee cup to her mouth, but her hands were trembling too hard, and it spilled, splattering on the counter.

"Come on," I said, guiding her over to the couch. "Let's sit for a second and just think. Is there anywhere else she might've gone? Any friends she still hangs out with?"

"No. There was Amy Albright up the street, but they haven't seen each other since Neil was arrested. Her mother won't even look at me in the supermarket." This last seemed like a bitter afterthought.

Footsteps came down the stairs, and the forensic tech gave us a small wave as he filed out, carrying his bulky equipment hardcase in one hand. When he was gone, I said, "I never asked, but I'm sure Kenny doesn't have a phone."

"No. That was one thing Neil and I always agreed on—no phone until she was twelve. But she can text from her tablet, though, so maybe it's like all the rest of our rules we set up and tried to enforce—worthless." With that the tears came, and Tess wept into her hands. Outside, the wind gusted, spinning old leaves in dry pirouettes, nudging grit against the windows. When Tess quieted she said, "She's punishing me. For keeping her from him. I'm losing her."

I stood and went to the back door, looked out half expecting to see Kenny peering from behind one of the trees, watching to see if her rebellion had made a dent in the adult world so set on destroying the remains of her childhood.

"But I don't care what they say, he has something to do with this," Tess was saying. "He said something to her on the phone, and she either mistook it, or this was planned. I have half a mind to drive up to the cabin right now and search it. They might buy his bullshit, but I—"

"I know you broke the glass," I said without turning around.

Dumbstruck silence. You could've heard the gears in a wristwatch meshing. "What?" Tess said.

I shifted toward her. She looked small on the couch, and for the first time I saw how much she and Kenny resembled one another. "You threw the rock through the door and got upstairs before I came out of my room."

She tried an incredulous laugh and looked around. "What are you talking about?"

"You changed and got your gun. You tried drying your hair off from the rain, but it soaked into the shoulders of your T-shirt. I saw it while we were waiting out in the driveway. I'm guessing you didn't think anyone would notice in all the commotion. I almost didn't."

For another beat she attempted to keep the charade going, then crumbled. Her tears were gone, a shocked paleness invading her face. "Are you going to tell anyone?"

I let out a long sigh. Until that point I was 90 percent sure she'd done it. "I don't know. You fucked up, Tess. Bad."

"What else was I supposed to do? Just let him have her?"

"You don't have a choice."

"But it worked. We've got a restraining order now. He's being charged with something. Finally."

"And Kenny's missing."

Her lip curled as if she'd smelled something rancid. "We'll find her."

"Of course we will. But you need to realize what you're doing isn't going to end well. She'll never thank you for it."

Tess wiped her nose and stood. "At least she'll be alive." She headed for the front door. "I'm going to go look for my daughter," she said, then was gone.

34

As if Lowe had tempted fate by speaking of good weather, the sky filled with ruddy clouds in the afternoon and the temperature dropped.

I sat behind the wheel of my car like an automaton. Making turns when I should. Signaling. Glancing in the mirrors. But I was miles away. Thinking of Kenny out there somewhere in a light jacket and knitted hat that wouldn't keep her dry or warm when the sun went down and the mountain air grew teeth.

First off, I'd called Abe, asking if the staties were aware of Kenny's status yet. They weren't, but he said he'd find the local report and amplify it any way he could. He didn't ask if this had anything to do with the information he'd given me, and I offered nothing. Didn't have to; we both knew the answer.

Then I got my feet moving, canvassing as much of town as I could, stopping at all the open businesses to show them a picture of Kenny I'd taken at the boat landing before our kayaking. No one had seen her. I drove in concentric circles, extending outward street by street, avenue by avenue, cutting down side alleys and up dirt tracks leading to desolate county roads. All the while my mind ratcheted through possibilities.

Kenny had gotten lost making her way through the woods surrounding the neighborhood.

She'd been picked up by some creep on the highway.

She'd fallen and broken a bone.

She was hiding in plain sight somewhere we weren't looking.

The last was as comforting a thought as I could muster, especially seeing the weather shifting as afternoon tipped toward evening.

And in that moment I experienced a center-melting dread so powerful it felt like physical cramps. I gasped with it and had to guide the car off the highway into a residential smatter of homes, where I parked and took several deep breaths. Suddenly the car was too close. Suffocating. I got out and walked around an entire block as the wind came up and nipped at the back of my exposed neck. Tess was right, I wasn't a mother. I couldn't know what she was going through. But goddamn it if I hadn't fallen in love with the kid, and it was like acid in my heart not knowing if she was safe or freezing or injured or dead.

When I got back to Tess's, she wasn't there. I texted her with no response. Didn't expect one. I ambled around the house aimlessly for a time before fixing a sandwich I only picked at. Then I made coffee a spoon would stand up in, put it in a travel mug, and went back out.

At the neighborhood entrance I paused, just like the first time that morning, trying to fathom which direction Kenny might've gone. She hadn't taken the direct route onto the highway because there was no traffic-camera footage of her leaving the development. That meant she cut through some of the brush and timber to the east or west and continued on from there.

I put myself in Kenny's young shoes, taking in the landmarks, what everything would've looked like in the middle of the night. But more than that, I tried feeling the emotions she would've been carrying. The anger and frustration. The disappointment. The urge to just *do* something.

A car honked from behind me, and I glided forward into traffic, taking a right. I cruised the lakeside until nearing the first crossroads where I hung a left, letting instincts and some other unnamed internal compass guide me. The paved road was narrow and soon gave way to gravel where the foothills began. A glance at the odometer read one point two miles from Tess's house.

Even as the road became long sweeping curves climbing the side of the mountain overlooking the lake, a surety of where I was going to end up loomed. It wasn't long until the cabin I'd only seen in an online newspaper came into view on the right through the trees.

Neil Grayson's home was even more quaint in person. The yard was tidy and inviting, and the grade the house was built on was steep and picturesque. There was no car in the front yard, and I hadn't expected there to be one. An urge to pull in and poke around was tempting, but I kept the vehicle rolling. This wasn't my destination.

It was another half mile up the road, which degraded into a dirt track posted with warning signs of dead ends and no maintenance, before I saw what I was looking for. A break in the trees on the lakeside where a small drive emptied into a clearing. And when I pulled in, I saw I wasn't alone, but it wasn't who I'd hoped for. Apparently, he'd followed the same line of thinking I had.

Neil's blue crossover was parked beneath a towering pine, and the man himself stood at a rough wall of cobbled rock lining the lookout's edge. I spent half a second debating, then pulled in and parked a few spaces away from his car. He glanced once over his shoulder as I climbed out, then went back to looking at the valley as if he'd been expecting me. I took in the solitude of the overlook, how remote and silent it was here at the end of a dirt road most people wouldn't bother with in exchange for the view. I was alone with a man accused of murdering a young woman. My hand tightened on the mace in my coat pocket.

I ambled up to the rock wall and stopped, all my initial thoughts swept back by the view. It was beyond breathtaking.

The drop was as sheer as it had seemed from the water the day before, and the entire valley sprawled below. The water was a blue bruise fading to black with evening's shadows while the moraine caught a final burst of sunlight, so it became a gorgeous emerald sweep, the likes of which were only found in nature. It might have been the most beautiful view I'd ever seen.

"Thought she might show up here at some point," Neil said, breaking me away from the vista's pull. "It's one of her favorite places. I guess she told you that too."

We stood there for a while not saying anything, watching twilight seep into the land below. Headlights crawled mute on the distant highway.

"Tess talked about you. A lot," Neil finally said. "When we first got together, she said you were like a sister when she was young. That in another life you would've been. She said you taught her how to swim when the swimming lessons her mom paid for didn't work."

"I guess I did."

Neil shifted in place, tucking his hands in his pockets. "You're all Kenny talks about too."

It was like someone turned on a space heater in my center. "She's a really special kid."

"She said you're terrible at cribbage."

I couldn't help but laugh. "Maybe she's just really good."

A faint smile that faded quickly. "I drove everywhere I could think of today looking. It was only a half hour ago I thought of coming here. I've had this strange feeling all day of just missing her. Like she's there in the corner of my eye and gone when I turn my head."

The wind swelled, and I waited until it had fallen. "I'm guessing yesterday wasn't the first time you and Kenny talked on the phone since all this started."

Neil's eyes found mine, and there was a hint of surprise there. Good. "So she knows."

"No. Tess mentioned a number kept calling and hanging up. She was worried Kenny might be answering her phone when she wasn't around. She was right."

He scuffed one booted sole in the dirt. "I knew if I so much as sneezed around her, she'd dream up something for a restraining order. So yes, I got a burner phone and called once in a while. I got through to Kenny twice. It was worth it before Tess blocked me."

"That's all fine and good, but hanging around in the neighborhood was a bad idea."

"I thought it was harmless." He paused. "Thank you again for letting me talk with Kenny the other night. It meant everything."

I didn't acknowledge this. "If you know where she is, Neil, you need to tell me."

"I don't know. I was dead asleep this morning when the cops came by. I spent the day looking for her whether you believe it or not." He studied me for a long moment that became unnerving. "It was you who set Jacob on the suicide route, wasn't it?"

I wavered. "Was I wrong?"

He looked away and I waited. It was darker, night coming on fast now, with stars shimmering out of the veil in the east where the sky had cleared. When he spoke, it seemed he was talking to those first specks of light. "I've had depression since before I knew what to call it. My father was . . . a hard man. Deeply intelligent, but cold." He paused. A bird settled in a rasp of wings somewhere in the trees. "When I was fourteen, he caught me cutting at my wrists and sent me away to a private academy where they employed 'tough love,' as he called it. He believed depression was simply weakness, and if it was beaten out of me, I'd be fine. So they used conditioning methods—strenuous exercise, isolation, starvation. When I came home, I pretended to be exactly what he wanted so I'd never have to go back to that place. I guess I never stopped pretending."

A boat horn sounded from the far end of the lake, carrying up the water like a funeral wail. I licked my lips, which were dry and cracked. "And you never told Tess."

He shook his head. "I used to wake up in the middle of the night and feel like I was afloat in an endless black ocean, an immense weight slowly crushing down from something I couldn't see. I'd get up and go to Kenny's room and watch her sleep to bring me back. She was my lighthouse. My beacon."

I absorbed this. "And Allie Prentiss?"

Neil grimaced at her name, half his features lost in the failing light. "A mistake. I never should have . . ." He turned toward me, and I couldn't help but take a step back. There was still ten feet between us, but he could cover it fast. Maybe faster than I could pull the mace and deploy it. "Last year everything got worse. The worst it's ever been. Allie was struggling in my class. She hung around during my office hours on the pretense of getting her grade up. I knew it was a mistake, but I thought maybe it would pull me back from the edge. We never—" He gestured weakly. "I couldn't get myself to do anything more than kiss her. I loved Tess. I still do." The last was so faint I could barely hear it.

A few pieces of what Tess told me began to mesh with the present. How Neil wouldn't answer his phone for stretches of time. His ring and wallet and note all stacked on top of his desk at the college. I looked over the wall at the vertigo-inducing drop and thought I knew where he came when he disappeared.

"Why are you telling me this?" I asked.

He was a long time answering. "Kenny trusts you."

We stood for a time, watching house lights come on in the valley, neighborhoods blooming like wildfires in the dark. "Did Kenny say anything to you yesterday?" I asked.

"No. She was angry. I told her things were going to turn around, to just be patient." He dropped a fist onto the stone ledge. Once, twice—the second time hard enough to make me wince.

It was time to go. I'd stayed much longer than I'd meant to. Night had fallen, and Neil was only a darker shadow. I was deeply aware of the yawning gulf past the wall. How easy it would be for him to grab me, force me over it.

Just as I started to move toward my car, Neil faced me and took a step closer.

My hand came out of my pocket, mace clenched tight.

"I love Tess, but I don't trust her. Not anymore. I wouldn't have done it if she hadn't forced me."

Before I could reply he'd set off across the clearing and climbed into his car. A moment later he was gone, leaving me alone on the side of the quiet mountain where there was only the lament of the wind.

35

At three in the morning I gave up searching.

After the encounter with Neil, I'd driven aimlessly, hoping fate would somehow cross my path with Kenny's. I deserved a cosmic break. When exhaustion became a back-seat driver, swaying the wheel too far onto the shoulder a second time, I went to Tess's, fully expecting her to be there and awake. We could talk over next steps, how to move forward. But the house was empty and dark. No note. No texts. Nothing.

In Kenny's room a pale swath of moonlight spilled on the floor across a pair of jeans turned halfway inside out, and Kenny was there asleep in her bed. For a second my tired, yearning mind really believed it was real. But then her small form became just a rounded fold of blanket, and the mirage dispersed.

I went to the window and looked out for a time before going downstairs and falling into bed.

Not dreams, but the suggestions of them. Massive shapes moving beneath the subconscious surface. Trying to break through and reveal themselves before submerging again. I was glad I couldn't see what they were. There was a sense that if I did, something would change, shift in an irreparable way. I woke in a sweat with the sun slanting hard into the room from the west.

Is there anything worse than waking up to remember the bad news you'd forgotten overnight? There's a unique cruelty in truth's respite.

The temperature had dipped to forty-eight degrees during the night. The hope that Kenny had returned while I slept was dashed upon a quick circuit of the house, and on top of that, Tess still wasn't home. Disquiet crawled in my lower belly. I called her phone, but it went to voice mail. "Very cool. First the daughter, now the mother," I said to the empty living room. The levity I hoped for didn't follow. My voice sounded flat and odd without anyone to hear it.

I ate a solitary breakfast of cold cereal and drank three cups of coffee to wash the last of the cobwebs away. It was already two in the afternoon, my weariness finally catching up with me from the night before. As I was debating exactly what the next moves were, my phone rang. Not recognizing the number, I picked up, hoping and dreading it was the local police.

"Hello, is this Nora?" the voice said. After a second I placed it.

"Hi, Gayle, how are you?"

"Um, we're okay. You're on speakerphone with Joel and I."

"Hi, Joel."

"Hi."

"So we're really worried, Miss McTavish," Gayle said. She didn't need to tell me. The tightness of her voice spoke volumes. "Mrs. Weisman still doesn't know when we're supposed to go to court, and she said right now my grandma is keeping Ivy."

"That's right. She explained about the continuance, right?"

"Yes, but we don't know why it's taking so long. We filled out all the papers, and the people from the state came to visit and everything."

"The fairy parade is pretty soon," Joel chimed in. "Ivy can't miss it, or she'll be really sad."

"We're trying very hard to get her back home."

"But we did what the judge said." Gayle's voice was a taut whisper. "Why won't they let her come home? Her bed is waiting for her and her stuffed animals. She needs to come home. *Please.*"

The raw pleading of the last word torsioned my heart, tried twisting it out of my chest. Within my helplessness I was reminded again how the word *broken* didn't describe our systems because that would imply their being whole at some point. The truth was they never were. They'd always occluded the most helpless, the most needful. They cut as many corners as possible in the name of budget and efficiency while slicing away at families in the process. If the system had been designed with true aid and mercy in mind, there wouldn't be heartbroken mothers asking *please* in a way that made you want to weep and burn everything down at the same time.

Tears equal parts sorrow and rage tightened my throat. "I promise you both, Ivy is coming home very soon. Before long this will all seem like a bad dream, and you won't ever have to think about it again."

We exchanged a few more words, mostly assurances from me I could tell they didn't fully believe. And why should they? I was another person with power and influence, the same as those who had taken their daughter away.

A quick text with Sharon confirmed the hearing had been rescheduled. Apparently, the judge was deeply interested in Arlene being at my office when she should've been taking care of Ivy.

This was all good. All positive. But I still felt powerless. At times all the oppression, the callousness, the utter selfish nature of human beings was like a tsunami rising up a thousand feet high. Too much to fight off. Too strong to ignore. Sometimes I just wanted it all to crash down, wipe everything away.

Shaking off the ennui since it served nothing and no one, I made an ill-advised fourth cup of coffee for the road. Already my chest was taut with caffeine, and there was the slightest tremor in my hands. But I needed the clarity to stay on track.

Kenny was out there somewhere, and I wasn't going to give up until I knew she was safe. Or if she wasn't.

The rest of the day drained away in hours lost on the roads. I stopped by more businesses and canvassed the neighborhoods bookending Tess's development. No one had seen Kenny, but the good news was almost everyone was aware she'd gone missing. The more eyes and ears on the lookout the better. I thanked all I spoke to.

Around six in the evening, after checking in with the local PD to no avail, I went back to Tess's. Still empty and quiet as a crypt. The comparison soured my mood even further. I could see the home as it was now as well as how it might be after tragedy. Nothing ever looked the same in the wake of loss.

Still no answer from Tess, either. An ember of fury at her stoked for a moment, then faded. I thought about making something to eat, but my stomach was a knot, and nothing sounded appetizing. Instead I poured a glass of wine and moved through the house, pausing here and there to gaze out a window.

Upstairs, Tess's room was unchanged. I'd noted small details prior to leaving to see if she'd come and gone while I'd been out, but everything was as it had been. In Kenny's room her essence seemed to be dissipating. As if the lack of her presence was leeching the color and light out of everything.

I poked through her things, moving clothes aside, smoothing out her bedspread, all the while searching for something that wasn't there. There was no note left behind saying where she was going, no clue to her direction or intentions. The police had swept the room thoroughly, and I doubted anything had been overlooked. Even her tablet had been gone through.

Her tablet. I picked it up and punched the wake button. The screen bloomed to life and opened to a page crammed with apps. There was no access code on the device, possibly some rule set by Tess or Neil. For the next half hour I went meticulously through the applications, opening each with much more shame than I had searching Tess's phone. Because as Neil pointed out, I had Kenny's trust, while Tess had lied to me.

Even as the thought came and went, I returned to the last thing Neil had said at the overlook. At first, I'd wondered if it had been a cryptic confession on his part. A classic shift of blame to justify the terrible thing he'd done to Allie Prentiss.

I wouldn't have done it if she hadn't forced me.

But what if he'd been talking about Kenny? What if he did know where she was and was planning on disappearing with her as soon as they could make it out of town safely? But they'd had the chance to run the night Kenny escaped from her room. By morning they could've been hundreds and hundreds of miles away.

Nothing tracked.

I scrolled to the last page of apps having clicked into every one of them, searching for something that might stick out, but there was nothing. As I was about to switch the device off, I hesitated and went back and found the settings function, moving down through the options until one caught my eye.

Device Location. It was toggled on.

I tapped it, and the screen opened to a map of the area rendered in greens and blacks. There was the sweep of the moraine and the rounded crescent of the lake below snowcapped mountains. Mutiny itself was a smattering of color, the buildings tiny dots and dashes at the overhead distance.

And there on the screen were three devices designated with pin drops.

A side bar listed them as KENDRA'S TABLET (THIS DEVICE), DAD'S PHONE, and MOM'S PHONE. I zoomed in, confirming the tablet I was using was at the present location, then swept over to Neil's phone. It was currently on a road a few miles away to the north. A moment later his pin shifted, indicating he was on the move. I swept the screen in the opposite direction, homing in on Tess's phone.

It was at a house on the southeast side of town a few miles away. I watched as it remained steady, unmoving. Tapping on her pin brought up the address, and I drew out my own phone, taking a few minutes to locate the county auditor's website and tax parcel information before punching in the address.

The search symbol spun and spun. Somewhere out in the street a child yelled to run faster. Then the screen changed and displayed the owner info for the address.

36

Jacob's home was a well-kept Tudor nestled between tall hedges separating it from its neighbors.

I took in the brick-fronted wall and the charming, rounded doorway as I made my way up the front walk. There were a couple of lights on farther back in the house, and I steeled myself for what was to come as I pushed the doorbell.

Seconds ticked by. Then a minute.

I rang again. Waited. Rang again.

Then footsteps came hurrying through the house, and Jacob's voice filtered out from inside. "Hold on! Hold on!" The door opened, and he stood there in the gap wearing only a pair of gym shorts, a towel hanging over one shoulder, his hair wet. "Nora?" He glanced past me at the street. "What's going on?"

"Sorry to bother you. I wondered if we could talk for a minute?"

He glanced back into the house as if checking someone else for permission, then stepped aside. "Sure, come on in."

Like Jacob himself, the house was sturdy and understated. A spotless kitchen led off the entryway, which connected to a dining room boasting a lofted ceiling. A set of stairs ran upward out of sight opposite the entry. Jacob bustled past me, gesturing at the dining table. "Have a seat. Would you like a cup of coffee?"

"I'll lift off if I have another drop."

"Tea?"

"Sure, that would be great."

He set a kettle to boil and gave me a sheepish look, draping the towel around his shoulders like a shawl. "Sorry, was just getting out of the shower when I heard the doorbell."

For the first time I noticed how chiseled his physique was. Lean muscles beneath a downy layer of dark hair. "Don't apologize." I caught how it sounded and followed it up with, "I'm the one barging in unexpected."

"Be right back," he said, disappearing through the entry. A moment later a washing machine lid banged down and its cycle started. Jacob reemerged and gave me a tight smile on his way upstairs. I sat for a few seconds alone before the kettle started a low whistle. I turned the burner off and set the kettle aside, then wandered a little deeper into the house, listening for movement from above.

A cozy living room opened off the dining area. Lots of hardwood and leather furniture. A large flatscreen. Black-and-white abstract art on the walls. And on all the tables and shelves were strangely pointed sculptures fired in off-putting shades of green and red. Closer up they resembled some kind of fungi, so deeply glazed they appeared to glisten.

"Kinda weird, aren't they?"

I kept from flinching. Barely. Jacob had entered the room without me hearing him. He'd changed into a pair of sweatpants and a threadbare T-shirt sporting a Jolly Roger, the Ridgewood University mascot.

"They're, uh, unique," I said.

"My ex made them. She was into her art. I've been meaning to get rid of all the stuff she left behind, but then the place would be pretty bare. I'm not sure what's worse." I followed him back to the dining room, where he poured two cups of jasmine tea. "I offered to send everything to her but never got an answer." He laughed, settling opposite me. "Sorry, didn't mean to give you the mundane details of my failed marriage."

I blew steam off the cup. "Totally fine. Tess mentioned you were divorced."

"Yeah, four years now. Almost as long apart as we were together. Neil and Tess really helped me through the worst of it. Tess especially." He rose and returned with a small bottle of honey. "You ever take the plunge?"

I laughed. "No. I'd say I haven't met the right someone, but I think *I'm* not the right someone."

"My aunt was single her whole life. Took vacations when she wanted, changed careers, never asked anyone permission for anything. She was the happiest person I ever knew. Being solitary has its benefits."

"Cheers to that."

We drank in silence for a moment. The house was very quiet. Still.

"So, what brings you my way?" Jacob asked. His eyes widened. "Is it Kendra? They didn't find her, did they?"

"No. Nothing yet. I was out all yesterday and most of today looking."

"Me too. Actually, I'd just come back from a search party right before you showed up."

"A lot of people out looking?"

"Thirty or forty at least. I hope she's okay. It would absolutely destroy Tess if something happened to her."

"So that's kind of why I came by," I said, turning my cup in slow circles. "I know the last few months have been pretty rocky, but did Tess seem herself before that?"

Jacob's brow furrowed. "I guess so. Maybe a little down overall. Why?"

I thought about how to begin. "It's strange because there's this little girl I remember from being a kid, and there's this woman I'm getting to know now with a whole lot of blank space in the middle. And that middle is where she became who she is."

"I'm not sure I'm following you."

167

I hesitated at yet another line there was no going back from. "Do you think Tess is capable of something . . . violent?"

"Violent? Tess?" Jacob barked a laugh. "I mean, she can get a little irate if the service is slow at a restaurant, but violence? No. Absolutely not." Some of his humor slowly faded. "Why? What's this about?" When I didn't respond right away, he said, "You don't think she had something to do with Kenny going missing?"

The thought had crossed my mind, but I shook my head. "No. She loves Kenny. I don't think she'd ever hurt her. Not intentionally anyway."

As I circled what I was trying to get at, Jacob sat back in his chair and rubbed hard at a crease between his eyes, then froze. "Oh God. Tell me this doesn't have anything to do with the break-in." When I said nothing, he released a long sigh. "The chief of police just emailed me this afternoon. They compared the security company's record for when the alarm went off and the video time stamp of Neil leaving the neighborhood, and there was only a ten-second gap between the two." I stayed silent. "So there's no possible way Neil broke the glass, got back in his car, and left the area. It had to have been someone else." He stared at me. "Was it you?"

"No."

"Did Tess ask you to do it?"

"No."

"So she did it." I fell quiet again. "Jesus. And you knew?"

"I figured it out later. I wasn't fully sure until yesterday."

"I should've known—" He stood and paced into the kitchen and back. "We had half a dozen conversations after Neil was released. She wanted a restraining order, and there was no precedent. She asked if she should make something up. Say Neil had choked her or hit her before. I told her absolutely not, and if she mentioned it again I couldn't represent her, but I should've known. Damn it." I thought back to her suggestion of forging a suicide note. He closed his eyes. "I probably shouldn't have said anything."

"Well, my concern goes a little beyond that. I think she's been tracking Neil's movements through their phone location data. They must still be shared even if their plans aren't connected anymore." Jacob settled back into his seat. "That's how she knew when to break the window—Neil was in the neighborhood, except he was just cruising through. But it made me think of something else."

"What?"

"Allie Prentiss's last text was to Neil, demanding he come see her."

"Wait, how do you—"

"Not important. But we have Neil in the vicinity of the crime scene around the time of Allie's murder and a text from her asking him to come there." I waited a beat. "What if Allie didn't send the text?"

It took a moment for Jacob to realize what I meant. "You think her killer sent Neil the message?"

"Time of death is usually narrowed to around an hour. If Neil was seen anywhere near her place within that time frame . . ."

Jacob sat back in his chair. "And you think since Tess tried framing him for the break-in, she did the same thing for the murder?" A long pause. "You think Tess killed Allie Prentiss?"

Did I? Until that moment I'd kept the sickening idea at my periphery. Couldn't believe my friend would be capable of something so brutal. But each person is a universe unto themselves. Unfathomable. Unknowable. "I don't know what I think," I finally said.

"No." Jacob was shaking his head. "No, I don't believe it for a second. You asked me since I know Tess, and I'm telling you she couldn't have done it."

"I know there's something between the two of you, and I hope that isn't clouding your judgment."

He blinked as if I'd slapped him. "Why do you say that?"

"Tess told me you were together in college." When he didn't respond I went on. "She said you kissed her the other night."

Jacob let out a half laugh and looked away. "That's so Tess. Always shifting responsibility. She's the one who kissed me." I absorbed this. "I suppose she told you about the proposal, then, too."

"Proposal?"

A flush had crept from the collar of his T-shirt, staining his features. "We were dating, and I was young and stupid and thought I was in love. So I bought a ring and asked her to marry me, and I cringe to this day thinking about it. She was way too kind, even then. Instead of saying no, she said she couldn't give me an answer, which was all the answer I needed. God, I was so naive." He laughed but it faded just as quickly. "I love Tess, and I loved Neil too. I know them as well as anyone can know other people, and there's only one of them who's capable of murder."

———

The evening was clear and cool when I stepped outside. The temp hung at fifty degrees with a promised low of forty that night. Damn cold for a kid outdoors.

I glanced back once at Jacob's home before climbing into my car, half expecting him to be watching, but the windows were all empty. I hoped I hadn't overplayed my hand or burned a bridge with him. I could tell he really did love Tess, and no matter what he said, love wasn't only blind. It was blinding.

We arm the ones we love the most with the weapons to destroy us.

I punched in the address from Tess's phone location and pulled away from the curb, leaving the dark stare of Jacob's house behind.

37

The clearest memory of my mother is of her standing above me on a hiking trail, the summit outlined behind her.

She's there, locked forever in that snapshot of time, hair tied back in a bandanna, something akin to a challenge shining in her eyes, urging me on, telling me if I went a little farther, then I'd be at the top, and everything would be revealed.

The image of her rose and fell away as I followed my phone's directions and turned onto a street elevated a few hundred feet above Mutiny. The houses here were middle class, mostly vinyl siding with a smattering of brick or stone, all on acre or more lots. The neighborhood itself was nestled into one of the smaller foothills, and the grade was short but steep.

As my destination neared, I kept an eye out for Tess's vehicle. Given how careful she'd been so far, I guessed she parked a short distance away and walked. But there was no sign of her car anywhere on the vacant street, and then the app was telling me I'd arrived.

Devon Wilson's home was a low modern ranch style perched at the top of a small rise against a density of pines. A newer pickup sat before double garage doors, and a mountain bike leaned in a breezeway.

Without braking, I glided into the drive and coasted to a stop. My headlights died, and the yard took on a hushed green-black tone. Part of me wished I'd brought Kenny's tablet along to confirm Tess was still here. Regardless, there were things I wanted to ask Devon Wilson anyway.

Tugging up the zipper on my coat against the breeze, I stepped up to the front door and peered in one window flanking it. A nice open concept with a dining room leading to a kitchen against the back wall. A light was on over the sink, and a bottle of wine sat open on the counter. My friend was definitely nearby.

I knocked, hard and fast. The sound echoed in the yard, and I glanced around. The next nearest house was several hundred paces away, only partially visible behind overgrown evergreen shrubs. I knocked again, stacking up my responses if Tess were to answer the door. I could feel a little of my will leeching away, feel all the reservations pulling like gravity back toward my car. But I forced myself to knock again.

No answer.

A faint tingling began at the base of my neck and spread. Soon my arms were alive with gooseflesh, and the coming night seemed so much more pronounced.

Something was wrong.

It was one of those undeniable sensations like being watched. I thought of Neil saying how he'd felt he was lagging behind Kenny, that she was there at the corners of his vision and then gone whenever he looked.

A loud chatter of birds came from somewhere behind the house, their calls harsh and amplified by the breezeway's alley. I moved in that direction, squinting through the dim corridor.

The mountain bike at the forefront, then deeper shadow and a humped pile of something near where the backyard began. A shovel leaned beside it. I reached into my pocket and squeezed the mace. "Hello?"

No answer. The pile didn't move.

I started through the breezeway, searching the garage through the main door's window as I passed. Nothing. The birds called again, a high chitter needling the eardrums. The pile was an oblong shape beneath a rumpled tarp stirring slightly in the breeze. In the low light I saw a head, shoulders, legs at the bottom. Swallowing acidic spit, I nudged the tarp with one toe and met something solid and hard.

I gathered myself and reached down, grasped the tarp, and ripped it back.

A low stack of firewood sat underneath.

My breath whooshed out, and relief rushed in to take its place. Along with it came embarrassment. The sense I was somewhere I shouldn't be. I resettled the tarp and was turning to go back to the car when the birds called again and there was a flush of many wings.

The backyard was alive with movement.

I paused at the breezeway's mouth and stood watching. There were dozens of brown thrushes and finches picking at seeds covering the ground like carpet. Four large feeders overspilled with chickadees and brilliant yellow birds I couldn't identify. They preened and pecked, their black beaded eyes twitching, until it seemed they were not separate but a single undulating entity. The illusion continued as I stepped into the yard and they burst into flight en masse, whirling up into the pines hemming in the property. They sat looking at me from their perches. An interloper. An intruder. It was time to go. I turned to head back down the breezeway and glanced into a wide set of windows near the corner of the house.

You never get used to the aftermath of violence. There is no barrier between your senses and the naked horrors of the world. But the more you're exposed to them the sooner you can reconcile the irreconcilable.

The windows looked onto the primary bedroom. White walls with high ceilings, sparsely decorated, a king-size bed at its center. Devon Wilson lay in the bed, nude, his skin pale. There was a small red hole on the underside of his chin while his face remained remarkably untouched. He may have been sleeping except for the blood and chunks of matter fanning up the headboard and wall behind him.

A pistol rested on his chest, hand slack around it, one finger still looped through the trigger guard.

38

"Tell me again."

The interview room at the police station was no more than a large closet. No windows, a narrow door with squeaky hinges, and the lingering scent of cheap coffee and dust. I guessed they didn't have much call for interrogations in Mutiny.

Detective Lowe sat across the comically small table from me, his phone out and recording. His casual demeanor from the day before had been swapped for a cold-eyed intensity. He chewed incessantly at the corner of his mouth.

"I was out canvassing for Kenny. I started a few houses down from Mr. Wilson's, and when I got to his place, I thought I heard someone in the backyard. When I went back to check, I saw him through the window."

It wasn't a lie. Not really.

After finding Devon and letting the shock and implications set in, then dissipate, I'd driven farther up the neighborhood and knocked on some doors, hoping against hope no one had spotted me pulling into Devon's place prior. Then I'd "found" Devon a second time and rehearsed the story before calling in the death. Now I was just repeating myself on the record after sitting down in this little room with the detective. And really, I'd had no choice. There was no other excuse for me to come rapping on Devon's door and find him like he was without implicating Tess.

As of someone gently rapping, rapping at my chamber door.

I brushed back the intrusive line and asked Lowe to repeat the last question I'd missed.

"You say you heard someone in the backyard?"

"I *thought* I did. It was just birds."

Lowe grunted. "Birds. Yeah, he loved birds."

"I could tell." When he didn't say anything else, I said, "Did you know him well?"

Lowe blinked slowly at me. "We worked together," was all he offered.

The next hour passed in the slow tedium of the questioner and the questioned. A dance trying to throw me off rhythm. Catch me in a mistake. Except my story was so simple it wasn't hard to keep straight.

All the while a part of me was back in Devon's yard with night falling, bird calls filling the air, and the sight of him lying on the bed, his head mostly gone above the hairline.

"Did you know who Mr. Wilson was before knocking on his door?" Lowe asked, throwing me a curve among steady softballs.

"I knew *of* him since he was involved in the investigation, but I didn't know it was his house when I drove up to it."

Lowe stared at me without blinking for a span, then nodded. "Well, I think that's all I need," he said, scooping up his phone. "And you'll be available in the near future if we have any more inquiries?" It wasn't really a question.

"Yes." He started to rise, hand reaching toward the door. "Detective? Can I ask—was it a suicide?"

Lowe eyed me for a time. "You said you were with CPS, right?"

"I used to be. I'm a family advocate now."

"What did you do at CPS?"

"Forensic investigation."

"Right. Well, I'm not at liberty to say since it's still an open case."
He paused, appraising me again. "But you saw what I did. Draw your
own conclusions."

———

It was pushing 9:00 p.m. when I turned into the development. Most of
the houses' lights were on, TVs flickering, people moving past windows
oblivious to all except their own lives. I idled down the street, keeping
my gaze everywhere but straight ahead until I'd pulled into the drive
and shut the engine off.

Tess was home.

I sat for a long moment, listening to the unnatural silence of the
car, my mind a maelstrom. I went inside.

Tess was at the kitchen counter, a glass of wine before her. She
perked up at my entrance, glancing past me as if she thought someone
else might be following. "Hi," she said.

"Hi." I stayed where I was, our last exchange hanging thick in the
gap between us.

"Have you heard anything?" she asked. There was no life to her
voice. She already knew the answer.

"No. Nothing." I prepared myself for what was to come—searched
again for another approach, all the while wondering what the hell I was
doing. Just as I opened my mouth, she spoke instead.

"I saw you earlier."

"When?"

A shrug. "You must've just left the house. I was at the gas station
down the street. I waved, but you didn't see me."

"I went out looking." She nodded, refocusing on her wine. "But
something happened." Her attention came back up.

I started talking and didn't stop, keeping my voice as natural as possible, pretending this was solely my story, something that only involved

me. A terrible footnote in an already terrible week. And I watched, gauging her reaction as it gradually registered.

Tess's color drained, and her mouth came open, one hand rising to cover it. Slowly she started shaking her head. I paused then, giving the natural response. "What is it? What's wrong?"

Tess kept shaking her head. "No. It's a mistake."

"He was a detective. The one who was helping oversee the murder case."

"It can't be."

"His place is in the foothills on the other side of town. There's all these bird feeders in the backyard."

With that, something shifted in her expression. Belief setting in. She rose, moving around the counter to stand over the sink. Her mouth opened, and she coughed dryly as she retched. Nothing came up, but she remained there, convulsing, over and over.

I went to her, rubbed her back, kept the confused mask in place all the while, asking what was wrong. After a time she swallowed and looked at me through bloodshot eyes. "It's a mistake," she said. "It has to be."

I got her to the couch and sat across from her once she was sure she wouldn't be sick. And waited. The seconds ticked out into minutes, and she seemed to drift away without moving, her prior horror and disbelief curdling into shock. "He was sleeping," she finally said, eyes resting on the floor. "When I left, he was sleeping."

"Hold on, you were there?" A slow nod. I'd seen videos of kids put under hypnosis before—some attempt at uncovering repressed memories—and Tess looked and sounded the same now. "What were you doing at his house?"

A long pause. "I stayed there last night after it got late. I was searching for Kendra, and I didn't want to come home. Couldn't."

I waited the appropriate amount of time. "You and Devon . . ." The faintest of nods. "How long?"

Tess blinked, glancing to her right as if she'd heard something. "January. We met through the crime-prevention committee. He—" Her throat worked soundlessly. "Neil was gone by then, even when he was here. Devon looked at me. Saw me. Touched me. I hadn't been touched like that in so long." She kept her gaze trained in the near distance. "The first time we were together, the birds were there outside the window. They were everywhere, moving so quickly. So vibrant. So much life." She fell quiet and appeared to drift away again.

I stood and got a glass of ice water. At first, she only looked at it as if it were something completely new and alien; then she put it to her lips and gulped it down in four long swallows. A hint of color returned to her face, and she seemed more aware of her surroundings.

"So you spent last night there," I said gently.

"Yes."

"And what happened today?"

"We drove around everywhere looking for her. We'd been so careful not to be seen together, but I didn't care anymore. We went to all her favorite places. We watched the cabin for a while."

My stomach tightened at this. "Was Neil there? Did he see you?"

"I—I don't know. He drove past us at one point. I'm not sure."

"Then what?"

"We went back to his place to eat. And we—made love. And he fell asleep, and I came home." She glanced at me, eyes shining. "Are you sure? Are you sure he's—"

"I'm sure." Her tears spilled free and ran in two heavy tracks down her cheeks. She didn't make an effort to wipe them away. "This is going to be hard, but did he seem disturbed to you? Was he different?"

"No, he was the same. He was himself. He wouldn't do this, Nora. He wouldn't. I know him."

I lowered my head and sat that way for a time, Tess's quiet sorrow the only sound in the room. "So there's a good chance the police will come talk to you at some point. I'm guessing you and Devon called or texted?"

She swallowed thickly and nodded. "Texted. But we always just talked about birds. That was our code when we wanted to see each other."

"Even so, they'll want to question you. You'll have to decide what you're going to tell them." When she still didn't seem to understand, I said, "You were the last one to see him alive."

Her small amount of resolve collapsed, and she wept again. I sat beside her, gave as much comfort as I could even as I squirmed internally. It felt terrible to lie to her when she was this vulnerable, hurting this much. But I'd gleaned enough from her reactions to know she hadn't had anything to do with Devon's death. She was hiding things from me, but this wasn't one of them. Which left two options. The first being it was exactly what it appeared to be: a disgraced former cop choosing a way out rather than spend time in jail for his actions.

Or someone other than Tess had been the last to see Devon alive.

39

I had no intention of watching the sun rise the next morning, but we experience so many things we never intend to.

Tess cried herself to sleep on the couch around 1:00 a.m. after vacillating from her worry for Kenny to the loss of Devon and back again. I did what I could but mostly just handed her fresh tissues and fetched a couple of extra-strength pain killers when she complained of a headache.

My own sleep was elusive, slipping away each time I felt myself succumbing. When I did doze it was to the cacophony of bird calls and the flutter of a thousand wings. I woke for good while it was only vaguely gray outside and made myself a cup of coffee as silently as possible while Tess slept on.

I sat on the front step and watched the neighborhood gain definition and color. It was chill, and I shied away from thoughts of Kenny outside all night in the cold, alone in the dark. Instead my mind turned what I'd seen at Devon's over and over like a rock in a tumbler. Not making anything smoother, but jagged. Raw.

Each detail was an HD snapshot.

The red hole on the bottom of his chin.

What had been his skull and brain painted on the wall.

How white his skin had been.

I wondered if certain people were like magnets when it came to trauma. Attracting the worst life had to offer. We saw reality through a darker lens. Spoke a silent language most would never understand. But I was kidding myself if I thought these things came out of the nether to find people like me.

It was the other way around.

The day never fully dawned, only grew to a smoky hue straight out of an apocalyptic film. Low clouds skimmed the mountains, and an unkind wind shoved the trees.

Inside Tess was awake, hollow eyed, and chewing absently at a piece of toast. "Get some rest?" I asked.

"Some. Had bad dreams."

"Understandable."

She set her toast down and was quiet for a time. "It's so strange you were the one who found him," she said finally.

I'd expected this, but not quite so soon. "The whole thing is strange."

"Yeah, but what are the chances? You happen to stumble onto the man I'm seeing right after he . . ." She trailed off but stared at me.

Tess's phone rang, but she didn't look away. The air tightened between us with each ring. Finally she reached down and answered, listening intently before saying, "Tomorrow morning is fine." When she hung up, she stood and threw her remaining toast away, then headed for the stairs.

"Who was it?" I asked when it seemed she wasn't going to offer anything.

Without looking back she said, "Lowe. He wants to speak to me. You were right again, Nora."

———

In the afternoon, mist started to fall from the ashen sky. It drifted down the mountains like smoke and swept over the foothills, turning the pines to green smears as the streetlights bloomed prematurely.

I sat in a fast-food parking lot at the western edge of town eating a surprisingly good burger and passable fries. Outside the streets sat idle. It might've been a painting. Occasionally a car would drift by, taillights red streaks in the murk.

I'd left the house before Tess could come back down. Much better to leave our aborted conversation where it was than try picking it up again. Especially with the unsaid accusations between us.

The radio issued an update on the report of a missing toddler, and I turned the volume up. I'd heard it half a dozen times since yesterday morning. Apparently a two-year-old boy named Thomas had wandered away from his family's campsite one valley over. And because of the low temps and lack of outdoor clothing the kid had on when he disappeared, search and rescue were working tirelessly to find him. More bad news. I wished Thomas all the luck in the world and clicked the radio off.

I considered checking in with Abe to see if there'd been any hits statewide on Kenny's whereabouts, but it was just perfunctory. He would've called if there were. A great part of hope is busywork.

I got busy.

On my phone's map app, I identified which parts of the valley I'd already searched and what was left. There were a few neighborhoods on the outskirts of Mutiny, but they were almost ten miles from Tess's house, and there was no reason for Kenny to be there. Inversely I studied the map nearest their home, looking for anything that stood out, a place where she might've dug in with continued access to the house for food and water when no one was there. But there was nothing. Nothing except the long sweep of the moraine growing from the mouth of the neighborhood.

Surely someone had checked there. Walked the hiking trails. Searched out any campsites for a girl who knew that area well. It would be an obvious place to look. Yet I hadn't thought of it until now.

A gust of wind rocked the vehicle on its springs, hooted in its voids. I turned the key and drew away onto the street, flicking on the high beams as I went. It was already getting dark.

40

Nora pulled out of the parking lot and drove down Main Street, heading toward the lake.

Where was she going now? She'd crisscrossed the valley earlier, driving seemingly without aim, but now she was heading somewhere. This seemed purposeful. The turn to the southern corner of town came and went. She kept going. Then the turnoff to the development appeared, but she didn't slow or signal. She was heading away from town. Away from other buildings and people and cameras.

This was promising.

A half mile later she swung into the moraine's access road and drove up to the parking area. There were only two other vehicles there given the foul weather. Her taillights flickered, then steadied, as she pulled into a parking space at the main trailhead. For a time nothing happened, then she emerged and went to her trunk, pulling out a weatherproof poncho and a pair of hiking boots. Donning both, she surveyed the landscape for a moment as if looking for something, then set off up the trail.

This was the best chance. Probably the only chance to keep things from unraveling even more than they already had. Or everything might be lost.

It was time to follow. And wait. And watch.

And do what needed to be done.

41

The trail ran like the hollow of a spine along the moraine's back.

To the left the grade descended gradually to the valley floor and the checkering of farmland in the distance. On the right the land swept away dramatically to the lake below, a pool of melted steel matching the sky.

I'd been pleased my heavy poncho was still in the trunk from the last time I went out in inclement weather and relished its warmth and waterproofing now. The wind was stronger on the moraine's open ridgeline, and the mist had graduated to a light rain. From the info I'd consulted online while sitting in the small parking lot, several trails branched off where the nearest mountain began in earnest. And on those trails were a dozen or more campsites. I could see Kenny, emotional but determined, setting off the same way I was now with meager makings for a shelter, and hoped I was wrong.

The going was easy at first since I hiked year-round, and the trail was well kept. But as the terrain gained attitude, my legs began to burn. I drank from the small bottle of water I'd brought but paced myself, realizing the walk was going to take all the time I'd allotted myself before full dark.

Just before the mountain trails diverged up into the heavier growth of pines, I met the owners of the two vehicles coming back down. They were a couple of men in their early twenties, fully kitted out for camping, who said they'd been up in the higher elevations for the last two nights.

"Anyone else up here you know of?" I asked.

"Not that we noticed," the taller of the two said.

"And you never came across this girl?" I panned my phone between them. Both looked closely, eyes squinting against the rain.

"No. Was she with anyone else?"

"She would've been by herself."

"Then we would've remembered her. There were a couple families on day trips, but no one alone."

I thanked them, and they hustled away, eager to be down and out of the wind. Five minutes later they were out of sight.

The trail I chose was the least traveled as far as I could tell. Steep. Narrow. Difficult. Exactly the one I thought Kenny would pick. The path wound upward through moss- and lichen-covered rock, trees growing impossibly from stone gaps, their tops lost in haze. Rain pattered from branches, and the wind lost its strength as the woods thickened. It became still.

There's a refuge in being alone in the wilderness. An innate peace left over from before we decided farming and putting down roots and capitalizing on cheap labor was the way to go. The connection is still there if you're open to it. At least that was always what my mother said.

She was the one who introduced me to the outdoors. Alongside being an artist, she loved the mystique of nature. She'd wax poetic on our link to the sea, how the salt in our veins moved with the tides. She said if you listened closely when you were completely alone in the wild, you could hear your sacred heartbeat. The one outside your chest. The one intertwined with all things.

For me it was the order nature offered. There was no sleight of hand in the wild. There was no deception. No lies. Just ecology forever seeking balance. It offered simplicity in an artificially complex world.

I shook free of the thoughts. The last weeks with Tess had reopened the closed wound that was my mother. And right now that was the last thing I needed.

A flicker of movement on the edge of my vision.

I turned and stared back down the trail. Something had been there a second ago. I'd caught only an impression of motion, probably an animal, no idea of how big or small. I listened, but there was nothing. I moved on.

Ahead, a pocket in the forest opened, revealing a leveled area large enough for a small tent. Empty. No sign anyone had been there in weeks. I kept going.

Around the time I should've been turning back, I crossed a bridge over a gushing stream, the water crystalline and cold a dozen feet below. There were two more camping sites not far off I wanted to check before giving up for the day. At least I thought there were two. My phone's service was there and gone as I moved upward, the signal weak when it did appear.

At the crest of a ridge I paused, surveying the land ahead and below. The trees were sparse in places, given way to rocky scree. Faintly there was the sound of flowing water. The rain had all but stopped, the wind only a vague notion. So quiet.

A branch cracked somewhere behind and above me.

Some blackbirds took flight, careening away down the mountain. I tried finding where the noise had come from, but the acoustics were strange with the incline and moisture. I waited, breathing shallowly, listening. Nothing.

Another hundred yards up the trail and around a bend, the ground leveled again, opening in a meadow where a building stood. Its sudden appearance stopped me, and I tried recalling something like this on the map. A sign near the trail's edge said only **Ranger** in faded block letters, the rest borne away by time and weather. Maybe an old ranger station, then. It was dark and looked empty.

The sky was filthy gray, night coming on fast. I knew I should turn back, but the building was probably the most promising place I'd seen so far for an angry runaway to take refuge. I pulled out my phone and turned on the flashlight.

The building was revealed in dingy browns and dirty whites. A dilapidated front porch yawned in rotting and missing boards. The front entrance was locked, and the two windows flanking it were covered from the inside. I moved around the exterior, picking my way past overgrown shrubs and low seedlings. My heart gave a hopeful surge as I spotted a door in the back that was open a few inches. I nudged it the rest of the way and shone my light inside.

Some animal had made the station its home. Leaves and branches littered the short hallway, and a faint rotting smell drifted out from one of the few visible doorways. "Kenny?" My voice was scratchy and low. Did I think she'd respond if she heard me? Yes. I was sure of it. By now she would be cold and hungry and lonesome, and wanting to come home no matter how angry she was at her parents. But there was no reply.

I stepped inside, boots crackling on the peeling floor. The doors inside led to cramped offices scattered with animal droppings and more leaves. Something small and curled decayed in one corner. The front of the building was a lounge stripped of everything but its outdated wallpaper. Water damage had partially crumbled one wall, revealing a slice of meadow on that side. I stood breathing in the stinking air, feeling the disappointment seep in. I'd been almost sure I'd find Kenny here. It seemed to fit too well. But there was nothing. No one had been here in a long time.

Something moved past the hole in the wall.

My chest cinched painfully as if all the air in my lungs had vanished. Whatever it was had been there and gone before I could get more than an impression. But it wasn't small. Thick saliva gummed my mouth and throat. I turned, staring down the hallway toward the open back door, which was now just a bluish rectangle, waiting for something or someone to step into view.

The seconds drew out, one into the next, my heart beating twice as fast.

"Hello?" I said, my voice dying in the narrow corridor.

A twig snapped. Then an expectant silence.

I sidled two steps to the front door, keeping the light shining down the hall. My hand fumbled for the knob and found the lock. I twisted it and dragged the moisture-swollen door from its frame with a tired squeal. One more look back, then I slid through the narrow opening and nearly fell through a hole in the porch. A gust of wind came up, bending the trees as I caught myself and picked my way down the bowed steps, dragging in the clean open air. It was past twilight, and the meadow was closing in, shadows growing beneath the trees like black mold. All at once I wished I'd turned around much earlier, gone back while the light was still strong.

I panned the phone in a half circle, eyes straining against the dark to make sure I was still alone. I took a step in the direction of the trail, telling myself I didn't need to run, no matter what my nerves were saying, and noticed something near the corner of the building.

It was a deeper shadow hunched close to the wall. Unmoving. My mind scrambled to recall if there had been a bush in that particular spot or not. I leaned to one side, trying to get a better look. There was a flash and something tore through the air next to me.

The pain was a thousand wasp stings dipped in acid.

It cut along the interior of my left arm and my side in a line of fire. My poncho tugged slightly, and I heard the gunshot rolling down the mountainside, both deafening and very far away.

I sat down hard, landing on a boulder near the trail and glancing off it to the ground. Warmth flowed down my side, running toward my waistline.

I'd been shot.

Any second the real pain would hit. The life-ending kind where you knew some crucial thing inside you had been irrevocably damaged. My right hand was a frightened bird, pecking and pulling at the wound, fluttering across my chest, feeling for a hole over my heart. But there was only a small, ragged tear a few inches down from my armpit. My pulse was fast but steady. I could breathe. I could move. I could run.

I did.

42

Down the trail.

Feet skidding over rock. Moving first left, then right, trying to make myself a hard target. Ahead the path widened, a bald spot on the side of the mountain.

A second shot rang out, the bullet singing away into the dusk. For a moment after I fled, a wild hope persisted that it was all a mistake. A hunter misidentifying his prey, overwhelmed by the fever of the hunt. But the second shot confirmed what I already knew.

I was the prey.

In between ragged breaths I realized my phone's light was still on, a beacon in the dark. I tucked it away and on instinct dodged off the trail at the next turn, trees flying past on either side. Down over wet rock and muddy ground. At the border of a small clearing, my boots slid out from under me, and I went down on my good side, the skin on my palm abrading away on a stone shelf. Then there was only open air beneath me, and I was falling.

Just as quickly the ground was there again, steeper than before, and it took every ounce of balance to land on my feet and keep pace with momentum, legs super-striding, arms pinwheeling.

I fell again, slid, rose, fell, skidded, got up. My breath came in short bursts, lungs heaving, burning. A washout appeared to the right, and I leaped down it, praying not to turn an ankle.

The washout emptied into a ravine where a river raged. I could hear the water spraying off stone more than see it. On the banks dead pines lay across one another like fallen matchsticks. I scrambled down and across the trunk of a tree, dropping low to slide underneath another pitched the opposite way. If I could get across the river, maybe whoever was hunting me would stop. Or I could lose them on the opposite side. A dozen yards downstream, a narrow tree had fallen across the water. I sprinted toward it, sweat burning in the wound on my side.

The tree bowed disturbingly when I placed my weight on it, the far end short of the other bank by a foot or so. It was only eight inches wide at its broadest point. I took a breath and started across.

One step.

Two.

Three.

Another shot, and water exploded a few feet to my right. My balance wavered. The tree shifted and broke free.

I fell.

The water was impossibly cold. I gasped, clinging to the tree, trying to keep my head from going under. My boots snagged on something below the surface, then pulled free. The tree turned, picking up speed in the current. I couldn't hear anything over the rush of the river, no way to tell how close the shooter was. I wasn't going to make it to the opposite side. I had to get out of the water.

Shoving away hard from the tree, I kicked toward the closest bank, feet touching bottom after a couple of strokes. I slogged out of the river, pulling myself up by a handful of dried roots. I rolled, onto my back, onto my side, then I was on my feet and into the nearest cover of trees. My boots squelched loudly, and my poncho flapped like the sodden cape it was. Night had closed in fully, and I could barely make out the tree trunks ahead. Something cracked behind me, and I ducked reflexively. But it was only a branch. He was closer. I needed to hide.

The grade steepened ahead, and a rock shelf appeared out of the gloom. A perfect alcove to conceal myself in. Exactly where he would look. I passed it by and climbed upward instead of going downhill like my body ached to.

Beyond the shelf was a smattering of young pines growing tight to the ground. I wove between them, moving as silently as possible, finally making out one large enough to hide beneath. I crawled under the lowest branches, curling in on myself until I was as small as I could be. My skin screamed against the cold wetness of my clothing. The bullet wound throbbed sickeningly. A hard rectangle pressed into my side and elation hit a second later as I fished my phone free. But even as I pressed the wake button, I knew it was useless. Just a waterlogged piece of glass and electronics. I took several deep breaths, willing my heart rate to come down, and tried focusing on staying calm, tried listening for whoever was chasing me.

There.

Footsteps coming from below. They paused at the alcove. Moved on. Paused again. He was deciding which way I'd gone. The darkness was now my friend. Silence my ally. I had to stay still.

I started to shiver.

The cold was undeniable. Voracious. It ate me up. My body shuddered, crying out for warmth. I gritted my chattering teeth, bit down on my lip hard enough to taste blood. And still he didn't move.

A breeze swept down the slope, nudging the trees, making the leaves and needles whisper against one another, and I took the opportunity to shift more behind the tree's trunk, tightening in to become part of the landscape, willing myself to disappear. Willing the shooter to move on.

But he stayed.

I listened as hard as I could, searching for footfalls over the flow of the river. Wondering if I'd made a mistake by hiding. Wondering if I should try creeping away now that it was dark.

A flashlight snapped on.

The beam swept out in a flood of white, sending shadows scuttling away, illuminating what felt like half the mountainside. My hiding place suddenly felt paltry. I felt insignificant. All my efforts were futile if they led to this. Gunned down in the wild where no one might ever find me. I thought of the people my father had shot and killed, how terrified they must have been meeting the last seconds of their lives. All their intentions laid aside.

The flashlight panned across the slope, stopping here and there to spotlight a tree or rock before moving on. Slowly it crept upward, closer and closer to where I lay. My heart picked up speed, and black flowers bloomed at the corners of my vision. I was going to pass out. If I passed out, that would be it. Even if he didn't find me, I'd become hypothermic and probably freeze to death before ever waking up.

A small, splintered twig rested beside my hand, the flashlight catching the white of its broken end. Before I could think it through, I picked up the splinter and jammed it as hard as I could beneath my thumbnail.

The pain was iridescent.

It traveled up my thumb and spread through my forearm like something alive. All at once I was very, very awake.

The beam hovered on a large tree a few yards to my left, sliding up and down its length before traveling on to my hiding place. I tucked my head down. Closed my eyes. Held my breath.

The inside of my eyelids glowed bright red. A shiver twisted up my spine. I shifted slightly, and the sliver sticking from my thumbnail caught on something and broke off.

Bile rose in the back of my throat.

The light held for another beat, then fell away, sweeping down across the grade before it winked out. A minute passed. Two. Three. He didn't move. Didn't leave. He was hoping I thought he'd gone, and I'd come out of my hiding place. A part of me knew this was exactly what would happen if he stayed too long. I had to move, had to get the blood flowing, or I would go under for good.

The seconds ticked by. Individual eternities.

Somewhere far away a car horn honked, there and gone on the wind, and what I wouldn't have given to be in my own vehicle with the heat cranked up and blasting over my freezing skin. Delicious, delicious warmth. My body strained against shivering, every muscle crying out to move. Soon there was no resisting it.

I shuddered, breathing out as slowly as I could, trying to hold on to control. My muscles ached to move more, then just ached.

Time passed. The darkness thickened, became a physical thing blocking out my senses. Nothing was visible. No sound. The earth was barely there beneath me. I started to float.

My fingers found the broken sliver beneath my thumbnail and plucked it like a guitar string. The pain registered, but it was muted. It was happening to someone else, and they were describing it. How low was the temp supposed to go tonight? I couldn't recall. How long since I'd fallen in the river? Twenty minutes? An hour? Two? I couldn't gauge that either. Time had lost meaning. The cold was different, too, not warm but not uncomfortable anymore either. My skin was velvety, the ground soft.

I sighed, still conscious of the gunman, but now the threat wasn't quite as real. It was all unimportant. A dream of a dream of a memory.

Dreaming. I was dreaming. All my life was a dream. I was warm and drifting further and further away.

43

Transcript of *Poe, the Man and the Myths: A lecture series with Professor Neil Grayson,* Part 11—presented by Ridgewood University in coordination with College Partnership Programming.

What was Poe's fascination with death? We can surmise where the obsession came from given the losses of his mother and father at a young age and later the succumbing of his wife, Virginia, to tuberculosis. Amid this recurrent darkness and hovering reminder of mortality, how could it not find its way into his work?

But we can also see another angle of his imagination in regard to death. In multiple stories he explores a fascination with murder and the madness he associated with it.

It is two sides of the same coin. On one there is dying and experiencing the loss of a loved one, while on the other there is the imposing of will and the infliction of death on another. The dying and the dead. The murdered and the murderer.

Which raises the question: Is there a greater intimacy than those bonded by death?

44

A bell was ringing.

Far away, but shrill. And there was light. Red light.

Everything red and warm. I turned my head away from the light. Sleep was tidal, irresistibly pulling me under, and I wanted to go. Wanted to roll in its undertow forever.

But the light was gorgeous, and I followed it.

At first it was nearby, bright and alive, then it swept away and dimmed. I floated forward, wanting to go faster, to catch up to whatever was casting the glow, but it retreated until it was only a suggestion in the dark.

A sharp snap startled me, pulled me from the warm cocoon of mental mist. It took a long moment to understand I wasn't dreaming. I was standing on an angled stone set in the mountainside, shaking uncontrollably. With each passing second more and more details established themselves.

I was in the woods above the moraine. Someone had shot at me. No, that wasn't right. They'd shot me. The wound was very faint now, but that was because I was being eaten alive by the cold. And I'd drifted into unconsciousness only to be woken by the shooter's flashlight.

Leaving. The shooter was leaving. Giving up. He hadn't found me.

And I'd been following him without realizing it. Following his light.

Through the violent shuddering I made sure I couldn't see the flashlight anymore, that I wasn't hallucinating, and tried regaining my bearings.

I drew in a painful breath. Another—deeper. A stick cracked in the distance, and I blinked, feeling darkness trying to rush back in and drown my consciousness. The worst was wanting it to.

I tried moving again. My limbs were filled with icy glass, joints rusted together. A deep throbbing pain in my fingers and toes. Far away a shaft of light rose up a rock shelf before disappearing completely.

He'd gone over a ridge.

High above, the stars screamed in the sky, their points knife tips piercing black fabric.

I took another tentative step forward, willing a clarity to my muddled thoughts. What did I need to do? Anything I'd read about hypothermia was shrouded in fog.

Move.

It was like a voice had spoken beside me, and I startled. Maybe it had been in my head but hadn't felt like it.

I moved.

Slowly at first, taking a single steadying step, then another. And another. The starshine was so bright the ground was ghostly visible, sticks and rock set in relief of their shadows. Each movement was agony and at the same time got easier and easier. The false warmth began receding, and the cold returned in full, biting and aching. But I welcomed it.

It proved I wasn't dead.

At the base of the incline was a game trail, which I guessed the shooter had followed. I went slowly in the same direction, pausing every few steps to listen and make sure there were no hurried footsteps returning.

Gradually I realized the lining of my poncho was still soaking wet, and I pulled it free, turning it inside out so the relatively dry weatherproof side was against my body. I tried picking up the pace but slowed again at the slamming of my heart.

For a while after that I dipped in and out of my surroundings. I'd climb an entire grade before realizing I hadn't stopped to listen in some time. Then I'd be moving again, warm blood venturing farther and farther out from my center. The ache in my muscles and joints began to ease. My fingers and toes continued to thud like rotten teeth, but even that was bearable.

I didn't know how long it took me to reach a trail or exactly which one it was, but I released a quiet sob when my feet hit its well-worn surface. I rested then on a stump at the trailside, breathing deeply, continuing to move my fingers and toes, and when I forced myself to rise, the eastern horizon was smudged with gray. The very first suggestion of dawn.

———

The sun had appeared by the time I made it to my car. There were no other vehicles in the parking lot, and I wondered where the shooter had stopped so I hadn't seen him following me. Unlocking the driver's side door I fully expected another shot to ring out, a round to punch through my center and that would be that. I was too exhausted to be afraid. All tapped out.

It took five minutes for the heat to start pouring from the vents, and it was as wonderful as I'd dreamed on the mountainside. My poncho lay in the back seat, and my phone, useless and dead, sat in the center console.

My hands shook as I passed them back and forth over the warm air. The heat was a miracle. Divine. When I could move without trembling, I put the car in gear and left the parking lot.

The rational part of me said I needed to go to the hospital. Make sure there weren't any lasting effects from being hypothermic and that the bullet hadn't grazed anything crucial. Though if it had I wouldn't have made it through the night. And I needed to alert the cops. Let them know someone hadn't intended for me to leave the mountains alive. But right then all I wanted was a shower. I wanted to be fully warm and clean. After that I could face the rest.

When I arrived at Tess's, I knew something was wrong. The driveway overflowed with vehicles. Her own was askew with two tires on the lawn, a police cruiser beside it, and Jacob's was parked on the street.

My stomach fell.

I pulled up behind Tess's SUV and debated what to do. A wild, irrational part of me murmured to just drive away. Enough was enough. I'd absorbed plenty of pain and trauma for one night and couldn't take any more bad news. I gave myself a once-over, straightened my damp jacket, and went inside.

Crying.

It was the first thing I heard stepping inside, and my heart darkened further. I swallowed, moving through the entry into the kitchen.

A uniformed officer stood at the border of the sitting area, hands thrust awkwardly in his pockets. He turned my way as I came in and gave me a cursory glance, taking in my disheveled state, then nodded solemnly. Jacob sat in the chair opposite the couch, his tall form hunched forward. He wore a pair of jeans and a rumpled T-shirt, looking like he'd rolled out of bed and thrown on the first thing on his floor. Tess sat on the couch, her back to me, shoulders heaving with sobs. Jacob glanced up then, but his expression seemed wrong. He wasn't somber or crying.

He was grinning.

"Nora," he said, and stood. I moved forward, rounding the corner of the couch.

Tears leaked in steady streams from Tess's eyes, and she choked out a small laugh when she saw me. "She's home."

Kenny looked up from where she lay cuddled on her mother's lap and smiled.

45

"You look really tired," Kenny said between bites of egg and bacon.

I sat at the end of the counter sipping coffee and worshipping whoever had originally invented the brew. It was steaming liquid gold in my throat and stomach and dispelled the last lingering chills. "I would've been getting more sleep if a certain young lady hadn't up and disappeared," I said. Kenny lowered her eyes and shoveled in a bite of toast.

For the time being I was thankful she'd been the only one to comment on my appearance. I needed to find the right time to explain what happened the prior night. Once I told Tess, we could take next steps now that I'd showered and knew I wasn't going to die from my wound.

The bullet had bored a split tunnel in my flesh—one half on my arm, the other on my side. Both were shallow and had clotted fairly quickly, but there was still a sheet of gore running from armpit to waistline that I scrubbed off in the hot water. The round had been meant for my heart, and leaning slightly to the right at the last second saved my life. The immensity of how close I'd come to death was too much to consider. I knew from experience I'd suffer later by pushing it back now. But I didn't have any other choice. I was just thankful no one had made much of how I'd looked. If anyone noticed my damp clothes and the hole in my jacket, they'd been too preoccupied with Kenny's reappearance to mention it.

"I am sorry," Kenny said, bringing me back to the present.

"We're just glad you're all right," Jacob said from the opposite end of the counter. Tess hummed quietly to herself at the stove but added nothing.

"So you left in the middle of the night and headed for the cabin . . . ," I prompted. I'd only heard the briefest of explanations before going to shower.

Kenny barely nodded. "It didn't take that long to get there, only a few hours. I waited up in the trees above the cabin until I saw the cops come and go. When my dad left, I went down and let myself in. The basement door key is still under the flowerpot," she said, directing this mostly at Tess, who had turned to listen.

"You know he was going to look for you," Tess said. "There were all kinds of people out looking for you."

Kenny's face colored. "I know. I'm sorry."

"Then what?" I asked.

"I grabbed a few things and made a little fort up in the trees and waited there until I knew Dad would be sleeping. Then I went in and slept on the downstairs couch until right before he woke up and went back out again."

"And how long did you plan on doing this?" Tess asked. A half shrug. "You're lucky you didn't catch pneumonia or get eaten by a bear."

"Well, I'm glad your father found you when he did," Jacob said in a lighter tone. Kenny didn't acknowledge this.

"How did he figure out you were staying in the basement?" I asked.

"He noticed some food missing and pretended to go to bed. Then he waited up in the dark," Kenny said. She pushed a last bite of egg around her plate with her fork. "He was pretty mad."

"And he really had no idea you were there that whole time?" Tess asked, eyes narrowed.

"No," Kenny said, glancing at all of us. "He didn't know. He called the police right away. He told them where I was, and they came and got me. He didn't do anything wrong."

Tess turned back to the stove and finished flipping the last of the eggs. Jacob sipped his coffee. Kenny looked at me, then down at her plate, shaking her head. "I know you all hate him, but he doesn't deserve it." She pushed back from the counter and started away. Jacob gently caught her arm.

"Hey, we were very worried, and it was stressful while you were gone, that's all," he said.

Kenny jerked away. "You act like you aren't trying to keep me from seeing him." She struggled with something, then blurted, "Mom will never love you like she loved Dad."

"Kendra!" Tess thundered.

"It doesn't matter," Kenny said, backing toward the stairs. "It's all going to be different soon."

She spun and was gone a moment later, leaving a vacuum behind. Jacob raised his eyebrows. "Well, she's still very upset. She'll calm down."

Tess stared at the floor, gaze tired and haunted. "What did she mean by that? It's all going to be different soon?" she said after a moment.

Jacob let out a long sigh. "Neil must've mentioned something to her." We both looked at him. "I received notice late last night that he's filed for sole custody."

The quiet deepened. Took on weight.

Tess blinked. "What?"

"His attorney said in the filing that new information has come to light that supports the petition."

"What information?" Tess asked, stepping forward.

"I don't know. We won't know until the court date."

"Well they're not going to set one, right?"

"The judge has no reason not to."

"What about the restraining order?"

"It's been dropped, Tess. Neil was cleared of all charges."

She shook her head. "I don't understand how this is possible."

"Just because he filed doesn't mean he's going to get full custody."

"He wasn't supposed to get partial custody."

"Let's stay calm."

"Stay calm, right. Easy to say when it's not your kid."

"Hey, that's really not—"

"Fair? No, it's not. None of this is. It's wrong. All of it. He's a murderer, and he's turning my daughter against me, and no one's doing anything to stop him."

"Tess—" I said, but she was storming away, up the stairs and gone, following Kenny's lead.

Jacob rubbed his temples. "Wow, that's not how I wanted it to go at all."

"No easy way."

"There never is with family, right?"

"No," I said, looking into my empty cup. "There never is."

———

Kenny's door was open an inch when I went up a short time later. I knocked, then gave it a nudge when there was no answer. She was curled on her bed, a pillow tucked tightly to her chest. "I don't wanna talk," she said without moving.

"That's fine. I just wanted to say goodbye."

She turned her head and studied me, maybe to see if I was bluffing, then sat up. "You're leaving?" I nodded. "Why?"

"Because you're home and safe, and I'm not helping by being here."

Something changed in her expression, a fragile wall of anger crumbling down. "What I said before, I didn't really mean you. You've been . . ." She swallowed, and tears rose in her eyes.

I crossed the room and hugged her close. It was the first contact we'd had since her reappearance, and it felt good. None of my usual hesitation when wanting to embrace someone. Holding her solidified her presence here, that she really was alive and safe. When we parted, she swiped at her tears, her breath hitching. I rubbed her back with one hand. "I know it doesn't feel like it, but things will be okay."

"Will you come back?"

I thought of Tess and how much I'd been hoping the bond we shared as kids could be renewed. How each passing day seemed to be drawing us apart instead of together. "I'm not sure."

"It's my fault. I shouldn't have run away."

"I'm not leaving because you ran away. I probably would have run away if I were you."

She was quiet for a long time. "Are you running away now?"

Damn it.

I squeezed her shoulder gently and rose. I needed to talk to Tess and the police, then be gone. Gone from this place of winnowed hope and suspicion. Gone from the shadows of the valley and cold rivers and bullets in the dark. Gone from this beautiful tender girl the world had no sympathy for.

"Nora?" I paused in her doorway. "Thank you for everything. You made it better."

Had I? I wanted to say she was welcome but couldn't form the words.

"And thank you for looking for me. I saw how dirty and wet you were when you came in. Mom said that's where you were last night. Out searching." The cold and darkness tried swallowing me whole in a mouth of panic. I staved it off. Barely. "You both were."

For a second I started to move again but stopped. "What do you mean?" I asked. "We both were?"

Kenny looked up. "No one was here when the officer brought me home. He had to call Mom, and she got here a little while later." She glanced down, shame heating her face, fingers toying with her pillowcase. "She said she was out looking for me all night."

46

Limits—we all have them.

I prided myself on knowing my own and trying to obey them. All the therapy I'd undergone said it was healthy. Know your limits. Abide. That was what I told myself I was doing as Mutiny shrank in the rearview mirror, then vanished completely as I headed for the coast.

But it felt like running away.

Before I turned off the radio, there was an announcement—Thomas, the two-year-old boy, had been found only hours ago. Miraculously he was okay overall. A few scrapes and bruises from where he'd fallen down in a small ravine, but alive and recovering in a hospital. *Good for you, Thomas, good for you.*

For the next few hours I went somewhere else. A place I only visited when I needed to escape. It was a sprawl of sand so white it hurt your eyes to look at, and the turquoise of the water was supernatural, just waiting to swallow a body in its cool embrace—its only reason for being. I sat on the beach and didn't feel the slow throb in my arm and side, didn't taste the dank cold of the mountain river, didn't think of the fleeting surprise in Tess's gaze upon seeing me after Kenny's return.

I sat on the shoreline my mother had described to me. Sat near the water's edge I'd only ever dreamed of.

———

Merrill literally leaped into my arms. Walking through Stephen's front door, I was mostly ready for it, but his bulk nearly bowled me over, and I couldn't help but laugh as he lavished me with kisses on my neck and chin. Stephen appeared barefoot in the kitchen doorway, wearing a cashmere sweater and a worn pair of jeans, a glass of wine in one hand.

"I think someone missed you," he said as Merrill wriggled with so much delight he slipped out of my arms and rebounded back into them.

"You sure?"

"It's starting to make me feel bad. I'm the fun uncle."

I set Merrill down, kissed him between the ears, then went to my brother. Hugged him harder and longer than I meant to. He held me, and all of the last weeks came rushing forward at once. "Hey, are you okay?" he asked, pulling back to study me. I nodded, blinking hard.

"What the hell happened to your thumb?"

"Slammed it in a door. It's fine. I'm fine."

"Our definitions are not the same, I'm afraid. Sit down."

He guided me into the kitchen. I sat. He poured wine. I drank. Merrill flopped on my feet and fell asleep. Stephen reclined in a chair across from me, gazing out at his backyard oasis, savoring the merlot. It was afternoon already, and the sun broke from behind a scudding cloud and poured onto the grass and trees, maxing out the volume of color and texture.

"So . . ." I finally said.

"So."

I started talking, slow at first, then faster. Filling him in on everything I'd only alluded to in our infrequent texts. Stephen listened, refilling our wine when the glasses got low. I excised the prior night's events from the story, fast-forwarding to Kenny's reappearance and Tess's meltdown at Neil's petition.

"And she didn't say goodbye?" he asked when I'd finished.

"No. But to be fair, neither did I."

"It sounds like you were the only one being fair. Especially to the kid. My God. People never think about the most vulnerable, do they?" Stephen glanced away. "But why would they when they're the easiest to step on." Merrill raised his head slightly, and I scratched his ear. He resettled with a dramatic groan. "So what are you not telling me?" Stephen said.

I hesitated, then sipped my wine. "Nothing."

"Look, I know you're hurt. And I don't just mean emotionally. It's in your eyes and the way you're holding yourself." I looked down, turned my glass in a circle. Stephen laughed humorlessly. "You think you're sparing me, but the imagination is so much worse than reality. I'm sitting here thinking of all the shit you probably got yourself into and how close you came to dying, and I'm hoping it wasn't that bad, but I guess I'll never know. I'll just keep looking after your dog while you galivant off into danger." He shook his head in disgust and drained his glass.

I reached across the table and took his hand. "You're the best uncle Merrill could ask for."

"Oh, fuck you." But the corner of his mouth twitched upward. "You're the worst sister in the world."

"Do you have any more of this?" I said nudging the empty bottle.

"There's a decent malbec by the fridge."

I set about opening the wine while Stephen fussed over a burr tangled in Merrill's fur. When I was seated again with both our glasses topped off, he said, "I do worry you see certain boundaries as challenges."

"Isn't that what they are?"

"No. Not always. Sometimes they're warnings."

We fell silent again. The sunshine outside faded behind another cloud. The kitchen darkened. The wine was silk sliding through my veins. Before I knew I was going to speak, I said, "What would you do if you knew where Mom was?"

"What was that line from *Aliens*? The one about the only way to be sure?" When I barely smiled, he sat back, staring at me. "What brought this on?"

"Seeing Tess. We talked some about the old days."

"I see. And what—you're feeling nostalgic?"

"No, I'm . . ." I sighed. "Just humor me."

"So, hypothetically speaking."

"Right."

"I don't know. Usually I try to see how long I can go without thinking about her. Like a little game with only one player."

"You don't have anything you want to say to her?"

"Like what? Why did you forsake us to a psychopath? Tell her she's the reason Paul's dead? I think she knows." He looked down at his long, delicate fingers. Our father's hands. "It doesn't matter anyway. It won't change anything."

"It might change things for us."

"I don't want anything to change." He leaned forward. "We escaped something horrific mostly intact. We both have our fractures and scars, but we're here. We've built lives for ourselves beyond what happened and didn't let it define us. I won't waste my time worrying about some woman who never really loved us. There's nothing she could say to make anything different. It could only cause harm. And I've had my fill of harm."

He started to say something more, but stopped and shook his head. I watched the wine swirl near the rim of my glass as I turned it, almost but never spilling over.

"So what would you say to her?" Stephen finally asked. His voice had softened.

I thought of Stephen as a child, running on the beach, hair pressed back from his forehead by the wind. Thought of us all as children, our futures still unsure but coiled and waiting. Thought of our footprints in the sand, their depressions losing definition with each wave that washed over them.

"Nothing," I said. "There's nothing to say."

47

A quick stop at the local cellular outlet, then home.

I opened the front door, and Merrill barreled past me, nails clicking on the floor as he raced through the hall, the kitchen, and back again. "Happy to be home? Me, too, buddy. Me too."

I dumped the plastic bag from the cellular place on the counter and set my new phone beside all the paperwork and cardboard boxing. Getting a new device had been painless (except for the price), and the customer-service rep had done all the updating, chattering on about features and promotions while I nodded at the right places and hovered somewhere outside myself.

For a time I stood at the counter, listening to Merrill happily rediscover all the toys we hadn't brought to Stephen's, then opened the new phone and pulled up the call log, stomach an icy nest of snakes. I stared at the log for what felt like hours, but it was only seconds. Plenty of time to confirm my fears.

Tess's number was the last to call my phone.

I tapped on it and saw there'd been two missed calls from her—one the night before, then another in the morning's early hours. I brought the phone with me and sat on the couch, implications settling with me.

Tess's first call had come around the time I'd been crawling beneath the pine tree to hide. I could see her standing there in the dark, searching for me, then having an epiphany and dialing my number, listening for the ringtone to betray me. Only afterward she must've realized my phone was down and out from being in the river. The second call would've been to cover her tracks after Kenny had been found and brought home—proof she'd attempted to let me know the news. And there was something else.

It slid around the edges of my mind, something vaporous and crucial, slipping away each time I tried grasping it. Something to do with the cell phone.

Wait.

Not my cell phone. Hers.

The bell I'd heard while I was still in a hypothermic stupor, it hadn't been a hallucination—it had been a ringtone. She'd gotten a call. A call telling her Kenny had been found safe and she was waiting at home. That was why she'd left. And if she hadn't, I'd still be there, frozen to the ground beneath that tree.

I breathed deeply, trying to calm the heavy rap of my heart against my breastbone. The unreality of the last twenty-four hours washed over me, and I had to reassure myself I was home, I was safe, wasn't still drifting in a frozen haze, wasn't dead.

So if Tess had been the one who shot and chased me, why then. Why would Tess want to kill me?

On the surface it seemed apparent: I knew too much. Was too close to understanding her true nature. And what was that exactly? Who was my long-lost friend really? Was she a spurned wife driven to murdering her husband's lover? A woman overcome in the heat of the moment, then left to deal with the fallout of her actions? But why reach out to me then? She would've known any benefit of my presence and expertise would've been outweighed by having another person involved. Or had she thought I would be an unquestioning ally. Someone she could mold to her advantage. Only after reconnecting she realized I wasn't the same little girl she once knew.

But of course neither was she.

I went out on the deck. The wind was light and coming straight off the ocean. The spring scent of new growth was fading. Soon it would be summer, the days expanding while night constricted.

I must've seen something. Or heard it. Something I wasn't supposed to. That was why she'd decided to follow and hunt me down when the situation presented itself. But what could it have been? What had I seen and not known it?

I kept trying to imagine Tess there in the dark, gun in hand, waiting for me to make the slightest noise—and failed. She was flawed and emotionally unstable, but did I really believe she was capable of not only killing Allie Prentiss, but me as well?

I didn't know. And that was what kept me from implicating her when I'd filed a police report in Mutiny. The officer who took my statement hadn't seemed overly concerned with someone shooting at me. He'd even floated the idea I'd been mistaken. Maybe it had been someone target shooting? A lot of guys did target shooting up there, and it could've been a ricochet. I waded through the bog of misogyny and told him unless target shooters typically tried hunting down people they accidentally wounded to finish the job, it wasn't likely. In the end he said he'd pass my statement along to Detective Lowe. Maybe Lowe would follow up. Maybe he wouldn't. I couldn't think anymore. Every bone in my body was made of lead, pure exhaustion leaking from them into my system. My thoughts kept plowing into one another like cars on a slick stretch of highway.

Merrill wandered onto the deck and peered up as if asking what was wrong.

"What if it's me?" I said. "What if I'm wrong?" He licked his chops and whined. I scratched behind his ear. "Dinner time, isn't it?" He did his hungry dance, spinning once in a circle. "Okay. Let's eat."

We did.

After a light supper I started resettling into the house, threw in a load of laundry, watered the plants. The routine soothed me on a deeper level, one that appreciated the comforting mundanity of household chores. Twilight had descended, and sleep was on the very short list of things to do when I thought of the mail and went out to retrieve it. Bills. Bills. Junk. More bills.

And one thin, crisp certified letter.

Generally you don't need to worry about envelopes with multiple pages. They're bloated and wordy because they don't have anything to say. But ones with a single page—they're to be wary of. They mean fucking business.

I opened the envelope, so narrow it was like a razor blade, and pulled out the letter, part of me already knowing what it was and dreading it. I only needed to skim the first few lines.

As the last light left the sky and darkness rushed in to fill its place, I wished Tess had never found me and called for help.

Started to wish I'd never known her at all.

48

"All rise."

The courtroom was cold and drafty with the added frigidity of systemic functional architecture. No frills or comforts, no windows to let any natural light in, just fluorescents buzzing like hungry flies above hard bench seating and paint the shade of old oatmeal.

Gayle and Joel rose beside me. We stood at a long table on the left of the courtroom's main aisle. Sharon Weisman glanced my way from her position on the far side of the young couple before giving them each a reassuring nod. It had been over two weeks since I'd returned home, and we'd spent much of that time preparing them for today. They seemed to be ready. I hoped we all were.

The judge strode in, not looking at the small congregation on this Tuesday morning. Another day for her. A day of reckoning for people this side of the bench.

"Be seated," the judge said and shuffled through a sheaf of paperwork as we sat. Hushed silence fell.

Gayle leaned close to me and whispered in my ear. "You said Ivy was going to be here, but she's not."

"She's in the building. There's a playroom for kids to wait for their parents. That's where she is."

"And she'll come home with us when we're done, right?" It was the fourth time she'd asked me that morning.

"That's right."

She smiled like all the other times. It was radiant.

———

While the clerk and judge rehashed the necessary information for the case, I went back through all the notes Sharon and I had made, all the questions and proper responses we'd worked on with Gayle and Joel to make sure the system didn't make a liar out of me. That was what I didn't want the two of them to worry about. The system had already failed them, and they'd suffered enough for it. But that didn't mean the suffering was over. This fact was punctuated by the person across the aisle.

Arlene Jones sat several rows back on the opposite side of the courtroom. She wore a cranberry sweater above a dark ankle-length skirt. Her left foot was encased in a hard supportive medical boot. Beside her a woman roughly the same age with unruly red hair looked around with eyes so wide they seemed to protrude from her head. I surmised this must be the esteemed Willamina Gustafson.

Arlene glanced my way, and her eyes narrowed. I smiled and held her gaze until she finally looked away.

"All right," the judge said, placing her hands together. She leaned forward over the bench to take in Gayle and Joel. "I think we can get started. Are we ready, Mrs. Weisman?"

"We are, Your Honor," Sharon said.

"And you, Mrs. Valchek?"

Lila Valchek stood from the table opposite ours. She was a tall, hawkish caseworker I'd dealt with dozens of times before. A veteran in state services. From my experience Lila had always been rigid but fair. Beside her, representing CPS, was my old coworker, Richard Jackson. Jackson the slacker. I was surprised to see him since he wriggled out of as many court appearances as professionally possible. He twiddled his fingers at me and winked. I kept from rolling my eyes. "We're ready as well, Your Honor," Lila said, and took her seat.

We began.

"Correct me if I'm wrong, Mrs. Valchek, but it appears all the necessary requirements set by the state have been met by Mr. and Mrs. Pearson in the interim period."

"They have, Your Honor," Lila said. "But the current guardian has requested to speak to the court. She has further testimony to add to the record before the court makes its ruling."

The judge slid a paper to one side. "Mrs. Jones, are you present?"

"Yes, Your Honor," Arlene said, then winced as she stood, putting weight on her good foot.

I did roll my eyes then.

"Mrs. Jones, you are Mrs. Pearson's grandmother, is that correct?"

"That's right."

"And you wish to give testimony in effort to retain custody of your great-granddaughter?"

"Yes, Your Honor."

The judge raised her eyebrows. "All right. Please take the stand." Arlene hobbled to the small boxed seat beside the bench and eased down, wincing again. "You were sworn in earlier and are still under oath. Do you understand?"

"Yes, Your Honor."

"Please proceed."

Arlene adjusted herself, eyes sweeping out across the sparsely populated space. She never looked at our table. "Well, I'd like to start by saying that Ivy has been very happy with me and well looked after. She's—"

"Your Honor," Sharon said, standing. "This is pure opinion, and with all due respect, Mrs. Jones doesn't speak for Ivy."

"Mrs. Jones, you'll please keep the testimony pertinent to the matter at hand and forgo your own sentiments," the judge said. Arlene sucked at her teeth, nodding curtly.

"In that case I thought you should know that my granddaughter has a history of neglect and irresponsibility. My daughter Josephine, who is no longer with us—may she rest in peace—wouldn't allow Gayle to have a pet. Not even a goldfish. She knew as well as I did that Gayle doesn't have the attention span to care for another living creature. And here we are, the exact situation I always feared. I'm just glad I'm still around to take care of the little dear."

Quiet fell. The judge tilted her head. "Is that all, Mrs. Jones?"

Arlene glanced around, lips pursed. "Well, no, no, it's not. There was another . . . incident with Ivy." She finally looked at our table, fixing on Gayle before turning back to the judge. "When Ivy was only a year old, Gayle left her alone in the bathtub."

There was a sharp intake of breath beside me and suddenly Gayle was on her feet. "That's not true, Grandma! You were watching her! I went to the bathroom, and you were watching her!" I put a hand on Gayle's arm, trying to guide her back to her seat as the judge banged her gavel. "You're lying, Grandma! And you swore not to, that's what *under oath* means."

"Gayle, honey, sit down," Sharon said quietly, helping me to get Gayle back in her seat. Joel rocked forward and back in silence, eyes cast at the floor.

"Order, please," the judge said as Gayle sat, tears forming, then falling from her eyes. "We can't move forward with proceedings if there's any more disturbances. Is that clear?"

"We understand, Your Honor," Sharon said, one hand holding Gayle's tightly. I held the other. She was trembling.

When the courtroom had fallen quiet again, the judge said, "Mrs. Jones, this is highly irregular to say the least. Why is it you've chosen to wait until now to disclose this incident?"

Arlene sniffed. "I was hoping it was a one-off. I wanted to believe Gayle could learn to be a responsible mother. But it seems I was wrong."

"Your Honor," Sharon said, "any testimony for the alleged incident is hearsay. I'd ask the court to strike Mrs. Jones's statement from the record."

"I'll hear the testimony first, Mrs. Weisman," the judge said, then focused on Arlene. "Proceed."

"Well, like I said, it was when Ivy was around a year old. Gayle was giving her a bath upstairs, and I was trying to tidy up their house as best I could, they're not the best housekeepers you know, and when I went upstairs to check on them, Ivy was alone in the tub."

Gayle's hand closed painfully on mine. I squeezed back.

"And where was Mrs. Pearson at this time?"

"Down the hall in her bedroom. She came back a minute later, and I scolded her for it. But of course it didn't register." Arlene raised her chin. "I just want what's best for Ivy. And she's better off with me."

The judge thanked her, and Arlene hobbled back to her seat. I leaned over to Gayle and whispered, "Don't worry. It'll be okay." She didn't acknowledge me. Her gaze had fallen to the tabletop, eyes blank.

"It appears a Mr. Linden wants to make a statement?" the judge said.

"Here, Your Honor," a middle-aged balding man said from near the back of the room. Linden was Gayle's manager at the greenhouse where she worked. He took the stand, and after a minute of describing Gayle's position and responsibilities, he said, "To keep this brief, Gayle is the best employee I've ever had, bar none. She is the kindest, most thoughtful person I know, and whenever she's brought Ivy by work she's been an attentive and doting mother." Linden beamed at Gayle. "An excellent mother."

"Thank you so much, Mr. Linden," Gayle said. There was a low ripple of warm laughter in the room. He nodded, smiling.

"Okay, Ms. McTavish. Looks like you're next," the judge said when Linden had left the stand. I gave Gayle's hand another squeeze before leaving the table. When I was seated the judge said, "Ms. McTavish, you're a family advocate representing Mr. and Mrs. Pearson, correct?"

"Correct."

"All right. Please proceed."

I took a breath. "I've seen some bad things while working in social services. Heartbreaking circumstances. Violence. Abuse. Neglect. Parents who are not fit to care for their children, and kids enduring unimaginable things at the hands of the people who are supposed to protect them. But the pain caused by wrongfully removing a child from their home is a different class of trauma. Because in this situation, the system is the abuser. And that's what we're seeing in this case."

Out of the corner of my eye, I saw the judge lean forward in her chair. I pressed on.

"Gayle and Joel are honest, hardworking people who *adore* their daughter. All statements and documentation support that Ivy is healthy, happy, and wants for nothing. The children I've seen removed from their homes for protection would be lucky to be placed with parents like the Pearsons. And the only reason we're here today is because of a deep-seated prejudice, nothing else."

"Ms. McTavish, you're walking a line here," the judge said.

I faced her. "I'm sure I am, Your Honor, but if so, it doesn't just need to be walked, it needs to be leaped across. What Gayle and Joel have gone through for the better part of two months is an offense designed by an antiquated system with cruelty at its core. No one, and I mean, *no one* else in this room would've lost custody of their children over riding improperly in a shopping cart." I looked across the faces—Richard Jackson stared at the tabletop while Lila had her head tilted like a curious bird. I held longest on Arlene. She was pale beneath her clumpy makeup. "It's beyond shameful. Gayle and Joel aren't just owed the custody of their daughter back—they deserve a profound apology. And that wouldn't even begin making up for the suffering they've endured."

My pulse hammered in my temples, and sweat rolled down my back. My anger was transcendent. I saw every kid who had fallen through the so-called cracks in the system when that was really all the system was composed of. Pitfalls created by flawed and shallow-thinking people in service of the status quo.

"Is that all, Ms. McTavish?" the judge said quietly.

"It isn't, Your Honor, but I think it better be for now."

"I agree. You may step down."

As I crossed to our table Sharon looked both exasperated and exultant. I knew I'd gotten carried away but couldn't help it. When I sat down Joel reached across and patted my arm, never making eye contact.

"Okay, well that concludes testimony," the judge said. "Before ruling—"

"Your . . . Your Honor?" Gayle said timidly.

"Yes, Mrs. Pearson?"

"Could I say something?"

The judge eyed Sharon, who shrugged. "All right. Come up, please." She made her way to the stand and repeated the oath as the bailiff walked her through it. On the stand she fidgeted for a moment, looking first at Sharon and then at me. I nodded.

"Um . . . hi . . . I just want to say that I miss my mom." Gayle looked down at her hands. "She died six years ago, and I think about her every day. She used to take me to the café by our house, and we'd have cocoa and lemon bars, and we'd pet dogs we met on the way home, and she was a really good mom. I learned to be a good mom from her, and I think Ivy misses us like I miss my mom." She paused. "I know my grandma is sad because Mom died and she couldn't do anything about it, so she tried helping us with Ivy, but she wasn't really helping. And it's not helping by taking Ivy away. So if we could please have her back, that would make it all better. Okay, thank you."

Gayle didn't wait for the judge to let her step down. She came back to the table where Joel hugged her, kissing her cheek twice before sitting down. Arlene suddenly rose and left the room, her shoulders hunched and shaking silently.

"All right," the judge said, and there might've been the slightest tremor in her voice. "Do you have any further recommendations, Mrs. Valchek?"

"None, Your Honor. Everything is in my report."

"Very well." She surveyed the courtroom. "This morning I had a fair opinion on what ruling I'd make regarding this case given prior circumstances and evidence. The only thing that could've swayed my decision was today's scheduled testimony. Surprisingly it was the *un*scheduled testimony that secured the following conclusion." The judge turned her attention to our table. "Regarding the custody of Ivy Josephine Pearson, I hereby rule in favor of—"

49

Tears.

Happy ones. Finally.

Gayle and Joel sat with Ivy held between them in the doorway of the courthouse playroom. I stood with Sharon, watching from a short way down the hall, trying not to ruin my own mascara. Sharon bumped my hip with her briefcase. "Good work, partner."

"You too."

"Ever think about going back to school? Getting your law degree? The firm's looking for someone with your—"

"Anger?"

"I was going to say *passion*, but yes, *anger* works, too, sometimes in this business." She turned to me. "It was a risk, saying all that today. Gears in the machine don't like being told the machine is broken."

"The gears can change or piss off," I said. "And I appreciate the offer, but I like what I do now. I want to keep it that way."

"Invitation stands," Sharon said, starting away. "And you're buying drinks next time." I watched her go, then turned my attention back to the little family down the hall. Gayle was cupping Ivy's face in her hands and kissing her on the forehead. Joel was talking excitedly about the fairy parade.

"Nora, Nora, Nora." Richard Jackson appeared at my side like some unwanted ghost. "You really like to stir things up. You know you're still the talk of the department. Just the other day I was telling Maureen—"

"Rich, you really fucked up on this one," I said, continuing to watch the Pearsons. "That removal never should've happened."

He laughed. "You are something. Just because you quit doesn't make you better than me. That cynical shit you spew only goes so far, you know? We live in the real world, not some idealistic la-la land. That little speech might've tugged some tears from the judge, but you and I both know nothing's gonna change. I didn't have any more choice about the removal than all the times you did the same thing. So don't talk down to me like you're on some higher level. We're all in the gutter together."

I watched him swagger away, then turned my attention back down the hall one last time like a cleansing breath after breathing smoke. Took the Pearsons' joy with me as I left the building. Outside, a trancelike Arlene stood on the courthouse steps, staring at the parking lot like it was her first time seeing it. She looked all of her years, a bone-thin hand squeezing a tissue over and over. I could've slipped by without her noticing, but I stopped and said her name. She turned to me, and it took a moment for her to realize who was speaking to her. "You," she said with more venom than I thought could be packed into one word.

Before she could go on I said, "I'm sorry." She blinked, mouth opening then closing. "I'm very sorry about your daughter. I can't imagine the pain of losing a child."

Arlene shook her head. "Don't . . . don't you . . ."

"But Gayle's right. You can't change that she's gone, and this isn't the way forward. You have to find another path. I hope you do."

I left her on the steps and didn't look back.

———

I drank too much that night.

First wine, then shots of tequila. A mistake, but I didn't care. Music followed. Old-school rock. AC/DC, Def Leppard, Ozzy. Dancing ensued. Merrill watched, head resting on his paws, eyes following my efforts through the living room and into the kitchen. He looked embarrassed for me. But it felt good to let loose after the last weeks. Even the burn of the bullet wound reminded me I was alive and had helped a little girl get home today. The only sobering thought was of Kenny, still caught in the thresher of her parents' intentions.

And tomorrow. Tomorrow.

I almost called Stephen but didn't. Considered texting Daniel Stellsgard, the assistant DA, and finally finding out if his stomach was as flat and hard as it looked beneath his dress shirts. But I didn't do that either. I settled for an order of General Tso's, a stupid rom-com, and more wine.

Merrill cuddled beside me on the couch. Blue light and shadows danced away from the TV. Our reflections in the glass of the big windows felt more tangible than real life. I fell in and out of sleep, my mind like a plane doing touch-and-gos.

Around five in the morning I woke, gathered my things, and drove the short distance down to the beach. The waves were dark copies of themselves, rolling in without enough light to see the white of their foam. I paddled out, dunking my head a few times in the cold water to quench the molten ache of my evening's debauchery.

Only one suitable wave came in, and I waited a second too long to stand up. It tossed me, and the ocean roared angrily in my ears, the leash yanking hard at my ankle, spinning me over. I came up sputtering and blinking the salt out of my eyes, wondering if this was a portent. A single chance blown by hesitation. I hoped not.

Back at the house, a shower as hot as I could stand it. Then coffee. Lots of coffee and breakfast. Merrill and I went on a walk, then I filled up his water and food.

I bent and petted his head, and he looked at me with way more knowing than a dog should be capable of. "Yes, I'm gonna be gone for a little while. Not like before. Uncle Stephen will come check on you." I hugged him. Kissed his snout. Then went out the door.

Behind the wheel of my car, a familiar urge overcame me. I could go back inside and turn the locks. Shut my phone off. Pretend I didn't have to be anywhere. Hide. But Kenny had been right to ask. She'd seen more clearly than I had.

Are you running away now?

I backed the car out of the driveway and aimed it east. Toward the ascending sun.

Toward Mutiny.

50

A storm pursued me over the mountains.

A squall coming off the Pacific that built itself in stacked thunderclouds, bellies lanced with knives of lightning. It followed for a time, then fell away the farther east I went. When Mutiny came into view, the sky was clear, the air humid. I'd actually had to use the AC most of the drive. I was early and spent several hours cruising around the town's outskirts, letting my thoughts drift. The lake was a sheet of glass, the mountains peering down into their own reflections. The moraine rose to the side, much greener than when I'd last seen it a few weeks ago. The bullet wound itched.

It was late afternoon when I drove slowly through the center of town, making the necessary turns, and pulled into a parking space. The first clouds had appeared in the west, and fog crept up from the ground in a low haze. I studied the courthouse for a moment before shutting the car off and heading inside.

The courtroom was already partially filled when I entered and found a seat in the back of the gallery. A few spectators were press and had their tablets and phones out while others huddled together, speaking in low voices.

Tess and Jacob sat at the left-hand table before the bench, Neil and his lawyer, Yolanda Beech, opposite them. Tess wore a sleek blue skirt and matching top. Her hair was piled up and pinned, simple but nice. She stared straight ahead while Jacob murmured something in her ear.

She nodded. Neil wore a suit I recognized from his YouTube videos and kept drumming his fingers lightly on the tabletop. The air was stuffy and expectant. A second before the judge entered, Tess turned and saw me. Her eyes widened and she blinked. My mouth was dry and my pulse thudded dully in my ears. Then the judge was striding in, and there was the rustle of clothing as we all stood.

"Be seated," Judge Rein said. We sat. The clerk droned off Tess's and Neil's names and the reason they were here. Tess threw another look my way I couldn't read before facing ahead. Beech touched Neil on the shoulder and said something to which he nodded. Then she turned and spoke to someone seated directly behind their table.

Someone forgettable. Someone familiar.

A man with a dark mole on his left temple.

My breath caught.

The man I'd chased from the block party shook his head, replying to Neil's attorney; then they both returned their attention to the judge as he spoke.

"Okay, folks, it's late in the day, and no one wants this to drag out into tomorrow or the next day, so we'll jump right in. Are counsels fully briefed on the filings?"

"I am, Your Honor," Jacob said.

"Yes, Your Honor," Beech said.

"Very good. We're here because you've petitioned for full custody given new circumstances. Please proceed, Mrs. Beech."

"Thank you, Your Honor," Beech said. "To start off we'd like to call Mr. Benjamin Pellum for testimony, please." The man with the mole stood and sauntered to the stand.

"Mr. Pellum, you've signed an affidavit swearing to tell the truth here today," Rein said.

"Yes, Your Honor," Pellum said. He had a low, nasally voice that barely carried to the back of the room.

"Go ahead, Mrs. Beech," Rein said.

Beech remained seated and said, "Mr. Pellum, can you tell the court what it is you do for a living?"

"I'm a private investigator."

My stomach curdled as I felt a slow dawning.

"And did my client, Neil Grayson, hire you earlier this spring?" Beech continued.

"He did."

"And what did he hire you for?"

Pellum leaned back in his chair. "He wanted me to keep an eye on his wife and daughter."

"You're referring to Tess Grayson and Kendra Grayson."

"That's right."

"Did he give you a reason why he wanted you to do this?"

"Not really. Just said he was concerned about his wife's behavior."

"And what did your services entail?"

"Observation from my vehicle as well as from other public spaces."

Beech turned over a piece of paper. "Can you tell the court what occurred on the night of May sixth?"

Pellum sucked his teeth. "I observed Mrs. Grayson and her daughter attending a neighborhood get-together. Kind of an outdoors potluck thing."

"And was Mrs. Grayson drinking alcohol that evening?"

"Yes. It appeared so."

"And do you believe she was intoxicated?"

"Objection, Your Honor," Jacob said, standing. "Mr. Pellum has no proof or qualifications to determine my client's level of intoxication."

"I'll rephrase, Your Honor," Beech said, cool as a daydream. "Mr. Pellum, did you notice Mrs. Grayson speaking loudly or slurring her words?"

"Yes."

"And did you attempt to record her interactions with several of her neighbors?"

"I did."

"Your Honor, with your permission I'd like to play the video taken by Mr. Pellum on the night of the sixth, please."

Rein surveyed the room. "Very well."

Beech stood and moved to a digital screen mounted in the left-hand wall opposite the empty jury box. She fiddled with a small control for a moment, and then the screen filled with a still image of a bonfire before jumping into motion.

The night of the block party played out on the screen from Pellum's perspective. There was Tess speaking to the group of neighbors; there I was in the background hurrying toward her, trying to stop her.

So he was a liar and a cheater? So what? Lots of people cheat. But not everyone kills their lover.

Tess's words boomed loudly across the courtroom. Tess herself watched the screen, mouth slightly open, features bloodless.

You'll see, it's a huge mistake. He's a fucking monster.

The view swung away from Tess as I finally caught her. Shifted to Kenny standing wide eyed and staring.

The video ended.

There was a short collective murmur through the spectators, and Rein called for quiet. "Nothing further," Beech said.

"You may step down," Rein told Pellum. He returned to his seat.

Jacob leaned toward Tess, speaking fast and low, then stood. "Your Honor, could we take a short recess, please, so I can confer with my client?"

"We're in the middle of proceedings, Mr. Leighton, so no."

"But, Your Honor—"

"Mr. Leighton?" Rein raised his bushy eyebrows. "I've spoken." Jacob lowered himself to his seat. "Mrs. Beech, it looks like you have one more testimony?"

"Yes, Your Honor," Beech said, turning slightly in her seat. "We'd like to call Ms. Nora McTavish to the stand."

51

I knew it was coming, but preparation never fully outweighs fear.

From the second I saw where the certified letter had come from and read the subpoena it contained, I knew I'd be returning to Mutiny. Knew I'd have to be in this courtroom. Knew it would culminate in this moment.

But in this case Stephen was wrong—reality was worse than imagination.

Tess's expression, the pure astonishment, was hard to look at. I made my way forward feeling every eye in the place pressing against my skin. I was sworn in and took the stand. For a second the room blurred, all the people and colors running together. They snapped back into focus as Beech said my name.

"I'm sorry?" I said.

"I asked if you could state what it is you do for a living," Beech said. Neil sat beside her, watching me. Impassive. I could feel Tess's stare like heat on the other side of my face.

"I'm a family advocate," I finally said.

"And prior to that?"

"I worked at state child protective services."

"And what is your relationship to Mrs. Grayson?"

She said you were like a sister.

"We knew each other as children. We're friends."

"You were staying with her off and on over the last month, is that right?"

"Yes."

"And is it true she asked you here to help her with the custody case against my client?"

"Objection, Your Honor," Jacob said. "Ms. McTavish was here solely for personal support. There was no payment or contract."

"I'll let her answer the question," Rein said after a pause.

I tried swallowing, but my mouth was smooth and dry. "She asked my advice several times, but I came for personal reasons."

Beech nodded. "And in your time staying at the Grayson residence, did Mrs. Grayson ever say anything derogatory about my client?"

"Yes."

"And did she ever make any of these statements within earshot of their daughter, Kendra?"

I finally looked at Tess. Her features were an amalgam of emotions. Anger. Disbelief. Pleading.

"I can't recall," I finally said.

"But you obviously remember the night of May sixth. That was you in the background of the video, was it not?"

"Yes."

"So in your opinion, did Kendra hear what Mrs. Grayson was saying about my client?"

A long pause. "Yes."

"Did you speak with Kendra afterward?"

"Yes."

"And what was her emotional state?"

I took a deep breath. "Distressed."

Beech surveyed me for another moment, then looked to the judge. "Nothing further, Your Honor."

I stepped down and returned to my seat, not looking at either table as I passed. Beech made a show of shuffling some more papers before standing. "Your Honor, as we've shown, there is a clear case of parental alienation against my client perpetrated by Mrs. Grayson. On top of the video evidence gathered by Mr. Pellum, there have been several unsubstantiated accusations made by Mrs. Grayson, as well as a restraining order that has now been suspended. My client is deeply concerned about his daughter's emotional and psychological well-being, and at this time we ask you remand her into his sole care. We also welcome recommended parameters for Mrs. Grayson to regain shared custody at a later date. Thank you, Your Honor."

Rein scowled down at his desk. An expectant silence gathered. Someone coughed quietly. Rein glanced at Tess and Jacob. "Mr. Leighton, do you have anything to add?"

Jacob whispered something to Tess, who didn't respond. Didn't move. Jacob waited another beat, then looked at the judge and stood. "Not at this time, Your Honor."

"Very well," Rein said. He adjusted the neck of his robes and looked down from the bench like a buzzard on its perch. "Mrs. Grayson, parental alienation can be highly damaging to children in cases of divorce or separation, and the display shown today is one of the most egregious I've seen." Rein paused, scowling even deeper. "Therefore, it is my ruling that effective immediately Kendra Grayson be remanded into sole custody of the plaintiff."

Tess crumpled forward with a low moan and started to cry. Jacob placed a hand on her back.

"I will forward a series of requisite contingency actions and schedule a custody reevaluation at a date later to be determined." Rein swept the courtroom with a glance. "This hearing is adjourned."

———

The sky had become dark and tumorous by the time I stepped outside. The air was still heavy but cooling fast, the fog gone, leaving behind an odd clarity to everything. There were too many angles, too many edges. All of them sharp.

I headed for my car, ears attuned for the voice I knew would come, so when it did there was no surprise.

"Nora!" Tess was striding across the parking lot, which was mostly empty now. A perfect stage for this last scene to play out between us. She stopped a few paces away. Her hair had come undone from a couple of pins and wisped down to her shoulders. She was trembling, faint tear tracks shining in the strange pre-storm light. "Why?"

"I was subpoenaed. I didn't have a choice."

"You could have said anything."

"You mean lied."

"I mean you could have defended me. You're my friend, for God's sake."

I looked past her and sighed. "Tess, from the first time you called, you haven't been honest with me."

"What are you talking about?"

"There was no way you didn't know Neil was going to get partial custody. Jacob told you that, and you're not stupid." I took a breath. "You didn't want an ally; you wanted a weapon against your husband. And that's what you thought I was. And when I couldn't stop him from getting custody, you used me as a witness to your plan. You used Kenny."

Something changed behind her eyes. A darkening. "I'm keeping her safe." Her voice was deadly soft.

"Is that how you justified helping Devon frame Neil?"

Tess blinked and took a small step back as if she'd been pushed. "What?"

"Kenny told me she saw Devon at your house in the middle of the night on the weekend Neil was arrested. You were already seeing each other, and my guess is he was sure Neil was guilty. He probably convinced you."

"You don't know . . . anything," Tess said breathlessly.

"Neil was going to be released, and Devon needed something damning. You told him where to plant the book with Allie's blood on it. The nook beside the fireplace at the cabin? That's where Neil hid your engagement ring, right?" She shook her head, jaw working, but no sound came out. "How far did it go, Tess? You framed Neil—so did Devon kill Allie?" I let the words hang for a beat, then pushed on. "Did you?"

Tess barked a hoarse laugh. "You're crazy, aren't you? Just like your father."

The barb glanced off me. I could feel the anger thrumming like some mainlined drug in my veins. "That's why you followed me into the mountains, isn't it? I knew what the two of you did."

"What are you talking about?"

"Where were you the night Neil found Kenny? Because you weren't home."

Tess straightened, her chin coming up. "I was out looking for her, then I went to Devon's."

"Why?"

"Because I loved him!" Her voice rang off the courthouse wall. She was shaking, tears spilling once more. "I spent the night there. I have no idea what you're talking about."

"You called me that evening."

"So? We argued before you left, and you didn't come back. I was worried."

"And you called again in the morning after Kenny was found safe."

"To let you know."

Behind her Jacob appeared outside the courthouse doors. He scanned the parking lot and spotted us. Headed our way at a fast walk.

Tess shook her head. "I can't believe you've done this to me. To my family. I trusted you."

I studied her, trying to sift through the lies for the truth. "We used to know each other," I said after a beat. "But we don't anymore."

"Tess?" Jacob reached us and touched her shoulder. He gave me a look that fell somewhere between annoyance and sorrow. "We should probably go."

Tess hadn't taken her eyes off me. "When something terrible happens, know that it's your fault."

We stood that way for a moment, both anchored in place by the other.

Then Jacob said, "Come on," and ushered her away. Tess glanced back once, and I had the fleeting memory of her being driven away from her mother's funeral, looking out through the dark tinted glass of the town car, a hollow-eyed mask of loss.

They climbed in Jacob's car and pulled out. Gone from sight a moment later.

I stood in the parking lot alone. Thunder came from the west as if the clouds were grinding off the mountaintops.

The poisonous day darkened.

52

I'd seen the little motel a few times while traveling back and forth to Mutiny.

It was a two-level building set a short distance off the highway only a half mile out of town. A partially lit vacancy sign thrummed in the evening air like a siren's call. I heeded it.

A room for the night cost ninety-two dollars. The bed looked clean. No mint on the pillow, though. I found a small bar attached to the far end of the building, a weathered man with a gray beard sitting behind it absently watching a baseball game on the TV in the corner. He poured me a glass of wine so tall only surface tension kept it from overspilling. I took my drink outside onto a patio littered with four tables and a dozen chairs. Alone.

I didn't know why I'd pulled off here. Maybe it was the idea of the long drive ahead into the storm. Maybe I was just tired. Maybe it was the hollow feeling in my chest, like something vital had been scooped out.

My suspicion about Tess's involvement in framing Neil had formed around the time I'd tracked her phone's location. As the days and weeks unfurled, the idea had coalesced into a clear picture.

Devon and Tess's affair.

Devon's late-night visit to their house.

Tess's proclivity for snooping and knowing a perfect place to hide incriminating evidence.

Her reaction today had confirmed it. She hadn't been able to conceal the shock and shame. She'd helped her lover frame her husband. But did that really mean Neil was innocent?

When something terrible happens, know that it's your fault.

What if Devon had been right about Neil and just hadn't possessed the evidence to charge him? What if I had helped a murderer regain custody of his child? What if I'd taken Kenny out of a bad situation and put her someplace much worse? My stomach roiled.

The patio door opened, and four men strode outside holding tall beers. They all wore what looked like matching forestry uniforms. One of them had long blond hair curling down past his ears and cool-blue eyes, which he turned my way for a second, marking me. He smiled and sat down with his friends. I sipped my wine and let my gaze linger on the storm crawling closer, shadowing the valley like a blanket being pulled over the sky.

What kept coming back to me was Tess's declaration of love for Devon. It was the truth. I could tell that much. She had truly cared for him. And if that truth supported her alibi of spending the night at his house mourning, someone else had been in the mountains with me.

I drew out my phone and did a quick search of Devon's name and Mutiny. Quite a few hits came up. I touched the latest article in the town's main newspaper. As I read, the churning in my stomach worsened.

Devon's death had been ruled a homicide.

There weren't many details except what had initially appeared as a suicide was recategorized late last week by law enforcement. The murder was under investigation and leads were being followed up.

I put my phone away and stared blankly at the patio bricks near my feet.

"Mind if I sit down?"

I startled, glancing up into the handsome face of the blond forest ranger. "Whoa, sorry," he said, taking a step back. "Didn't mean to scare you."

"Uh, no, it's okay. I was . . . miles away."

"I could see that." He nodded toward the chair opposite me, eyes questioning.

What the hell.

"Be my guest," I said.

He sat and extended a hand across the table. "Jeff Holden."

I shook with him. "Nora."

"Good to meet you, Nora. I'm gonna wager you're not local."

"Winner winner."

"What brings you to our little corner of the world and its finest drinking establishment?"

I sipped my wine. "Besides the excellent selection of vino?" He laughed. "Helping out a friend."

"That's nice. You live nearby?"

"On the coast."

"Whereabouts?"

"Easton."

"I've been there. Gorgeous coastlines." He gestured at my diminished glass. "Buy you another?"

"No, thank you."

Jeff sipped his beer. "So what does one do in Easton?"

"One does family advocacy."

His eyebrows shot up. "Really? That's great."

I laughed. "Is it?"

"Well it is when the bulk of your childhood was saved by a family advocate who got your parents the help they desperately needed."

I reassessed him. "I'm glad."

"Me too. The world needs more people doing what you do."

"I'd like to believe that." I polished off the last of my wine, its effect finally erasing the last of my lingering hangover. "And what keeps you busy, Jeff?"

"Search and rescue." He tapped a patch sewn onto the breast of his shirt.

"Interesting. How did you get into that?"

He shrugged. "Always liked helping people, I guess. And I didn't have the dedication for medical school, so here I am." He laughed again. "It's gratifying. And there's the adrenaline too. I guess I get off on that." There was a slight twinkle in his eye before he looked away.

"So you must've been out searching for Kendra Grayson when she was missing a couple weeks ago?"

"The runaway, yes. We were for the first day, then we got pulled off to look for a little boy who went missing."

My memory spun for a second, then clutched the name. "Thomas, right?"

Jeff grinned. "That's him. Little guy had fallen down an embankment not too far from his parents' campsite. Got banged up and couldn't get out. When I found him, he was snuggled in under a rock shelf fast asleep, if you can believe it."

"*You* found him?"

"Well, me and my team. You can't really take credit in searches, it's always a group effort." I couldn't tell if he was actually humble or only good at playing it. Either way, it was charming.

"All's well that ends well, right?"

"I'd say that's right." He sat back and looked at me, and something passed between us. A question. One involving several more drinks, more small talk, flirting—the answer in the form of us alone in my room later. I considered it for a second, wondering if Jeff, with his lean frame and calloused hands, was exactly what I needed right now. But only for a second.

"Jeff, we're goin' in," one of the other men said as the rest of his group headed for the patio door. "Gonna get wet here soon."

Jeff glanced my way. "I'd love to buy you a drink inside."

I stood. "I don't think so. Not tonight."

He smiled. "Well, I'll hope to see you a different night, then. It was very nice talking with you, Nora." He held out his hand and squeezed mine gently when I shook with him.

"You too."

I walked the length of the building and ascended the outdoor stairs to the second floor and let myself into my room. It was cool, and I turned up the heat before going to the window. The storm hovered somewhere over the lake, blue-white lightning arcing down every so often. By now Neil would have picked Kenny up from school, and they would be at the cabin. Their first night alone together in months.

The run-in with Neil at the overlook haunted me. I turned over all the things he said like artifacts, looking for a deeper hidden meaning in them. A warning. *I wouldn't have done it if she hadn't forced me.* His last words were less threatening now, knowing he'd been referring to the petition for full custody. At least I was pretty sure that was what he'd meant.

I went to the bed and lay crosswise on it. Watched the light from the storm dance on the ceiling. During my time away, Mutiny felt like an open wound whenever I thought of it. Unhealing. Unresolved. Things were still in motion here, but I couldn't discern exactly what they were. An irresistible urge to speak to Kenny flooded me, and I reached for my phone, just as quickly dropping it back on the bedspread. I didn't have her tablet's number to text to or email. Ditto Neil's. And getting it from Tess wasn't an option.

My frustration filled the room like a suffocating smog. Part of me wished I had asked Jeff up. At least then I'd have been distracted. I considered returning to the bar to see if he was still there but dismissed it. He'd been cute and pleasant and courteous, but a one-night stand wasn't going to fix anything.

I chewed absently on a ragged edge of cuticle. Jeff. Something about him kept turning my thoughts to the birds in Devon's backyard. I could hear them now, their chatter and calls in the seconds before I turned and saw Devon through his bedroom window. It shook me even more knowing someone had killed him and attempted to make it look like a suicide. At first it had fit. The disgraced cop taking the easy way out. But now his murder only raised more questions. I thought of Tess describing their last day together. How they'd searched for Kenny, then gone and staked out Neil's cabin. Her uncertainty if Neil had seen them. I pictured Tess and Devon returning to his house, where they drank wine, made love in his bed—all of it in plain view from the backyard where the birds fed and fluttered. I thought of the thick woods behind Devon's home and how anyone could have been watching them. Waiting for the moment Tess left and Devon fell asleep. Then stalking in silently to his room, placing a gun beneath his chin—

But what was the association between Jeff and Devon? The two men looked nothing alike. Had different professions. It was probably because I'd just read about Devon's death being deemed a murder before Jeff approached me. That was it.

But it wasn't.

I sat up on the bed, lightning the only intermittent illumination in the room. With each flicker and answer of thunder, what I reached for came a little closer.

Jeff was nice. Jeff was attractive.

He did search and rescue.

He'd searched for Kenny.

He'd found Thomas.

Wait.

Go back.

I leaned forward, feeling a precipice. A veiled border where something waited on the other side.

What was it?

Kenny. He'd searched for Kenny the first day she was missing.

The next lightning strike might as well have been inside my head. I jerked, lungs crimping off oxygen. Then I was rushing out of the room, leaving the door open in my wake. It had started to rain, but I barely registered the cold drops as they soaked into my shirt. Down the stairs and along the building back to the patio and inside the bar. I was sure they'd be gone, moved on to another watering hole where I'd never find them again. And I was having trouble remembering Jeff's last name. He'd be so much harder to track down without a last name. But the four men were there at the bar, gazing up at the TV, laughing at something someone had said.

I was only a few steps inside when Jeff turned and saw me, his whole face lighting up. "Hey, change your mind about that drink?"

"You said you searched for Kendra the first day," I said, grasping his forearm.

"What?" Jeff glanced at his friends, who were eyeing me like I was some kind of maniac. I sounded like one. Probably looked the part too.

"Kendra Grayson—you searched the first day for her but got pulled off to look for the little boy."

"Yeah, it's a priority thing," Jeff said uneasily. "Resources go to the most crucial missing party. Thomas took precedence since Kendra was older and a runaway. Why?"

"Were there other search parties organized and looking for Kendra even though you weren't?"

Jeff surveyed his crew. "Not anything substantial, no."

"Not like thirty or forty people?"

"No, anything like that would've been run through us. A couple volunteers might've gotten together, but we organize all private searches so they're done correctly. Otherwise it's kind of a waste. Are you okay? You're shaking."

"You're sure?"

"Yeah, I'm sure."

I think I said thank you. Or goodbye. Maybe not. I don't recall the trip back to my room through the rain, only suddenly standing at the window again, dripping wet, sure of two things.

I'd been a fool.

And Jacob had lied to me.

53

Transcript of *Poe, the Man and the Myths: A lecture series with Professor Neil Grayson*, Part 12—presented by Ridgewood University in coordination with College Partnership Programming.

Now, while we're still on the topic, I'd like to examine another type of obsession associated with Poe's work—the obsession of love.

The theme of love is woven into many of his short stories and poems, but perhaps not more so than the poem "Annabel Lee," which most believe—once again—to be about his late wife, Virginia. The love he describes in this poem is mythical. It is transcendent. It is coveted by the angels themselves, and the narrator believes their jealousy is why poor Annabel is taken from him. But even death can't keep them apart because their love is destiny.

(Recites from poem)

And neither the angels in heaven above
Nor the demons down under the sea

*Can ever dissever my soul from the soul
Of the beautiful Annabel Lee*

The narrator fully believes they will be reunited despite death's separation, and this is where some might say his interpretation of love becomes obsession.

And to them I would say, what else is love but an obsession of the soul?

54

Streetlights muted in rain flashed by overhead as Tess's number went to voice mail for the third time.

"Fuck." I tossed the phone aside and concentrated on the mostly empty road. The drizzle had graduated to a cascade, like the entire town was at the base of some cyclopean waterfall. Ahead the buildings fell away, and the lake began, a vast open darkness on the right side of the car, mountains leaping into definition with each lightning strike. I pressed the gas down a little more, hoping I was wrong. As wrong as I had been so far.

The day I'd gone to see Jacob to talk about Tess's state of mind and what she was capable of, I hadn't considered who I was talking to. I'd known Jacob was probably still in love with Tess—even she had alluded to the fact. But if I was right, it was so much worse than a long-standing infatuation.

It was obsession.

The moraine loomed in a muted flicker—the back of some great slumbering beast—and I swung the car into Tess's neighborhood.

I recalled how disheveled Jacob had looked when he'd answered the door. He'd just gotten out of the shower and thrown a load of his clothes in the washing machine while I waited, since he'd only recently returned from a major search effort for Kenny.

Except he hadn't.

And if Jacob hadn't been out looking for Kenny, then where had he been? And why had he lied?

My headlights washed over the dark face of Tess's home. No glow from inside. No cars in the drive. I cursed again and pulled to a stop before the garage door. Outside the rain instantly plastered my already damp clothes to my body. The garage windows were slightly above my line of sight, but I managed to pull myself up enough to confirm the interior was vacant. The front door was locked. At the house's rear entry, the greater view inside revealed only empty darkness. I pounded on the glass anyway.

"Tess!" Nothing. No lights. No answer. She wasn't here.

Back in the car, the rain so loud on the roof it was like being trapped in a static-filled speaker. I could barely think over the noise. After a couple of deep breaths, I called Tess's phone again. Voice mail.

I started the car and backed out, blasting the heat on my face and hands. Saw no one as I sped out of the neighborhood.

The timing was right when I thought about it. Or wrong, depending on your point of view. When Tess had left Devon to finally come back home, I'd been considering my options, wondering if I should go and confront her. At the same moment I could see Jacob entering Devon's house, stalking closer and closer to the sleeping man, trying to gauge the right angle and distance for a suicide shot without waking him. When it was done he'd gone home, beating me there by only minutes.

Now his house loomed ahead.

I glided past, slow enough to see there were no lights on and his car wasn't in the driveway. I drove around the block and parked on the eastern side where an alley cut through the backs of the properties.

Out in the storm again, hunched and running low.

A dog barked viciously from under a porch awning but wouldn't brave the weather for a taste of me. Down the alleyway until I was even with the back of Jacob's house, his yard hemmed in by a low hedge and a single weeping willow—its leaves flared white in a sweep of lightning. I sidled through a gap in the hedge and stayed low all the way up to the back entry, peering in through the glass.

Someone stood inches away on the other side of the door.

My heart blotted out the thunder overhead, and I sagged with relief seeing it was only a bulky coat hanging on a rack. Edging around to the left I looked in the living room window—vague shapes of furniture. Jacob's ex's weird art. No movement. The back of the garage was around the next corner. Jacob's car was absent. I didn't know if this was a comfort or not.

They weren't at Tess's and they weren't here. I made my way back to my vehicle and climbed inside, shivering hard. Checked my phone. No missed calls. I pulled up the number for the local PD and punched it in. After a moment a calm voice said in my ear, "Mutiny Police Department, Officer Reynolds speaking, how can I assist you?"

I cringed, realizing Officer Reynolds was the person who took my statement about being shot. "Hi, I can't find my friend, and I'm worried she might be in trouble."

"Okay, what kind of trouble?"

"I'm afraid someone might be trying to harm her."

"And your friend's name?" I told him Tess's name and address, to which he responded, "And you're concerned about her ex-husband, I'm guessing?"

"No, I'm . . ." How to frame this so I didn't sound completely unhinged. "She's not at home, and I think she might've been taken by someone she knows. Someone she trusts."

"And this person is?"

"Jacob Leighton."

"Ooookay," Reynolds said, drawing out the word in a way that made me want to scream. "And why do you think Mr. Leighton would want to hurt her?"

"Is there any way to just start checking with patrols to see if they can locate either of them?"

"Well, not without good cause, ma'am. And so far, I'm not hearing it." I exhaled into the mouthpiece, and Reynolds said, "Listen, I'll send a car by the address you gave me in a while. We've had a couple accidents tonight with the weather, and all officers on duty are occupied at the moment. Try not to worry, and we'll call if we find her. Have a good night, ma'am."

He was gone before I could say anything else. I chucked the phone at the passenger door. It rebounded into the seat and lay still. I sat, breathing hard for half a minute before putting the car into gear and aiming it toward Main Street. There was one last place to check. If she wasn't there, I had no idea what to do.

How far could love drive you? I suppose that depended on how strong it was. For Tess, her love for Kenny had driven her to help frame Neil to keep him in jail for the crime she was sure he committed. Drove her to stage a break-in to keep him at bay once he was free.

But Jacob's had driven him so much further.

I could imagine the years between his proposal to Tess and now. Never actually getting over it. Watching her fall in love with and marry Neil. Watching her have his child. Watching her slip beyond his grasp while the yawning gulf of desire widened and became something else. Something darker and desperate.

As I drove into the foothills above town, the rain tapered, its curtains drawing aside until Devon's driveway was revealed in my high beams. I sent up my last hope and turned in.

The windows were blank eyes reflecting my headlights. No vehicles. No sign of movement. I checked the garage anyway. Empty.

Back in the car, dripping wet, my fear growing exponentially with each passing minute. Tess had left the courthouse with Jacob. Now both of them were nowhere to be found. What was a person capable of whose love had twisted them over years and years? What form could that love take?

And what would they do when denied the one thing they wanted?

I knew all too well from dealing with the aftermaths of other obsessed and violent men. Walking through carnage left in the wakes of denials. All because they couldn't accept the word *no*.

Images of desolate rainy fields flashed through my mind. Tess on her knees beside a shallow grave, crying, pleading with the figure standing above her holding a weapon. Telling her he loved her. Saying it had all been for her.

My stomach clenched, and I thought I might be sick. I had to calm down. Had to think. They couldn't be far away. I just needed to figure out where.

Slowly my head came up, and I stared at Devon's darkened home. I knew how to find Tess.

I'd known all along.

55

There was a single light on in the cabin when I pulled into the short driveway.

The rain still fell, turning the windshield into a blur as soon as the wipers quit moving. Neil's crossover was parked beside the small garage. I hurried past it through a dozen puddles and up the stairs to the front door, punching the doorbell once before stepping back.

Neil appeared in the small decorative window a moment later, brow furrowed, eyes wary. The outdoor light came on, and I blinked in its glare. Neil cracked the door a few inches. "Nora? What are you doing here?"

"I need to come in."

"Why?"

"I think Tess is in trouble." He surveyed me, and I imagined what I must look like. Soaked and wild eyed. Hair plastered to my head. "Please," I said, trying to keep my voice level.

Neil hesitated, looked past me as if to make sure I was alone, then let me inside.

The cabin was blessedly warm. A fireplace crackled brightly in one wall, and the single light in the main sitting area was a tall curved lamp overhanging a well-worn recliner. A mug of tea steamed on an end table, and a hardcover was propped open beside it. A savory smell lingered in the air from whatever dinner he and Kenny had eaten earlier.

I stood dripping on the entry rug while Neil brought me a towel from the kitchen.

"What's wrong with Tess?" he asked as I dried my hair and face.

"I need to use Kenny's tablet."

"What? Why?"

"So I can see where Tess's phone is. She's missing."

"Missing? How do you know she's missing?"

"I don't have time to explain, I just need the tablet, that's all."

"Well you're not making any sense, so I think I'd like you to leave." When I didn't move, he started ushering me toward the door.

"It's Jacob," I said, standing my ground. "I think he may have done something to her."

He stopped. "Jacob? What do you mean?"

"You knew he proposed to Tess in college."

"Sure. It was kind of a running joke between the three of us."

"Did you ever get the feeling he'd never moved on?"

Neil crossed his arms, a line creasing between his eyes. "I think maybe he still loved her on some level, sure. But I never faulted him for it. He got married and divorced. I guess I'm not understanding what you're talking about."

"I think Jacob killed Allie Prentiss."

He blinked and shook his head. "What?"

I set the towel down as a gust of wind keened in the eaves. "I don't think Jacob ever moved on from losing Tess to you. All these years he tried living his life, but the feeling never went away. You were friends, and when he noticed a change in your behavior, I think he started following you. He saw Allie and you together. I spoke to Allie's landlord, and she mentioned someone skulking around their neighborhood before Allie was killed. I think it was Jacob, coming and going without wanting to be seen."

Neil frowned and took a step back to lean against an antique dresser. "What would he want with Allie?"

"To bribe her into telling Tess about the two of you."

"But we never—"

"I know that, but if Allie needed money she might've lied for the right price. Except I think there was some disagreement, maybe she asked for more cash or threatened to blackmail him instead, and Jacob snapped. He killed her, then thought he could frame you. My guess is he texted you from her phone the moment she was dead so you'd be seen in the vicinity near her time of death."

Neil laughed and shook his head. "Listen, this is really bizarre. I don't know who killed Allie, but it wasn't Jacob. He's harmless."

"I'm sure that's what he wanted you to think. But I bet if you're honest with yourself, you noticed things over the years. Maybe the way he looked at Tess when he thought you weren't watching. Or maybe he bought overly personal gifts for her birthdays or Christmas?" Something changed in Neil's gaze, a faint recognition. "I think he was waiting for an opportunity to destroy your relationship, and when it presented itself, he took it, but it went sideways. Except he was able to blame you. But then Devon Wilson came along and tampered with evidence, and you were out again, and—" I paused, trying to decide whether to continue or not, and plunged ahead. "Then Jacob found out about Devon and Tess."

I watched Neil's reaction, feeling the pressure of precious seconds slipping by. He looked away, chewing on the edge of his lip. "I knew she was seeing someone. Just not who. Not until they found the book in the hiding place. She was the only other person who knew it existed."

"And you never said anything." He shook his head. I took a breath. "Jacob must've gotten suspicious and seen them together. He killed Devon and tried making it look like a suicide, since Devon was another barrier between him and Tess. But she's not in love with him, and I'm afraid he might've told her how he felt today, and she rebuffed him. I'm afraid of what he might do to her. What he might've already done."

"Dad?"

Kenny stood at the rim of light, mostly in shadow. She wore pajama pants and an oversize T-shirt, which made her look even smaller and more delicate than she was.

"Go back to bed, mouse," Neil said.

"Kenny, I need your tablet," I said.

"No, just go back to your room, and I'll tuck you in as soon—"

"I heard." Kenny came closer. There were dark circles beneath her eyes. She looked ghostly in the low light. "I think Nora's right, Dad. I don't trust Jacob." Without waiting for a reply, she disappeared into the gloom of the hall.

"Listen," Neil said, facing me again. "I'm thankful you told the truth today on the stand, but this is insane. Tess is probably at a bar. That's all. Now you need to leave, or I'll have to call the police."

He tried herding me toward the door again, but Kenny was suddenly there between us, one hand holding out her tablet to me, the other pressed against her father's chest. "Dad, just wait." Neil sighed, staring at his daughter, then gestured to me in a "hurry up" way and paced into the kitchen.

I took the tablet from Kenny as the house groaned again, settling with a resigned thump near its center. I pulled up the tracking menu and hit the map feature.

"How do you even know about the tracking thing?" Neil asked, coming back to the entry.

"How do you *not* know about it, Dad?" Kenny said. "You're such a Luddite."

The progress wheel spun. And spun. And spun. The map partially loaded, more and more of the surrounding area appearing. Thunder grumbled somewhere over the lake. The cabin creaked. Despite my soaking clothes a bead of sweat ran from temple to jawline.

The map updated, dropping Tess's pin.

I stared.

My heart did a sluggish impression of a beat, then double-timed.

"What the hell?" I breathed.

"What is it?" Kenny asked, straining to see the screen. Neil came closer, curious despite himself. I glanced up at them, struggling to speak.

"She's here."

"What?" Neil said, taking the tablet from me. I took a step back, grasping Kenny's shoulder, drawing her with me toward the door. Neil noticed and looked our way, clocking my expression. The fear. He looked down at the tablet and back up at us. "I don't know what you're thinking, but—"

A short creaking came from behind a door beside the kitchen. Until then I'd thought it was a closet or pantry. But with another squeal something clicked into place. The sounds I'd been hearing hadn't been the house shifting in the storm.

They were footsteps on old stairs.

I grasped Kenny's shoulders tighter, mind screaming to run, but couldn't get myself to move.

All I could do was watch the basement door as its knob turned and it slowly swung open.

56

Jacob stepped into the light, the gun in his hand leading the way.

His eyes flicked to all of us individually, holding on me last. He offered a faint smile. "Sorry to interrupt," he said.

"Jacob, what the hell are you—" Neil began walking toward him, but Jacob met him with the barrel of the gun in his face.

"One more word or move, and your daughter will watch you die, right here." Neil's hands came up to shoulder level, and he took a step back. "This is what's going to happen—I'm going to talk, and you're going to do exactly what I say. Anyone does anything I don't like, I shoot Kendra." For emphasis he aimed the gun at Kenny, and she shrank against me. I turned, shielding her. The gun's muzzle was so large it looked like a black hole, eating the light in the room.

"Jacob, you need to think about what you're doing," I said in as even a tone as I could manage. Every terrible situation I'd ever been in flickered behind my eyes like a movie reel out of control.

"Oh I've thought about it," Jacob said. "It's actually all I've thought about for a long time." He motioned toward a row of coats hanging on hooks. "Put those raincoats on. We're going for a walk."

———

The storm swallowed us.

Beyond the cabin's glow the night was complete. The rain fell in drifting curtains that faded to drenching darkness as soon as we left the driveway.

"Turn right," Jacob said from directly behind us. He was walking with one hand gripping the back of Kenny's slicker, the gun nestled between her shoulder blades. Neil was on my right. He kept glancing back and swiping at the lenses of his rain-speckled glasses, his face slack like someone caught in a dream. I moved as slowly as I could, head erect, eyes forward. Mind whirring.

Could I duck off into the darkness and zigzag to avoid Jacob's bullets? Probably. But I also believed he would shoot Kenny the moment I was gone. Could I try spinning on him, wrestle him to the ground with Neil's help and get the weapon from him? Probably not. I'd seen him without his shirt on and knew he was strong. Besides, I wouldn't risk him shooting Kenny out of reflex. We were in his control.

"Jacob, please. Look at what you're doing," Neil said, over his shoulder. "Look at Kenny. Please, man, we've been friends a long time. We can talk about this." Jacob responded by nudging him between his shoulder blades with the gun barrel. Neil fell quiet.

We marched down the center of the dirt road, and after thirty paces I knew where we were going. A gutshot of acidic fear nearly crumpled me.

"Jacob," I said, "there's another way than this."

"Do you want her to die right here?" he answered. "Don't say anything else."

The landscape scrolled by, lit occasionally by a stutter of lightning. Ahead our destination appeared.

"To the left," Jacob said, steering us into the overlook's clearing.

Any hope of a vehicle or another person evaporated in the next fork of lightning. The area was empty. Of course it was. Who the hell would be out at a viewpoint when there was nothing to view? As we neared the low rock wall, time seemed to speed up. Each step came quicker, each breath more vital. I had to do something, or it would all be over before it really began.

"Stop," Jacob said. He shoved Kenny, and she gave a short cry, stumbling into her father's arms. I resisted the impulse to comfort her. We were balanced on the tip of a knife. "Any of you move while I'm talking, I shoot. And I can't miss this close. Do we understand?" None of us replied, but he took our silence as an answer and went on. "I know none of you wanted this to happen, but it's happening. This is reality. You need to accept it. Here's your choices. Neil, Kendra—you can hold each other's hands, climb onto the wall, and step off. It'll be over in a second, and you can go together. Or I can shoot you both, and everyone will think you did it, Neil."

"You know, Jacob, you're not too good at making murder look like suicide," I said. There was a tremor in my voice, but it was slight. A part of me was already walled off. Dedicated to these being the last moments of my life. I wasn't going to spend them begging someone who had no intention of mercy.

"What did I say?" Jacob said, turning the gun toward me.

"But, see, you can't just start blasting away. You really want to make this look like a murder-suicide, and going wild won't fit the narrative. How would you explain me being here?"

"You're wrong. I have no qualms about killing all of you right now. The weather will take care of a lot of evidence. And I'm creative, I'll come up with something. I've come this far already." In the next flicker of lightning, I watched for a waver in his gun hand, but it was steady.

"What did you do to Tess?" I asked, shifting an inch toward Kenny.

"Nothing. She's fine."

"You're lying."

"Why on earth would I hurt Tess? After everything I've done for her. After all the years I've waited."

"For the same reason you couldn't move on. You can't accept she doesn't love you."

Jacob chuckled. "See, you underestimate me, Nora. I'm not one of your lunatic fathers or husbands you encountered through the system. I'm not going to destroy what I can't have. That's not what this is about. This is about a second chance. You heard Tess, she said it herself. She wants to start over. I'm giving her a clean slate."

"You're destroying her life." Another half step toward Kenny.

"So I can help her rebuild it." More lightning exposed his placid expression. He was like a Buddhist monk. Calm. Peaceful. "When all this is over, I'm the one who'll be there for her. I've always been there."

"You crazy fuck," Neil muttered.

Jacob crossed the distance between them almost too quick to register.

The pistol lashed the side of Neil's head, and he grunted with pain. Kenny cried out. "You of all people don't get to tell me anything," Jacob said. "You shared a life with the most amazing woman in the world, and what did you do? You *squandered* it. You were too wrapped up in your own feelings to see what she needed. I watched you with that girl half your age, watched you come here and stand on this ledge over and over. Oh, how I wished you'd jump each time." Jacob laughed, and there was a manic energy to it. "I cheered you on! But you didn't have the courage, and you never deserved Tess in the first place."

"Stop it!" Kenny yelled. "Let us go."

"Kendra," Jacob said. "You're too young to understand the burden you are to her. You weigh her down. The way you treat your mother, what you put her through—you have no idea."

I sidled another step and stood fully in front of Kenny. "How long will you wait?" I said, jamming my words like a chisel into the gap I'd seen in his armor. "When she brushes you back and moves on to another man to comfort her like she did with Devon. Will you watch as she fucks someone else again? Falls in love with them? How much patience do you have? How many more people will you kill? Because at this rate it looks like you'd have to be the last person in the world before she'd consider you."

When he lunged I was ready.

The gun whistled through the wet air where my head had been as I ducked. Then I drove my hand forward, not in a fist, but with fingers extended, searching for the softness of his eye, and finding it.

I gouged. Felt skin tear.

"Run!" I yelled.

Jacob screamed and lashed out. This time I didn't move fast enough.

The hard steel of the pistol caught me on the jaw, and my lip exploded on that side, salty heat spilling into my mouth. The world tilted violently, and the ground came up to meet me. A second later a gunshot rang out.

I waited for the pain to set in. The same unbelievable sharpness of the last bullet wound, only this time in my center, boring through something vital.

Except there was nothing outside the ringing in one ear and my throbbing lip.

"Get up," Jacob said. I did after a moment, finding I could still gather myself.

Kenny was huddled at Neil's feet, sobbing. He stood over her, cradling her head against his leg. Jacob lowered the pistol from where he'd fired into the air, training it back on me again. A stream of blood that appeared black in the next flit of lightning flowed down from the corner of his right eye as if he were weeping it. "Stand by the wall, all of you. Now."

I moved to the low wall. Neil and Kenny did the same. Neil was still holding her, telling her it was going to be okay. That he was there.

"I guess you've made your choice," Jacob said, closing in. "It could've been so much easier."

Here it was.

Not how I'd intended to go out. Not like this. All of my life rushed forward, everything slamming together like a hundred-car pileup.

Running with Paul and Stephen and Tess on the beach.

My mother smoothing back an errant strand of hair from my forehead, smiling.

Every single child I'd helped.

Every one I'd failed.

All of it there and gone, a filament flaring bright and burning out.

Jacob trained the pistol on me, steadied it with both hands.

I tensed every muscle and prepared to strike one last time.

"Jacob, stop!"

The voice came from behind him, and he jerked, spinning around.

Tess stood in the downpour, arms extended, hands gripping her revolver.

"Mom!" Kenny cried.

"Tess?" Jacob said, dumbstruck. All the steel was gone from his voice.

"Put the gun down," Tess said. She was crying, tears mingling with the rain. The massive revolver nodded in her hands. Jacob looked down to his own weapon as if seeing it for the first time. I inched sideways, out of Tess's line of fire. "You don't want to do this."

"It's for you," Jacob said, taking a step toward her. "For us."

"I don't want this," Tess said. "They're my family. I know you don't want to hurt them."

"But they hurt you," Jacob said, taking another step toward her even as she retreated. "Over and over. They still are." He lowered the gun and placed his other hand on his chest. "I would never hurt you. I want to make you happy. I *can* make you happy."

"Not like this." Tess's gun bobbed again as she took one hand away to push wet strands of hair from her face. "Let's just talk, okay? We can work it out. We love you, Jacob. All of us. Please."

Jacob lowered his head. Rain fell from the hood of his slicker. When he looked up again, he was smiling. "Don't worry. It's going to be perfect. You'll see."

He raised his gun, pointing it at Neil and Kenny.

The shot was beyond loud. World ending.

A foot of flame leaped from the muzzle of the gun, nudging back the darkness.

Jacob's knees unhinged.

He fell almost at my feet, and I stepped away, standing in front of Kenny and Neil. For a second nothing moved but the wind and rain, then blood ran from Jacob's mouth in a steady stream. He tried raising the gun again.

Tess fired a second time.

The shot knocked him flat to the ground. He fell on his stomach, head turned to the side. Tess moved between us and him and stood looking down. Jacob blinked up through the rain pooling in one fluttering eye and reached toward Tess's feet, hand tremoring.

She stepped back.

His hand stretched, reaching and reaching. Then it slowly settled to the muddy ground. He lay still.

The rain pounded down. I sank to the overlook wall as Kenny made it to her feet and launched herself into her mother's arms. Tess clutched her, both of them beyond words, just holding one another. After a second Neil joined them.

I stared at Jacob's motionless shape and watched the dark river running from beneath it widen in the dancing stormlight.

57

A hundred fairies gathered beneath a trellised archway interwoven with a riot of flowers.

They ranged from a dark-haired girl in a wheelchair who must've been eleven or twelve, all the way to a toddling boy who couldn't have been more than a year old. Their costumes were store-bought, hand-sewn, mismatched, and every iridescent color in imagination. They carried wands of all kinds with pompoms and tassels and glitter floating in the handles. Almost all wore tiaras or crowns that caught the strong early-afternoon sunlight, refracting it in a thousand glittering points as they capered and ran.

I made my way down the short stairway to where the botanical gardens began in a dozen winding rows. Crowds of people lined the aisles, waiting for the event to start—phones out and ready to soak up as much cuteness as digitally possible.

Ivy Pearson pranced on the closest edge of the group as a half dozen frazzled-looking volunteers tried wrangling the kids into a semblance of order. She wore a tiny pink tutu and a wispy blue top with puffy shoulders. Her wand had streamers coming from its handle and a gold star at its other end. She waved it at her parents, who were in the front row of spectators. Gayle and Joel waved back enthusiastically. I turned my face up to the sunshine. Soaked it in. The gash on my lip ached in the heat, but even that felt good. Very real. Very alive.

It had been just under two weeks since the night of the storm. So little time, yet so much within it.

Jacob had been pronounced dead at the scene by the first paramedics who showed up. Not that you needed any medical training to see that. The four of us had huddled in the back of an ambulance until law enforcement was able to take statements, my lip held together with a butterfly bandage and an ice pack. Much of Tess's story I'd guessed at after realizing Jacob hadn't harmed her, and she confirmed it in a solid rush to the officers, all the while holding Kenny in her lap, unwilling to let her go.

After Jacob had brought Tess home, she'd lain down to nap, a plan to stake out the cabin already formed in her mind. Still fully convinced of Neil's guilt and terrified Kenny wasn't safe, she'd bundled herself in a rain jacket and kept watch on her family a short distance from the cabin as the night darkened and the storm wore on.

She never saw Jacob's approach from the opposite side of the house or his entrance through the basement door he'd learned of after Kenny's disappearance. Her first clue that something was wrong was my sudden arrival, then four figures instead of three trundling off into the rain a short time later. She'd followed but lost us in the storm. Only after hearing Jacob's warning shot had she sprinted to the overlook in time to see us lined up near the wall.

I moved along one of the garden beds and found a relatively vacant spot to stand as the parade started. Music played from hidden speakers near the ground, and the fairies danced out from beneath the arch. The crowd went wild.

There was no choreography to their movements, just a bunch of kids frolicking in the sun between rows of vividly blooming flowers. They hammed it up for their parents' cameras, posed with friends, and marched on. I clapped and whooped along with the rest of the spectators, yelling Ivy's name loudly as she went by. She grinned and waved, and I wasn't sure she remembered who I was since we'd only met one time, but it didn't matter. What mattered was the sunshine and her costume and the flowers. Her smile mattered.

As she paraded by, my gaze fell on someone across the aisle, and I froze.

Arlene stood by herself, a strange, dreamy expression on her face as Ivy danced away. She looked smaller, diminished in a way that wasn't solely physical. She finally glanced up and saw me watching her. There was a beat where I wondered if something terrible was about to happen, if Arlene had come completely apart since Gayle and Joel regained custody. But she only nodded to me and turned away, threading between the throngs of people and was gone.

The stitches in my lip itched. I scratched around them.

The doctor in Mutiny who'd put them in had done a good job. They were small and tight, and he'd promised a minimal amount of scarring. That was good. I didn't need any more.

After I left the clinic, Detective Lowe spent the better part of the day interviewing us separately before confirming our stories matched. I brought up my night in the mountains and how I believed it had been Jacob pursuing me, fearing I would eventually realize his alibi for when Devon was killed was faulty. What I kept to myself was the notion that I was simply yet another barrier between him and Tess—a potential pitfall in his imaginings of their future together. At the end his obsession had been all consuming, a wildfire that would've eventually burned everything and everyone out of Tess's life.

When we'd finally left the courthouse, there'd been little fanfare, since the story hadn't broken yet, and I wanted to be well away from Mutiny when it did. Before I left, we all went to Tess's—Tess herself still visibly uncomfortable in Neil's presence, though if it was because of lingering doubts or her own guilt, I couldn't say. I didn't ask.

Shell-shocked. That was the word that came to mind looking at the three of them sitting on the living-room couch, Neil on one side of Kenny, Tess on the other. They'd gone through something that wouldn't fully make itself known until later in the form of nightmares and ambushing panic. They would need therapy, need to talk about it. They would need each other. When they didn't think I was looking, Neil had gently brushed Tess's cheek with the back of his hand, and she smiled tiredly at him. I was glad to see it.

After I said my goodbyes, Tess followed me out of the house and stopped me before I could get in my car. I didn't know what to expect, maybe some sort of plea or justification from her. Instead she caught me in a hug that felt both desperate and earnest. We stood that way for a time, two women with the shadows of little girls on the ground beside us. When I drove away, all three of them waved from the front step. A family again. At least for the moment.

Now another family approached me.

The parade was over, had ended while I was adrift in the past. The Pearsons were all smiles, with Ivy hoisted high on Joel's shoulders. We talked about the parade and how Ivy had been the most beautiful fairy of all. She had a handful of poppies, and she gave me one. I slipped it behind my ear as we walked toward the parking lot together.

"I saw your grandmother here," I said quietly to Gayle when we reached their car.

"Oh, yeah. She asked if she could come and watch, and we said that was okay."

"You know you don't have to agree to anything she asks."

"We know. But she's still my grandma, and she's sorry even if she can't say it yet. Sometimes it takes people a long time to say they're sorry." Gayle turned her face up to the sun, squinting into the blinding blue sky. "Mom always said second chances were easy to give, but it was hard deciding who to give them to. I didn't understand that before, but maybe I do now."

I opened my mouth, then closed it.

Gayle leaned forward and kissed me on the cheek. "Thank you. You saved us."

I watched them drive away and took a last breath of the sweetly scented air. Tried holding it inside me all the way home.

———

Merrill hurtled into the lush greenery ringing the yard, then came loping back with the slobbery ball I'd thrown hanging out one side of his jaws. He dropped it at the foot of my lawn chair and sat down, watching expectantly.

"My arm hurts," I said. He didn't move. "You got it too slobby." He licked his chops. Stared at me. I made an exasperated sound and grabbed the ball, whipped it as far as I could, which wasn't very far given my seated position and the lull of wine running through my blood.

The afternoon was about as perfect as you could ask for—a light breeze from the Pacific rounding off the edge of the summer sun. The dappled shade of the backyard was the optimum spot for sipping booze and playing fetch. We did both until Merrill finally had enough and flopped at my feet. I refilled my glass and picked up the letter that had arrived while I'd been at Ivy's parade.

Seeing it was from Tess, I'd opened it before coming outside, but paused when the photo of my mom and Diedre at the beach slid out with it. I hadn't read a word, deciding to don some liquid armor before wading in. Now there were no more excuses.

Nora,

I guess I'm still a little bit of a coward since I wasn't able to tell you everything I wanted in person. But I'll cut myself a little slack given everything that happened right at the end. Writing it down is easier now, alone in the quiet of the house. Kenny is with Neil at the moment. We've agreed to share custody, and our lawyers are working out the details with the court. I'm still going to do the mandated parental conditions the judge laid out, though. I think it'll be good for me. Neil is seeing a therapist, too, and they're working on his depression. We've talked about it, and he's opened up more than ever before. I'm going to try to be there for him when he needs me in whatever capacity. If the last months have shown me anything, it's that I have so much more to learn about being a mother, a partner, a friend.

You were right. I did use you to an extent. Your experience was too tempting not to tap into, but I want you to know it wasn't the reason I called and asked you to come. You were the brightest spot in my childhood. The three of you were the siblings I never had, and I never forgot our time together. After Mom died, you were the one thing I clung to whenever I thought of her and started to cry. No matter what your expertise, I needed you, and you came. For that I'll be forever grateful.

I've met with a therapist who has agreed to see us as a family. I think it will be easier to work through this together. I definitely need to see someone. I've been having flashbacks, and sometimes I think I see Jacob in certain places, his face mixed in with a crowd of people. I'm having trouble eating, and sleep has been nonexistent. I spoke to Lowe again yesterday, and he said Devon had been shot with one of his own pistols. Jacob must've found it when he snuck in after I left—Devon hadn't been very careful about keeping his guns locked up.

I keep thinking I should've noticed something about Jacob, that he was capable of this, but there was nothing other than knowing he still loved me. You were right that people are unknowable, even the ones we love. Maybe especially them.

I worry about Kenny and find myself watching her sleep when I can't and making sure I'm there when she wakes up crying. Which is frequently. She misses you, by the way, and has been asking when we can come visit. I told her soon. I know you'd love to see her, though I'm not sure you feel the same about me.

You were right about something else, too—we used to know each other, but we're different people now. Maybe that's what growing older is—the fading of certain dreams. I'd always dreamed of being your sister, and you have a right to know our mothers wanted that too.

They weren't just friends—they were lovers. Right before Mom passed away, I walked in on them kissing when they thought we were all asleep. They wanted to run away together and join our families. The letters I gave you detail how much they loved one another and their plans for the future, but I have the feeling you haven't read them. If I know you at all, they probably don't even exist anymore.

Your mother ran away because she was heartbroken. But I also understand why you blame her for what happened afterward. I don't know what the answers are for something like this. All I can do is make sure you have a choice.

Maybe someday we can get to know each other for who we are now. People change. That's the beautiful thing about them. I hope you believe that too.

Love, Tess

My throat worked against a sudden tightness, and I blinked at the nodding leaves. When I could see clearly again, I drew out the picture Tess had included. Now my mother's and Diedre's body language made sense. How their hips touched, the casual way Mom held on to Diedre's waist, the way Diedre's head was tilted and how her lips were parted, as if she were leaning in for a kiss. I stared at the picture and finally turned it over. Seeing my mother's handwriting was like a ghost whispering in my ear.

Puerto Perdon, Feb, 2000

The best week of my life—I can't wait to spend the rest of it with you. This is where we'll bring the kids someday and never come back. It'll be our new start. Love you more than anything.

I set the photo down and stared into the middle distance. Back through the years to the times my mother would disappear, to the days wondering where she'd gone and when she would return. I thought of the beach again, of another life that might've been but never was. My hand reached out and traced the name of the town where they'd stayed. I said it quietly, letting the breeze carry the words away.

Tess was right. People do change. I don't know if it's beautiful or not. Change is painful. It's hard letting someone get close because it's so much harder to lose them.

There was still the same anger inside me, but now there was something else as well, something that made me think of sunrises spilling over water, and words spoken in the sorrow of missed chances and lost love.

Forgiveness is change, and there is beauty in that. But I didn't know how much I'd changed.

"Puerto Perdon," I said again, and thought that maybe I'd find out. Maybe.

ACKNOWLEDGMENTS

Eternal thanks to my family for your patience and love, I couldn't do any of this without you. Huge thank-you to my agent, Laura Rennert—your support and guidance are such a blessing. Thanks to my editor, Liz Pearsons, for the continued faith in the stories. Thanks to Jacque Ben-Zekry and Blake Crouch, I wouldn't be where I am today without you both. Thanks to Kevin Smith for the great rounds of edits. Thanks to Matt Iden for always having the time to read and tell me what's wrong and right in the story. Thanks to Richard Brown, Dori Pulley, Steven Konkoly, and Matt FitzSimmons—excellent writers and people all around. Thanks to the Thomas & Mercer team for continuing to believe in the books. And thanks to all the readers who keep making what I do possible; I am forever in your debt.

ABOUT THE AUTHOR

Photo © 2019 Jade Hart

Joe Hart is the Edgar Award–winning and *Wall Street Journal* best-selling author of fifteen novels, including *Where They Lie*, *The River Is Dark*, *Obscura*, *The Last Girl*, and *Or Else*. For more information, visit www.joehartbooks.com.